"If you were a man, you could be famous,"

Lacey said. "A teller of tales that entrances even the most unromantic of souls."

"If I were a man," Jenner reflected, "I would never have known you—not like this, anyway."

"Doesn't the unfairness of it make you angry?"

"I got tired of being angry about so many things. It's a terrible waste of effort. Besides, I don't want to be famous."

"What do you want?" he asked, expecting her to say she wanted him.

"I never think about wanting anything," she said slowly. "I never think much at all about myself. When so many possibilities have been taken away from you, the little things become more important—the feel of a strong young horse under you, a few weeks of the maddest life with the most amazing man." She laughed and looked up at him. "These become the great things in your life. You will be the last man I will ever love, Lacey. Of that I'm certain . . ."

Dear Reader,

Thanks to the success of our March Madness promotion during 1992 featuring four brand-new authors, we are very pleased to be able to, once again, introduce you to a month's worth of talented newcomers as we celebrate first-time authors with our 1993 March Madness promotion.

Teller of Tales by Laurel Ames. When free-spirited Jenner Page captures the eye of the bored nobleman, Lord Raines, their reckless affair causes a scandal that Regency London is likely never to forget, or forgive.

Riverbend by Mary McBride. Despite their differences, Lee Kincannon and the fiesty Jessamine Dade seem destined to cross paths at every turn, but the jaded gambler still can't believe that fate has finally dealt him a winning hand.

Snow Angel by Susan Amarillas. Katherine Thorn never expected to find herself stranded at the ranch of her unfriendly neighbor during a Wyoming blizzard, and she was even more surprised to discover that Logan McCloud was definitely not the man she thought he was.

Romance of the Rose by Claire Delacroix. Though Armand d'Avigny vowed that he would never again allow the lovely Alexandria de Fontaine to be taken from his side, Alex knew that as long as her enemy remained alive she would never be safe—even in the arms of the powerful knight.

We hope that you enjoy every one of these exciting books, and we look forward to bringing you more titles from these authors in the upcoming year.

Sincerely,

Tracy Farrell
Senior Editor

Teller of Tales

LAUREL AMES

Harlequin Books

TORONTO • NEW YORK • LONDON
AMSTERDAM • PARIS • SYDNEY • HAMBURG
STOCKHOLM • ATHENS • TOKYO • MILAN
MADRID • WARSAW • BUDAPEST • AUCKLAND

Harlequin Historicals first edition March 1993

ISBN 0-373-28763-1

TELLER OF TALES

LAUREL AMES

Although Laurel Ames likes to write stories set in the early nineteenth century, she writes from personal experience. She and her husband live on a farm, complete with five horses, a log springhouse, carriage house and a smokehouse made of bricks kilned on the farm. Of her characters, Laurel says, "With the exception of the horses, my characters, both male and female, good and evil, are all me and no one else."

Prologue

"Couldn't you see this was bound to happen, letting her run wild like that?" accused Bette Fallow as she paced the sitting room, stopping only to glare at her diminutive gray-haired sister, Milly.

"What do I know about raising children?" Milly pleaded. "You should have taken more of a hand with her. She was always hanging about the stables with you or taking off on one of your horses by herself."

"That is done with," Geoffrey Fallow said, rising with an effort from his chair. "She is ruined, and we cannot change it. What we have to worry about now is keeping Jen alive."

"You are right, dear," Bette agreed. "We should not be fighting amongst ourselves."

All three siblings turned toward the doctor as he entered from the hallway.

"The babe is dead, of course," he announced. "There was never a chance for it. It came much too early."

"What about Jen?" her uncle asked.

"I don't know. If there is no infection..."

"She's scarcely more than a child herself," fretted Milly.

"Losing her parents nearly turned her into a mute," said Bette heavily. "What will this do to her?"

"If she survives, which I don't promise you, she can never carry another child," the doctor answered. "And after her treatment at the hands of that brute, she may never again be able to tolerate a man's touch. It remains to be seen.''

The girl's family stood in shocked silence as the doctor bade them good day and saw himself to the door.

Chapter One

London Road, England
March 1815

Jenner pushed her head and shoulders up from the cold road and winced at the pain in her right hand. The inside of her glove felt warm and wet. There was just enough daylight left to see little splashes of blood hitting the damp ground in front of her. She watched in vague fascination, wondering where it was coming from and trying to remember what had happened. There was a horse grunting in pain somewhere close—Tallboy! Her boots scrabbled on the road as she got to her feet. A wave of dizziness hit her, and the knees of her buckskin breeches smacked the road again.

"How badly are you hurt?" a harsh voice demanded from beside her as she knelt, swaying. She had not seen his approach for the fog.

"I don't know," she whispered desperately. "I must get to my horse."

"My groom is with him." Strong hands helped her sit up, but she resisted efforts to push her backward, clutching at the man's sleeve with her left hand, until she realized there was a wall behind her that he wanted her to rest against. He pushed her chin up to get a better look at the damage in the failing light. "You are just a boy! What the devil were you doing riding about in this fog, and why didn't you clear off the road when you heard us coming?"

"My horse." She tried to rise, but he held her down firmly. She could see post-boys scurrying about trying to calm a steaming team. One figure detached himself from the hazy confusion and came over.

"Sir, it's a broken leg."

"Damn you, Hawes!"

"Not the team, sir, the lad's horse."

"Get my pistol from the coach. Lead him off the road first if you can."

"Let me up," Jenner pleaded, struggling against the arm that held her down.

"You could have been killed yourself, you little idiot. Collins, where the devil are you?"

"I have torn one of your shirts for bandages, sir."

"Thank you very much. Help me hold him."

The sound of the shot made Jenner flinch as though the bullet had gone through her and not her old friend. She groaned and quit struggling. What a disastrous mess—and all because she had not felt like riding to London in a stuffy mail coach.

Gentle hands were binding a length of linen around her head and wiping the blood from her face. "Where else are you hurt?"

"Just my hand," she said as she tried to raise it. She winced as the glove was ruthlessly stripped off by her first interrogator.

"That looks nasty. Do what you can for him, Collins— Hawes, lead the team off the road," he shouted. "We don' want the mail crashing into us."

Jenner bit her lip as the servant bound her hand. She felt like bursting into sobs, not for her own pain, but for the wicked impulse that had led to the death of her dearest old horse. Usually her fits and starts, as Aunt Bette called them, did not have such tragic results. The tears were hot on her cheeks as she took a shuddering breath and pulled herself up from the damp road. The one called Collins had her by the arm, but she could feel herself reeling again and leaned against the low wall. That's when it occurred to her that all the roaring was not in her head. They were on a bridge. The river was just below. That was why she had not heard the carriage overtake her.

The previous winter she wouldn't have thought of trying to ride the seventy miles from Thetford to London, but with the weather brightening, the trip seemed feasible at the beginning of March. She had not counted on the fog.

The one giving the orders came walking back, again conferring with the groom. Jenner noticed vacantly how the mists swirled about them and the damp air condensed on their coats. Or perhaps the swirling fog was partly in her head.

"Shall we turn back, sir?" the groom asked.

"No. We cannot be so very far from Halstead. We'll push on— You! I thought I told you to stay put." Picking her up, he handed her in to his servant. Collins tried to lay her on the seat, but she dragged herself upright in a corner of the carriage to look out the window for a last glimpse of her horse. The groom emerged from the fog with her saddle and valise. After a final conference with the coachman the gentleman entered the carriage and roughly threw a traveling rug over her. She then had to endure not only the bumping of the coach, but a lecture from her rescuer on the dangers of riding about in the fog. Had she felt slightly better she might have retorted that it was even more unwise to be tearing along in a coach-and-four in such conditions. But the loss of old Tallboy had damped her spirits to the point that she did not care what happened. She just wished the fellow would shut up. To this end she pretended to fall asleep, and very soon did so.

Efforts to pick her up again roused her to say, "I'm all right," in quite a normal voice. She jumped down from the coach only to hang dizzily onto the door with her good hand.

"Liar," the gruff voice said as he lifted her effortlessly, carried her into the inn and deposited her on a settle in the deserted taproom. The sight of the fire reminded Jenner that she was cold, and she started shivering belatedly. She got up gingerly and drew a chair closer to the generous blaze. Both her head and her hand had started to thump uncomfortably. She heard her assailant-benefactor barking orders to the innkeeper. "You are the most provoking boy," he said coming into the room. "What is your name?"

She looked assessingly at him and forced herself to stop shuddering before answering. "Jenner Page."

"What?"

"It's from Jennerian." The man was looking at her rather dubiously, so she continued in a rush, "I think he's a character in an Italian opera."

"I'm Lacey Raines. Give me your parents' direction so can write to them or, if it's not far, I will take you home." Raines had been stripping off his gloves and came to warm his hands.

"My parents are dead, and you can disabuse yourself of the notion you almost sent me to join them," she said bravely. "I have walked away from much worse falls than that. It's just..." She gazed into the fire with a troubled expression.

"If you are brooding over your horse, I will buy you another."

"Certainly not!" she said so vehemently it brought scowl to Raines' normally handsome countenance. He was of medium height and wore his straight brown hair rather

ong. Just now it was falling over his forehead in a boyish
way that robbed him of authority.

Jenner looked at Raines strangely. "He was not worth
much in terms of money but he was an old friend. It's my
fault he is dead. I should never have brought him." She said
this as stoically as she could, but the note of regret and defeat was unmistakable.

Raines drew himself up to take charge of the situation. "I
have procured a room for you..."

"If this is the George in Halstead I have a room reserved." She said it offhandedly, but observed with some
amusement Raines' color rising.

"I shall buy your dinner, then."

Raines looked so self-assured the temptation to taunt him
was irresistible. "I don't think I'm very hungry."

Raines' brown eyes looked piercingly from under knit
brows as he controlled himself with an obvious effort. "I
have sent for the doctor."

"What for?" Jenner panicked.

"You, idiot. Someone has to dress that hand."

"I don't want a doctor," she said desperately, for very
likely this would lead to the discovery of her true sex and she
didn't feel equal to explaining why she was traveling in disguise or to listening to any more lectures from Raines.

"Well, you are going to have one." Raines fumed and
compressed his lips so hard the muscles stood out along his
jawline and the creases showed around his mouth. Jenner
was thinking absently that he must have had dimples as a
child and that he looked young to be ordering her about so.

The innkeeper appeared to say the rooms were almost
ready. Raines picked up one of the glasses from the tray the
man left and walked over to Jenner.

"Drink this."

"What is it?" she asked tiredly.

"Brandy, and you will drink it." He gripped her by one shoulder and held the glass up to her.

"I don't think..." she started to say, but prudently decided she had pushed him far enough. "Thank you," she said lightly. "I am feeling rather chilled."

She sipped slowly at the potent drink, holding the glass awkwardly in her left hand. Raines downed his in one gulp.

He waited impatiently for her to finish, then came purposefully across the room. She half rose, not sure what he intended to do. "I'm going to carry you up to your room now."

"I only get dizzy when I stand."

"Exactly," he said, sweeping her up and carrying her up the stairs. It was strangely comforting to feel the strong arms sit her gently down on the bed. "Collins," he said to the middle-aged man unpacking her nightclothes from her valise. "Help the lad to bed. Collins is used to tending the wounded," he said to Jenner. "He won't hurt you as much as I would."

She let Collins help her off with her boots and coat. "I think I can manage the rest. I'm not used to being undressed," she explained. "Do you suppose there's any chance of some hot tea or soup? I'm still cold."

"I will see to it, sir," Collins replied, withdrawing discreetly. Jenner hastily got herself ready for bed. There was still the doctor to fool, but she might bring it off yet.

She had finished the broth Collins brought up and had just propped her hand comfortably enough to be able to sleep when Raines came in with the doctor, a rather elderly man whom Jenner speculated might not be all that observant. He unwrapped her hand and called for Collins to bring the basin and chair closer. To her horror he brought out a small brush with which he proposed to clean the dirt from the gash across the base of her palm.

"Someone had better hold the lad." He looked suggestively at Raines, who sat on the opposite side of the bed and pinned her shoulders while Collins held her right arm. Other than gasping now and then she handled the ordeal well enough, especially after Raines covered her eyes so she could not see what was going on. His touch was firm but gentle, not what she would have expected from the rough character who had ranted at her in the middle of a foggy road.

"Where is your home, lad?" the doctor inquired as he began to set stitches.

"Why?" she gasped.

"Because I have a feeling you are a runaway, as this gentleman suspects."

"I assure you, I am of age."

"Then where do you live?"

"North of here."

"Where?" Raines boomed so close to her he made her jump.

"I live," she said tiredly, "with two dotty old aunts, neither of whom would be able to do the slightest thing except worry, if they did know I had an accident."

"I will find out where you live," Raines assured her.

"Not from me—ouch."

The doctor bandaged her hand tighter than before and the entire operation had left her dizzy and weak. He probed the small head wound up by her hairline and decided it didn't need stitches, but almost knocked her out when he felt her bruised forehead. "How many fingers?" he demanded suspiciously.

Jenner had trained horses for years, so was no stranger to concussion. She squinted one eye shut and guessed correctly. "Now that is cheating," he complained. "What do you see with both eyes open?"

"It's a little blurry, but that could be the brandy," she said thickly.

"Who gave you brandy? No spirits for a head wound," he ordered but did not embarrass Raines by saying it specifically to him.

Jenner glanced accusingly at Raines, but his look of innocence was so boyishly convincing that she decided not to give him away.

"If you have not dined yet, Doctor, I would be glad of some company," Raines suggested.

"Delighted."

Jenner wished only for sleep and was glad to be rid of both of them. It did her peace of mind no good to hear the old practitioner say on the way out, "If he doesn't die in the night, he will probably be fine."

Jenner did not wake until there was full sun streaming in the window and noisy activity in the yard. She sat up carefully. Her head was still pounding but her vision was clear. In spite of a generally achy feeling and a badly bruised knee, she thought she could manage getting dressed. She swung her legs out of bed, pulled her riding breeches off the chair and was slowly and stiffly easing them on when Raines threw the door open.

"What the devil do you think you are doing?"

"I just remembered I left a dead horse on the London road. I had better do something about it."

"I have already taken care of that."

"You?" She smiled skeptically at him as she sat on the edge of the bed, embarrassed at being caught in her nightclothes.

"I should say I ordered my groom to take care of it," Raines said defensively.

"How enterprising of you. What will he do with it?"

"I have not a clue. You can ask him if you like. Give me those." She surrendered the breeches and swung herself back into bed, since she couldn't afford a struggle.

"Put down the tray, Collins," Raines ordered as the older man appeared at the door. "And remove Mr. Page's clothes to my room."

Jenner suppressed the objection that rose to her lips and arranged a pillow under her hand. She looked curiously at the bowl on the tray.

"What is it?"

"You are going to eat it," Raines informed her.

Jenner looked up in surprise. Only Aunt Bette told her what she was going to do, whether she liked it or not. "I see," Jenner said, stirring the unappetizing mixture. Raines took a determined step closer. "You mean it's a case of eat it or wear it?" She had the strength to smile challengingly at him, in spite of her bruises and aching head.

"Pretty much," Raines said flippantly. He risked his immaculate coat and approached the bed to loom over her threateningly.

"Oh, very well," she said placidly, as she began to eat the gruel.

"You little devil. You meant to eat it all along."

"Why not? It is pretty much the sort of thing my aunts might make for me if I were laid up."

"Then what was all the nonsense about?"

"I wondered how far you would go to get your own way."

Raines gave Jenner a warning glare, but had to chuckle when he was out of the room. He had trouble believing the boy was really of age. For all the lad kept a cool head, he was much too fragile somehow. The square jaw and firm lips were offset by a pointed chin and delicately chiseled nose. Plus the boy didn't weigh enough for his height, though his hands had seen their share of hard work. The lad was a puzzle.

Later, Collins gave Jenner one of the books from her valise and got himself roundly condemned by Dr. Scales when he arrived to check on his patient. "No reading until the headache is completely gone. If you are not running away from home, where are you going?" the doctor demanded.

"London."

"That may be, but not for a day or two yet."

Jenner hoped Raines would get bored and go off and leave her. But it seemed that once he had determined to do something, nothing could deter him. He had borrowed a chess set from the doctor and dragooned Jenner into playing him. It was a game she had been taught by her uncle when he was still alive, but she had not thought of it for years. It took her some time to sharpen her wits enough to give Raines any kind of challenge.

"Sacrificing a pawn, eh?" He looked over at her from his chair by the bed. "That won't work."

Jenner glanced at him, then back at the board. Rough and tyrannical he might be, but she could not bring herself to dislike him. He was not only handsome, but charming, and he knew it.

He studied the board suspiciously, then looked at her with a crooked smile to inquire, "What sort of trap are you laying for me?" He ignored her look of blank innocence and took so long over his move that she had plenty of time to consider her alternatives. It was true she deliberately threw away some pawns at the beginning to give her rooks and bishops space to move. She always saved the knights, her favorite pieces, to protect the king and queen. She thought her strategy must be sadly predictable to him by now. As soon as Raines moved, she moved, putting him on the defensive again. She smiled because he attributed a subtlety to her play that she did not in fact possess. And when she smiled at his machinations, he struggled even harder. He always won, of course, but it cost him a great deal more worry than it need have.

"I have your king in two moves," he said triumphantly. "Do you concede the game?"

"Gladly, since I have overtaxed your small store of patience."

She said it with a laugh but it caused him to demand accusingly, "What is the matter with you? You have lost all concentration. Is your head aching again?"

"No."

"Don't lie," Raines ordered.

"Very little, anyway. It's odd. I felt fine this morning."

"That's the way of it after a good long sleep, but the fever comes back toward afternoon." He reached over and felt her cheek, and she tried not to flush. His gentle touch was not unwelcome. Jenner looked at him in puzzlement. For an imperious young lord he seemed to know a good deal about illness and how to amuse a bedfast patient. She tried not to meet his eyes for fear of revealing too much, but the longer she knew Raines the more he stirred her desire and something else. She merely wanted to be with him. But a sense of guilt was beginning to grow in her at deceiving him so blatantly. This charade was much harder to carry off than she had expected. She had not thought to play a man for such a long time or in such close quarters to any but strangers. She wondered what sort of peal he would ring over her if he found out she was a girl.

A thought struck her and she asked, "Were you ever a soldier?"

"What makes you ask?"

"The way you play, as though winning was really important."

"Of course it is important." He raised his voice unconsciously.

"Were you in the army?" Jenner persisted tiredly.

"Only for three years."

"I thought so. My uncle used to shout at us in that disagreeable way and I was sure he picked it up in the army."

"I have always shouted in this disagreeable way," Raines said proudly. "The army had nothing to do with it. How is it you neglected to mention this uncle before?"

"He is dead now," she said sadly.

"How convenient."

"Carried off by an apoplexy in his early forties—how old are you?" she asked provocatively.

"Don't hold your breath. By your reckoning I have a decade yet to indulge myself, although you may shorten that span. I have no doubt you contributed to your uncle's early demise."

"I wonder if you may be right," Jenner said, suddenly serious and thinking of the scandal she had brought on her family. That she had been an innocent victim made no difference. They had all suffered because of her carelessness.

Raines watched Jenner's downcast eyes as he put away the chessboard. Ranting at the boy was no aid to his recovery. "I am sure you could never have done anything nearly as bad as I did to my family and they have not—the most of them—dropped over dead."

"Unless you have an illegitimate child to your credit, you are a paragon compared to me," Jenner said rashly, immediately regretting it.

Raines' brows came together and for the first time he believed the boy was older than he appeared. Jenner looked at him in some pain, her dark eyes troubled.

"No, so far as I know, I have no offspring. Do you support the child?"

"The child died," she said bitterly. "What is worse, I was glad it died—well, not entirely. But it would have been hard on everyone if it had lived." She jerked herself back to the present. "Why am I telling you this? I scarcely even know you."

"Just shows how fuzzy you are still in the head," Raines observed as he got up. "How old are you, anyway?"

"Twenty-three."

"I don't believe you."

She rolled her eyes. "You don't believe anything I say."

"Sometimes I think you are just trying to shock me, to get me to wash my hands of you. It won't work, you know. I am an expert at such tactics, and you are just an amateur."

Jenner looked surprised, then laughed weakly.

Raines thought he saw in the boy a shadow of himself a decade ago, and he hated his present life just enough to want to deter someone else from plunging down the same road.

Dr. Scales came the next afternoon and pronounced Jenner fit for travel, since it would be only half a day to London. Yet the old man still seemed uneasy at letting her go out of his reach until Raines promised to consult a physician known to him in town. Raines invited the doctor to dinner again that night and they filled the interval between courses by trying to wheedle out of Jenner where she was from, which had the effect of reducing her contribution to the conversation to monosyllables.

"If you are going to be churlish and not eat anything anyway you can take yourself off to bed," Raines said finally.

Jenner had been having the devil of a time trying to eat left-handed. "It's not for want of an appetite," she complained. "I just cannot manage most of this one-handed."

Raines looked so conscience-stricken she had to laugh at him, and she flushed when he came around behind her chair and reached over her to cut her beef. It was such a sweet thing for him to do when he could have called the waiter to serve her. He and the doctor patiently nursed the port while they waited for her to finish eating. She noticed Raines did not send the bottle her way, so he must still have doubts about her age. She was quite content with the glass of milk he ordered for her but, since she was not sure if he did it to bait her or not, she did not say so.

"Now, if you stop hounding me, I will talk to you—I know, I will tell you one of my stories. What do you fancy? Modern, medieval or ancient?"

"What do you mean by story?" the doctor asked.

"Here, let me give you Garth Griffen. It's one of my aunts' favorites, and it's a short one." She pushed herself back from the table and turned her chair toward the fire in the parlor. She began her tale of the child spared during the taking of a castle by the conquering baron and adopted into his household. The orphan took the griffin as his crest. The doctor looked receptive from the beginning, but Raines was still wearing an impatient expression. She put in all the color and music she had once imagined for that period. The pennants were scarlet and azure; the horse bridles jingled with silver bells. Gradually, as she told of Garth's fall from favor when Baron Malten had a son of his own, Raines' face took on a puzzled expression. She only glanced at the two men occasionally, but stared into the fire, and the direction of her gaze drew them to look there also. She made her voice low and hypnotic. She was an expert at pausing where she could create the most suspense.

"What happened then?" the doctor found himself asking.

"When Garth returned wounded from the encounter with Dumphries' men, and without Eleanor, her father's rage was uncontrollable. Malten had Garth beaten and thrown into the dungeon without even listening to him. He would have died there but for the compassion of his adopted mother. She helped him escape, but he was barely able to sit a horse. He couldn't imagine how he could rescue Eleanor from Dumphries if she had indeed been captured by the rival baron. He made slow progress until daybreak, since he kept falling asleep on his horse and waking to find it grazing. He had just decided to look for shelter in the woods when a troop of Dumphries' men overtook him, led by the baron himself. Garth halted his horse and tried to focus his eyes, then hung his head weakly. 'Where is the girl?' Dumphries demanded. Garth looked up at this vaguely and then smiled. 'You don't have her then,' and collapsed onto the ground.''

Raines was watching her intently now.

"When Garth awoke Dumphries was dangling a crucifix on a silver chain before his eyes. He could see after a moment it was the one his mother had twisted about his wrist before she was killed. He reached for it instinctively with the word *Mother* on his lips.

"'This belonged to my lady,' Dumphries said bitterly, 'how did you come by it?'

"'My mother gave it me,' Garth said in amazement. When Dumphries realized this was his own son, he had him nursed back to health. Garth's loyalty now was to his true father.''

Jenner glanced at her audience once during Garth's and Dumphries' assault on the castle and the gory fight with Baron Malten. She could make this part as horrifying as she chose. The doctor looked raptly at the fire, but Raines was staring at her with such scorching eyes she gave a start. His gaze did not follow her. Whatever moment her story had conjured up for him was engraved on his memory and not part of her experience.

"They found Eleanor at the abbey where she had ridden and taken refuge. She and Garth married and lived at Malten with Lady Malten, who was treated, even by Dumphries, with the respect and deference due to a noblewoman.''

"Is that the end?" The doctor seemed disappointed.

"For now, but I have not written that one down yet, so who knows what it will be like until it is finished."

"I wish I could remember that well enough to tell it to my grandson."

Raines said nothing, embarrassed perhaps at being drawn into such a childish tale, so Jenner merely bade him good night.

Jenner ate a sparing breakfast the next morning, only bread and butter and some tea. She shuddered at the pile of ham on Raines' plate and became aware of his scrutiny. "Did I mention I don't travel well in closed carriages? You would not want me to get sick on you, would you?" This was effective in forestalling the scolding he was about to deliver concerning her appetite.

His eyes narrowed. "I never really know if you are mocking me or not."

"Why would I do that?" she asked innocently.

"Holding you a virtual prisoner for three days could be provocation enough for a restless young lad. No matter how much you torment me, you have never condemned me for running you over and murdering your horse."

Jenner looked up in some surprise. "But that was an accident. You didn't mean for it to happen."

"I don't mean for a lot of things to happen, but so long as I am the only one hurt it makes no odds to me how I am punished."

"Punished? What are you talking about?"

"Content you that whatever evil may befall me, I have richly deserved it." Raines said this as though he took a certain amount of comfort, even pride, in the statement.

"What a strange philosophy for someone like you to hold. Why, it is almost—religious," she said, gazing at him.

"Please."

"No one is punishing you except yourself. Believe me, I know all about that sort of thing."

Jenner said this so confidently it caused Raines to trot out his life and examine it again. His father had abandoned him. His mother had castigated him with her tears until her death. The rest of his family, except for his nephew, found him an embarrassment. He had been left by three women in turn, each of whom he had sincerely thought he had loved. And he had not been killed in the Peninsula, which truly amazed him, for he had expected to be. He could only think his survival in the face of so many more worthy men's deaths some sort of cruel joke. Jenner's remark had done nothing to shift him from this belief. Though it did make him wonder what sort of hell Jenner had been through to make the boy sound so wise.

Raines brooded through most of the journey, and Jenner watched the countryside. What Raines would do to her if he now discovered she was a woman she could not imagine. It was tempting to let her mind drift along those lines, but no—not even one person must know the real identity of Jenner Page. She feared she had slipped once already in letting him discover a look of unguarded admiration on her face. But she had the countenance not to flush, and he only smiled in a self-satisfied way. That was the only annoying item about him, his complete confidence and self-control. But that's what made baiting him so much fun. She began to think the tenacity of his hold on her had less to do with her injury than her refusal to submit to his prying questions.

For his part, Raines was thankful the boy was not the sort of traveling companion who needed to be constantly conversing. He would not have been surprised to discover that everything Jenner had told him was a fabrication. But he would have been disappointed not to have gained the boy's confidence in some degree. Though Jenner had no reason to lie about most of what he claimed, Lacey had serious doubts about the lad's age. And there was something else that just did not ring true about Jenner. Eventually he would figure it out and see the lad delivered safe home again. He could not say why he interested himself in such a youth except that, without openly defying him, Jenner was proving to be the most stubborn person he had met in years.

After a time Jenner's head began to ache so fiercely from the motion of the carriage that she dismissed the knotty problem of escaping Raines' interference and concentrated on not being sick.

Collins sat across from them and had been watching Jenner during the last hour of the journey with a growing concern. Raines noted this and looked at Jenner, who was pale again and kept easing forward on the seat to reduce the effect of the rocking. Jenner blinked hard, stared pointedly out the window for awhile and didn't hear what Raines was saying. "I said, if you are going to be ill, we can stop."

Jenner gave a start. "No, it's not that. Just a headache."

"We will have a doctor to you when we get home."

"You can leave me at the Bull and Mouth. I wrote ahead for a ..."

"Certainly not!" Raines shouted, making her wince. "You will stay with me until you are completely recovered."

Jenner stared at him in a troubled sort of way but said nothing. When they alighted in Grosvenor Street she very nearly fell getting out of the carriage, but steadied herself and managed to make it up the front steps in spite of a spinning head. Raines watched her closely and took her arm to help her up the inside stairs.

"The front room, Edwards." The somewhat stout and impassive butler raised an eyebrow at this suggestion, but followed them up the stairs with Jenner's valise and opened the door to a large airy room. After placing Jenner's worn valise on the gold and green striped settee at the foot of the magnificent bed, he opened the cream-colored drapes and licked an imaginary bit of dust off the elegant dressing table. Before exiting he straightened the accoutrements of a trivial-looking writing desk and punched up the pillows in the two armchairs that flanked a small table in front of the fireplace. Jenner sat on the bed and, in spite of her aching head, watched with fascination, wondering how she could possibly conceal her identity from all three men until she escaped this magnificent haven.

Raines ordered Collins to assist her out of her coat and boots, and went off to command the presence of a physician.

"Does he always get his own way?" she asked as Collins got out her nightclothes.

"It's easier if he does, sir," Collins observed. Jenner thought the slightly graying Collins must be the possessor of nearly infinite patience to bear with Raines' imperious moods. Yet there was a certain tacit loyalty in his gray eyes. Collins was a man you could rely on. God grant he was not an overly observant one.

"I am feeling better now," Jenner assured him as she began to unbutton her shirt. "I can manage the rest, but if you could get them to bring me some tea . . ."

"Of course, sir."

Chapter Two

The next day Jenner slept past noon, which was unprece-
dented for her, but she felt so much better that, after carefully locking the door, she washed and dressed herself and
went downstairs to explore. The lower floor other than the
kitchen area, where she did not care to penetrate, consisted
of several large salons in the same light colors as her room,
an immense dining room, a friendlier breakfast parlor, a
music room that fronted on the street, and a cozy book-
room that also housed a collection of dueling pistols in a
large, glass-fronted cabinet.

She returned to the music room where the light from several tall windows in the east and south walls was excellent.
At one end was a portrait of a red-haired girl of astonishing
beauty and character. She was posed beside a piano, the one
in this room, in fact, as though she had just risen from
playing and was smiling her appreciation at her audience's
applause. She was just the sort of woman Raines would
love, and Jenner felt a spark of curiosity to know what had
become of her. Not dead, she hoped. Such a lovely creature
should never have to die.

There were other instruments there besides the pianoforte—a violin and a cello—and a tangle of music stands.
Jenner searched eagerly though the music for something
new to amuse herself with but was rather puzzled by the

mall, disarranged selection. The room was not at all what he had expected to find in Raines' house, and she began to wonder if he played any of the instruments, many of which looked to be expensive.

She sat down at the piano and idly began some exercises on the keys. Her hand was stiff, but it did not trouble her as much as her head. She extended her playing to some more elaborate exercises that used all the keys in order to loosen up her hand. She became so engrossed she did not hear the door open. She had been fiddling with a group of pieces over the winter that had evolved from these same exercises strung together with a marching tune she particularly liked. Sometimes it was soft and melancholy, sometimes strident and harsh. At the end it was fully ripened and victorious. There were no words to go with it, but it said that she would survive and that her life was worth living in spite of all.

Raines was no musician, but he knew talent. He would not be surprised to learn the lad was playing his own composition. When the lad stopped to massage the faulty wrist, Raines felt a stab of guilt. The boy could easily have been crippled because of Raines' recklessness in driving through the fog. That would have been such a terrible waste. The music took Raines away from everything for awhile and brought him back again. He didn't quite know what it made him feel like—not happy, but resolved.

When Jenner finished Raines stood up, and Jenner turned in surprise and smiled in that boyish way. "Why didn't you stop me? I should have asked before I went pounding away like that. It is the finest instrument I have ever touched. Do you play it?"

"No, I don't play at all. I bought it for Elaina when she was here." Raines nodded toward the portrait. "She was a singer. I suppose she still is, wherever she went."

"She's lovely." Jenner was curious and, she realized in surprise, oddly jealous of the woman, but she hesitated to ask more about her. "Do you mind if I play it?"

"No, amuse yourself as you like. Shall I get it tuned for you?"

"I hardly think I will be here long enough to make it worthwhile."

"What do you mean?"

"I only came to look for a horse and to see my publisher. I can't really be away too long. There's no telling what my aunts will be up to."

"I see," Raines said skeptically, fastening on the word *publisher.* "You came all the way to London to buy books."

"No, actually to sell." Jenner laughed. "My first book did fairly well for them, and they have the second one in type, but there are some last-minute changes they insist they have to see me about in person— You are not believing any of this at all, are you?"

"I have not said a word."

"No, but it's the way you look at me from under your eyebrows. Why would I lie to you about something like that?"

"Why won't you tell me the truth about yourself?"

"You already know more about me than most people," Jenner said resentfully.

"Is Jenner Page your real name?"

Jenner looked uncomfortable. "No, I chose it when I wrote *The Highwayman.* I cannot write under my real name."

"Not even a letter to let your dear aunts know you are all right?" Raines asked sarcastically.

"Not if you intend to post it. Then you would have my address and who knows what you would tell them."

"Then you are not leaving until you are fully recovered."

"What are you going to do?" she jested. "Lock me up?"

"If necessary."

"Now see here, I really do have to get out and see my ublisher."

"And who may that be? You need not answer. I shall now as soon as I pick up a copy of your book."

Too late Jenner realized she had given Raines an edge and he knew she had to devise a way to get to Hughes and Croft before he did. Her hand went to her head distractedly, and he heard his voice change to one of concern rather than derision. On a sudden inspiration she stood up and feigned a stagger. Without hesitation Raines pounced on her and carried her upstairs again, disregarding her protests that she was all right. He left her on the bed and went in search of Collins. Jenner grabbed her bill case and hat and was down the stairs and out the front door while Raines was still calling for his man. She ran only a short block before being able to hail a hackney, directing him to Hughes and Croft in Fleet Street. She was flushed and dizzy with the sudden exertion but elated with the excitement of the escape.

Jenner rather enjoyed tricking Raines, especially because she felt people seldom got the better of him. But he was no fool to be taken in by the same ruse twice. She would have to be careful. Her limited experience of men had not prepared her for Lord Raines. Her first encounter had been brief, violent and anonymous. And Rob, her only love, had been biddable and easy-going. Their association of four years had only ended because the district had gotten too dangerous for him. Much as she hated to let Rob go, she felt relieved that he was now safe in America. Whether he would find honest employment or take to the road again she would never know.

Raines was quite something else—a man used to having his own way. Though slight, he was fit and muscular. She would lose any physical struggle with him if it came to that. To bait him like a squirrel teasing a dog was dangerous and had already earned her an occasional playful cuff or a strong

restraining hand on her shoulder. His touch, after so man
nights alone, was comforting for all he thought he was di
ciplining an unruly boy. She shook herself back to the ma
ter at hand.

Mr. Hughes was not in that day, but Mr. Croft agreed
see her and she was shown into a large, pleasantly clutter
office. "There must be some mistake," the jovial-lookin
man said as he shook hands. "Are you Mr. Page's son?"

"No, I am Jenner Page. Sorry I am so late, but I had a
accident on the road. Got knocked off my horse."

"Well, I have the proof sheets here. We have made all th
changes we discussed by letter, but it is a question in thes
stories of yours of running the danger of accidentally re
vealing who the victims are." He seated himself behind h
cluttered desk as he indicated a chair for her. "You woul
not want any unpleasantness to arise." He looked at he
significantly.

"I have already changed the physical descriptions an
most of what they said. I would think only the actual peo
ple that were robbed might possibly recognize the rest of th
circumstances."

"Oh, in that case, if you are sure you changed every
thing identifiable—interesting idea, set of tales told by
highwayman. If I may say, you seem to have the dialec
down pat. They are all real, are they not?"

"Yes, they really are stories told me by a highwayman
not all his own, of course, and some of them happene
decades ago. I should not think anyone would even car
about them any more." Mr. Croft looked at her somewha
dubiously and she began to worry that she did not look ver
convincing as a man.

"I know it seems as though I keep odd company," sh
said to cover an awkward pause, "but the fellow is retire
now, and he never really hurt anyone. Half the time m
highwayman came off worse than his so-called victims."

"Yes, I particularly liked that one where the jewels turned out to be fake. That gave old Hughes quite a chuckle, too. Well, let me see, if you have changed the physical descriptions—certainly there are no names mentioned—I think we should be safe enough. I have the contract ready if you want to read it."

Jenner glanced down the page. It read much like the agreement for *The Highwayman* which had been sent by mail, except that, instead of a mere one hundred and twenty pounds, the amount agreed upon this time was two hundred and fifty. They had negotiated this as the revisions went back and forth, but Jenner got the impression the price and the publication of the book itself were contingent on her making a personal appearance.

"Are the terms satisfactory?"

"Quite," she whispered as she took up the pen, signed her name and accepted the check he had ready for her. She gazed at it a moment in disbelief. It was a third of the entire annual income of Fallow Farm and more than enough to replace their aging stallion. "There is one other thing," she said as she rose. "If anyone should inquire for my address I would like you to refuse to give it—especially to Lord Raines. I live with my aunts and I don't want them bothered."

"I would not give out your address in any case. By the way, are you working on anything else?"

"I have an idea, but I have not figured out an ending yet. Perhaps something will come to me while I am in town."

"Stop and see us again, please. I am sure Hughes will want to meet you. Where are you staying?"

"Actually I am staying with Lord Raines. His house is in Grosvenor Street."

"Oh, a friend of yours?" Croft asked, mystified.

"No, he is the one who ran me down on the road."

Mr. Croft looked a bit startled. "I was almost forgetting, there are a few pieces of mail for you. If anything else should arrive I will forward it to Lord Raines' house."

"Yes, that would be kind of you," Jenner said as she took the envelopes and left.

Next, she visited a bank, the receiving office, and spent an hour in Piccadilly Street choosing gifts for her aunts. She was not feeling particularly like shopping, but she thought a few hours might give Raines' temper a chance to cool. Jenner walked back to Grosvenor Street and was somewhat embarrassed to have trouble recognizing Raines' house, for there was little to distinguish it from the facade of all the other inscrutable stone-fronted residences along the fashionable street. She turned and looked back toward Grosvenor Square and the immense green of Hyde Park beyond. She was sure it was in the middle of the block and was about to backtrack when she recognized Edwards dusting the piano in the music room. When she knocked at the street door the butler took his time answering and evinced a tired surprise at seeing her again. He replied to her question that Lord Raines had gone out hours ago.

She passed the remaining time before dinner in the small book room. She opened the mail Croft had given her. They were invitations to events now past, and she discarded them and sat down at a small table facing the window to write to Aunt Bette and Aunt Milly. She confined her letter to a description of the countryside between Thetford and London and the news of the huge sum she had been paid for her stories. She cautioned them to write her in charge of the receiving office and asked them to let her know what treats to bring them. She did not think she would stay longer than it took to find Aunt Bette's new stud since the matter of the book had been resolved so quickly. Raines she did not mention at all. She had just read this over and was sealing it when an iron hand clamped down on her shoulder so hard it made her grunt in surprise and sent her heart pounding.

"If you ever pull another trick like that, I will know how to deal with you," Raines said into her ear.

"I wish you would not come up behind me like that. It cannot be good for me."

"Neither is chasing all over London good for me. Hughes and Croft!" he said jubilantly. "Too bad neither one was in. Now, come have your dinner. You have not eaten for more than a day. You should be perishing by now."

"I never get very hungry," Jenner said nervously, thrusting the letter in her coat pocket. Although being pounced on had been unsettling, she was puzzled that he was not more angry with her.

Actually, when Raines had returned home to find Jenner placidly writing in the book room, his overwhelming emotion was relief. There was some mystery about Jenner he had to solve before he was willing to let him go. In fact, nothing had interested him half so much in years.

Jenner was still sweating over the near miss with the letter. She had written no direction on it yet, but if Raines had been bold enough to wrest it from her and read it he might surmise the direction of her home.

They dined simply and alone. Raines seemed to be more amused by her trick than annoyed that she had bested him. She wondered what they would talk of with only the two of them sharing a meal, but Raines seemed quite capable of carrying the conversation so long as she paid attention and prompted him with questions. She particularly asked about buying horses in London. Raines volunteered to take her to Tattersall's and to introduce her to several of his cronies who could put her in the way of a good stud.

Jenner began to think that Raines had finally accepted her at face value until she caught him checking the level in her wineglass. She was used to him keeping scrupulous account of what she ate, but why had he given her wine if he did not think she could handle it? Suddenly it occurred to her that he might be planning on getting her drunk. Her suspicion was confirmed when he let Edwards fill her glass with port. She didn't much like it, but she downed it as best she could. It made her feel warm and sleepy but did nothing toward loosening her tongue.

After dinner they retired to the music room where Jenner played some pieces from memory. "That reminds me, I should buy some new music while I am here so I have something to learn this winter. I do not have much time to play in the summer when we are busy training."

"What do you mean, training?"

"Hunters and hacks—Aunt Bette raises them. Aunt Milly runs a pretty thrifty little farm. Between the two enterprises we manage to keep the place going. I am more use with the horses, of course. I suppose I have not the patience to deal with vegetables. Something is always chewing on them that should not. Do you have a country place?"

"Yes, near Kettering."

"What is the country like out that wa—" Jenner glanced up guiltily, and Raines smiled with satisfaction.

"So you are not from the Midlands."

"I must be getting tired."

"I should say so, to make a blunder like that. I suggest you go to bed. I have some reading I want to do." He waved *The Highwayman* under her nose.

Raines did not finish the book that night but did sit up late chuckling over Chad Bostwick's adventures and leafed to the back to make sure the fellow did not end on the gallows. It did not even occur to him that his valet and butler thought it strange for him to sit home reading his second night back in town, especially after the failure of his errand at Ingham.

* * *

"I expected him to take that young fellow's head off," Edwards confided to Collins, "when he caught him at Miss Claridge's piano, but he sits himself down and listens for a good half hour."

"The Page lad came along just at the right time. He seems to have charmed my lord out of the blackest mood I have seen him in these seven years."

"That Miss Dawson never turned him down!"

"She must have," Collins affirmed, "for he flung himself into the room in the middle of the day, gave me ten minutes to get his gear together and went off to order up the carriage himself. Let me tell you, that was quite a ride! I was afraid to so much as look at him. And he kept telling the coachman to move it along through the worst fog I have ever seen. We were lucky we did not kill the boy."

"Does he mean to keep him here?"

"I think until he's satisfied that the lad is recovered. A strange boy, to take Raines' interference and moods in such good part. Most lads would have flared up at him. But I expect he is still feeling knocked up from the concussion."

Jenner fell asleep trying to devise a way to discourage Raines' interest in her. If she simply left, she had no doubt he would be stubborn enough to hunt her down. That she had come back from her successful escape that day might throw him off his guard. Why she had come back was something that continued to puzzle her. She could easily have sacrificed her few possessions. But she had not said goodbye or thanked him. She could quit London altogether, disappear home again, but she really did want to find a horse for Aunt Bette. And even she knew she was in no frame to manage a stallion just yet, either riding or leading him. It was easy to persuade herself to tarry as Lord Raines' guest for a few days, even though it was unwise.

Jenner had another good night and in the morning tried the effect of ringing for assistance. She asked for a bath and lounged comfortably in bed sipping her tea until the tub had been filled by two able footmen. She carefully locked her door, then prepared to luxuriate in the steaming water.

It was at this moment that Raines, hearing the activity in Jenner's room, decided to wander over to discuss *The Highwayman*. He went through the common dressing room, but when he opened the door into Jenner's room he was arrested by the sight of the back of a slender well-muscled female wearing nothing but a bandage on her hand stepping into a tub. Ordinarily this would not have been an odd occurrence in his house, but he was nonplussed, which was an unusual sensation for him. He put down his first impulse and silently closed the door and went to his room to consider the situation. The thought that there was a woman so accessible and so completely at his mercy brought on a sudden rush of desire for her, but he still had trouble reconciling in his mind the fully mature woman he had just seen with the bothersome boy he had picked up near Halstead.

He lay down to get himself under control. It did explain many things, especially Jenner's reluctance to divulge any information about herself. But why she was roaming around dressed as a man was one thing he would insist on knowing before she got away from him. Thinking back on the past few days, he began to be amused by Jenner's predicament and was tempted to see how long she could carry on with it. But that would mean him behaving himself, and he did not intend to. Whatever Jenner's purpose, it could not be so innocent as to merely purchase a horse and, by her own admission, she was already a woman of some experience.

Raines was already seated in the breakfast parlor having coffee when she entered and he asked after her health. She replied, as always, that she felt fine. The meal proceeded as normally as any she had shared with him, except that he had a book open by his plate reading, a habit he deplored in her. The significance of this did not strike her until he looked up and said, "You are really not a virgin, are you?"

Jenner choked and spent a full minute attempting to figure out how to answer him and how he had found her out. But then he raised the book, and she said with relief, "How could I be and write that? But really, chapter twelve is a bit heavy going for the breakfast table. I thought you did not approve of reading during meals." She took a gulp of tea to clear her throat.

"Not ordinarily. But I really could not put it down. How did you discover what a woman actually feels? Did you ask her?"

She opened her mouth, but stopped when she realized she was going to lie to him for the very first time. It seemed a poor way to repay all the care he had taken of her. Then she saw that his eyes were laughing at her and she shook her head. "You know, don't you? What gave me away?"

By way of answer Raines rose, came around to her chair, bent down and kissed her. She was too stunned to either return or repulse his embrace. It was such an odd thing to happen in a breakfast parlor. He chuckled and walked to his seat. "It was an accident, actually. I walked in on you in your bath."

"But that is impossible," she said, blushing. "I locked the door."

"Not the one that connects with my room."

Jenner jostled her teacup with her still clumsy right hand and sloshed the hot liquid into the saucer. She shook her head. "I thought that was a closet."

"I had you put in the adjoining room so I could hear you if you got feverish in the night. You will observe that the door has a lock and a key if you choose to use it. I do play fair, you see. But you will not get away from me until I know your story. Now, finish your breakfast. We have things to do.''

Jenner was too stunned to do other than obey him. She was strangely relieved that she no longer had to deceive Raines, but even more conscious of her predicament than before in spite of Raines' assurance of fair play. In point of fact she was much less worried about what Raines might do than about what she might do.

It was a strange day altogether, for Raines treated Jenner just as he had when he thought she was a boy. She could not imagine why, now that he knew about her, he would flaunt her at his tailor's, visit his club, or take a drive in the park, where he greeted and introduced her to an alarming number of respectable-looking people. It took her the whole day to figure out what game he was playing. He was gambling, and the risk was fantastic. It was one thing for people to know he had a mistress in keeping, quite another for him to introduce her to them. If her identity was ever discovered it would not just be a famous joke, it would ruin him utterly. But perhaps that was what he wanted.

As they drove home she realized with a start that she had automatically classified herself along with his other mistresses. Stealing a look at his handsome profile, she thought there was nothing she would rather be. But she did have responsibilities, and her stay in London could not last more than a few short weeks. So she determined not to form an attachment to Lacey Raines, as though it was a thing she could control by an effort of will.

Dinner was suspenseful for Jenner, for she still had not decided what she was going to do. Lacey had to recall her from a reverie several times when she was getting behind him in courses. She had slipped away once. She might be able to do so again. But it seemed such a cowardly thing to do. If she locked him out, would he accept that decision?

What could he really do to her with servants all about? She could always appeal to them for help. This seemed more craven even than running, for in this matter he would be at her mercy.

Raines spoke, as always, of horses and hunting, wagers and matches, very much as though he were still talking to a country lad. Was that to put her at her ease, she wondered. Was he not even going to speak of love and seduction? Was he going to make no attempt to persuade her to become his lover? He seemed so terribly sure of himself. No—it was not that. He was not sure, she thought, as she watched him lounging in his chair, a smile lurking about his mouth. What he was enjoying was the uncertainty. In what must have become for him a rather boring daily routine, she had presented him with a unique situation. Whatever way she played her cards he would, as he said, play fair. But the outcome of the evening was entirely up to her.

She tortured him after dinner with the most religious music she could think of, then primly bade him good-night. As she undressed and got herself to bed she felt giddy, and not just from the wine. She had been without Rob for a year and it had been far from easy to give him up. Only her fears for the highwayman's life could have parted her from his companionship. It was not just sleeping by him during their stolen nights in the woods around Fallow Farm that she missed. Not having Rob to talk to had left a terrible void in her life. She missed having someone so close she could tell him anything and he would not think the less of her for it.

She got up and opened the door into the small dressing room. It was dark and airless with no window, and she detected a faint trace of scent as she held her candle aloft. It was feminine, yet dangerous, somehow. She finally decided it must be a residue from Elaina's clothes. Odd that it should linger here so long after the woman had departed. She wondered how much of Raines' love for the woman still

remained. She closed the door behind her and resolutely
locked it, chiding herself for how quickly Raines had re-
placed Rob in her affections. Would she have fallen so easily for just any pair of glittering eyes?

What she was contemplating was the height of foolish-
ness. She should consider herself well off from her previous dangerous affair and take it as a lesson not to involve
herself with another man, especially not one as unpredictable and high-handed as Raines. She could not believe that
she knew him well enough after one short week to have
fallen in love with him. He could easily grow piqued with
her and denounce her publicly. Yet she liked him and found
herself trusting him in spite of all the warnings from her
more sensible side. To lock this man out now was to close
the door on love forever. Such an opportunity would not
come again. Surely she was safe enough. She had been
careful to give him no clue to her identity or direction. She
could disappear at will, and he would never be able to find
her. That was her physical side talking.

Like a sleepwalker she must have gotten in and out of bed
half a dozen times to lock or unlock the door, and when she
heard Raines and Collins in the other room she was still un-
decided. Finally, in a half sleep, she couldn't remember if
the door was locked or not and was so tired of wrestling with
the dilemma that she convinced herself she did not care. She
knew she was trying to abdicate the responsibility for her
actions, and she lay there between the sheets with the blood
pounding hot in her veins wondering what would come from
her decision.

Then she heard the door open. With a short laugh Raines
threw off his dressing gown and slid into bed. He came up
against her naked flesh and groaned in expectation. He felt
her all over as though he needed to know every part of her.
She was almost drunk from his kisses and responded to
every stroke of his hands as though he was already inside

her. He was fully extended by the time he entered her and she was wet with expectation. She knew a moment's fear that he might actually hurt her, but her hunger was so great she only kissed him more passionately. It seemed to her she could not be close enough to him to satisfy herself. It was only by a great effort that she did not cry out, but she could not still the small gasps that escaped her as his rhythmic assault set off ripples of pleasure in her stomach. She gripped him with her internal muscles, and it was his turn to moan as he found release inside her. They were both panting and heaving for some minutes. They fell asleep in their locked embrace.

"Did I hurt you?" he asked some hours later when she turned in his arms.

"No, of course not," she whispered.

"I have a feeling you would always say that. How is your head?"

"Not thumping as much as the rest of me."

"Now tell me how you came to be doing such a madcap stunt."

"I thought it would be safer..."

"Safer?"

"To come to London as a man, rather than travel on the coach myself."

"You must be mad."

"I have been thinking that for quite some time. Does it matter?"

"Not a bit. Why were you coming to London?"

"I already told you. I had to see about my book. I would have had to put on men's clothes once I got here anyway, for Hughes and Croft think I am a man. I am not sure they would pay me so much if they were to find out who I really am."

"And who are you really?"

"Nobody."

"I will find out, you know."

"You might be better off if you didn't. I am not a respectable person. After all, I do consort with highwaymen—or one, anyway."

"How did that come about?"

"He stole my horse. Tallboy, in fact. I was out riding alone and he had a gun and took the horse. His must have been shot from under him. I followed him. It was not difficult for he was bleeding from a wound and the closer I got, the more blood there was on the track. He was collapsed in a ruined shepherd's cottage. Tallboy would have wandered home again if Rob had not been tangled in the reins when he fell. I had to bind up his wound or he would have bled to death. And he looked so helpless."

"Where is he now?"

"America, I hope. I gave him half the money from *The Highwayman*. I hope he has actually gone. Though he has never murdered anyone, if he were ever caught he would spend a long time in prison. And that would kill him."

"You paid him?"

"It was his story. He deserved something for it. And I wanted him to have another chance."

"Are you—do you love him?"

Jenner thought for a long moment. "I care about him, certainly, perhaps because he was the first man I ever really knew—no, I don't mean that. He was the first man I had even been around very much, so he was rather fascinating—and his scars. By the way, you have one or two that..."

"Don't ask," Lacey commanded.

"Anyway that is how *Bridle Lay* got started. He was telling me how he came by all of them. I learned a great deal from Rob."

"Yes, I agree."

She laughed. "And no, I do not mean just that. He taught me to fence, you know. I am not very good, I suppose, but it was fun. And he taught me to play cards. He even taught me to cheat, not that I would, but I think I would know if someone else were."

"Did he also teach you to hold up coaches?"

"No, he had very strict rules about that."

"A man of principle."

"No, he just liked to work alone."

Lacey chuckled. "But you are not in love with him."

"Is that important to you? No, if I had been I do not think I could have let him go. We both knew there was no way for us to be together forever."

"But you do miss him?"

"I get hungry for him at night," she said, sliding her hand down Lacey's thigh. "Does that sound selfish?"

"It is the kind of thing I would shock people by saying."

"I did think about going with him, but I have my aunts to look after. I owe them a great deal."

"You do have aunts, then?"

"Yes, I told you." She turned to face him. "Did you think I was lying?"

"I thought if you were, you were good at it."

"How am I to take that?" She laughed.

"Any way you like. I suppose you want to hear about my lovers now."

"I do not think so. They must have been stupid to have left you."

"You do not know me very well. I can be careless and cruel. I left them here for weeks at a time alone, came back when I felt like it, left again without telling them."

"It sounds to me as though you were bored with them and you wanted them to leave."

"I wonder if you are right. Not Elaina, though. I bought my commission in time to see the last few years of the Peninsular campaign. She was not waiting for me when I got back. At least she did not remove any of the furniture like the others.''

"Is that why you are so panicked when I go out? You think I might be making off with the silver?''

"No, I feel somehow responsible for you, even more so now.''

"Why? You owe me nothing. You have been kinder to me than I deserve.''

"After nearly killing you? I do have some shreds of conscience left. Besides, I do owe you something, a horse.''

"A horse, the other reason I came to London. We will soon have to retire our old stud. Aunt Bette has entrusted me to pick out a new one.''

"And take him the whole way back home yourself.''

"That's why I brought Tallboy, so I could lead the stallion. Besides, it's not all that—I'm going to have to watch myself. You are a lot trickier than Rob.''

"Yes, notice how masterfully I tricked you into making love to me—by daring you.''

"Perhaps I just forgot to lock the door and fell asleep.''

"You could have screamed.''

"And been throttled by you?''

"If I throttle you it will not be for that reason. You are the most provoking girl I have ever met.'' He kissed her.

She threw back the covers and crawled on top of him. Her warm weight brought him on again and he bounced her up and down on his shaft until she was gasping with delight. At the end he clutched her to him and she slid down beside him, basking in the warmth of his body.

"If there should be a child . . .'' Raines began dutifully.

"There will not be. I was pregnant once—not Rob's child. Mercifully, I lost the baby, but the doctor said I would never carry another one. Please do not ask me about it.''

Lacey covered her up, held her even tighter and kissed her hair. That is how Collins found them in the morning, Jenner curled up inside Lacey's strong arms. They woke when the tea tray Collins was carrying crashed to the floor. Jenner was appalled. Lacey was laughing in the most provoking way. Collins stayed only long enough to gather the debris.

"You have to tell him, Lacey. You cannot have him thinking that."

"Why not?" Lacey laughed.

"Much as you may enjoy shocking people, I do not think you would want such a joke to interfere with your own comfort. I do not believe he will stay with you or, if he does, he will treat you very coldly. Besides, if you will not tell him, I will."

"Oh, very well."

Lacey went to his room and rang for his valet.

"I wish to give notice, sir," Collins said coldly as he laid out Lacey's clothes.

"Why? Am I not paying you enough?"

"No, sir, you pay me very well. It is because of your...houseguest, sir."

"You did not object to the last mistress I kept here."

"Miss Claridge was a woman, sir."

"So is Jenner."

Collins dropped Lacey's boots to the floor so carelessly it caused his employer to remonstrate with him.

"I don't believe it!" Collins gasped.

"I am not going to ask her to strip for you." Lacey laughed. "I assure you she is a woman, and a rather attractive one under her male attire. You will just have to trust me on this one."

"But this is extraordinary."

"Yes, I think so, too. Now listen. I want you to follow her when she goes out without me. I must discover who she really is. Also, I do not want her roaming around London alone.''

"Won't she tell you?"

"No, nor why she will not tell me. There is some mystery about the girl, and I intend to solve it. In the meantime you are to treat her exactly as you always have. That should not be too difficult. Can you manage it?"

"I don't know," Collins said, wide-eyed.

"Well, you had better, for you will have to do for her as well as me. It is not as though we can hire her a maid."

Jenner had been in the bookstore some time and was so enjoying prowling through the dusty and cluttered aisles she did not realize it had started to rain until she chanced to look out the window. She stepped to the door then and called to Collins, who appeared sheepishly from between two buildings. "Come inside, man. Lacey will never forgive me if you catch cold on my account. Besides, I will need some help hauling all these books back to his house."

"He is not going to be happy with me that I was so clumsy."

"Then I suggest you not tell him you were clumsy. I certainly don't intend to— See if you can find the rest of this set, will you?"

Collins obediently scoured the opposite shelves for the missing volume. "But if you know I am following you, that means you could evade me at any time."

"Well, not any time. By the way, did it not occur to you that Montague House might have more than one entrance?"

"No," he said in helpless exasperation, "Is this it?"

"Perfect, Collins. Thank you," Jenner said, taking the volume. "Do you imagine I would leave without telling anyone? I could not—not with all these books, at any rate!"

At first Jenner could not imagine how this arrangement with Collins would work out, but as Lacey had told her, the man had served him through three mistresses and his whole time in the Peninsula, so pretending to serve a young gentleman who was actually a female was not much of a stretch for him. Her shirts and neck cloths appeared freshly laundered in her room as if by magic. Her boots and shoes were never unpolished, nor her coats unbrushed.

Each morning Collins tapped first on her door, since she usually awoke earlier. If it was locked or they answered him he entered through Lacey's room and gave them a decent interval to sort themselves out before returning with a tea tray. If they slept in Lacey's room Collins reversed the strategy. Jenner was amazed at how easily it all resolved itself. But then the arrangement was probably not much different when Elaina was here except for the presence of a maid.

They went to Lacey's tailor, where the black coat and breeches that had been so quickly produced received a final nip and tuck. Lacey smirked at Jenner's grimace as the tailor checked her measurements once again. She considered this almost as great a risk as being attended by a doctor. Lacey gloried in the audacity of it. Lacey had also ordered other coats, several pairs of pantaloons for her and an alarming number of shirts and neck cloths. Visits to his boot maker and haberdasher were equally fruitful.

Jenner was amazed at how quickly custom clothes could be produced. Lacey's taste was impeccable, and he had a flair for disguising her primary defect, her shortness. Five and a half feet was fine for a woman, but not very convincing in a man. Fortunately the current fashion for large, elaborate cravats disguised her slender neck. Her shoulders were square, requiring less padding than some gentlemen needed, and her muscular thighs did justice to the skintight pantaloons.

She had become used to Lacey showing her off in the parks and on the streets, but as they prepared to depart the house one night she said, "I don't understand what I want with evening dress. Surely I do not need it for the theater."

"You do if you are going with me."

"You think I do not know what you are about, but it is the excitement of deceiving everyone that has you so keyed up. Have you thought about what will happen if I am found out?"

"Not at all."

"I did not think so."

"Do you want to go to the play tonight or not?"

"Yes."

"Then hold still," Lacey demanded as he adjusted her cravat.

They did not cause much of a stir at the theater, at least not that Jenner perceived, but she became so absorbed in the play she scarcely noticed she was being pointed out occasionally.

"Did you like it?"

"It was wonderful, but we are heading in the wrong direction, are we not?"

"I thought we would call in at Lady Ember's ball. You did get an invitation."

"How did you know that?" Jenner asked suspiciously.

"I look over all your mail."

She laughed at this. "That will not get you anywhere. Do you think I am stupid enough to give my aunts your address?"

"Evidently not." Lacey was beginning to seethe a little.

"You can go on to this party. Let me go back to your house. I promise I will."

"No, you accompany me tonight."

"We could both go back to your house," she suggested provocatively, laying a hand on his shoulder.

"You tempt me, little vixen. That will come later anyway."

"Not if I am too tired."

"Then I will make love to you in the morning. But you are coming with me."

They went on haggling until they reached Lord and Lady Ember's well-lit house and Lacey stopped Jenner in the hall to inspect her.

"Remember, you do not look your age for a man, so do not go around saying you are three and twenty. They will have trouble enough believing you are a writer." Lacey gave her neck cloth a final adjustment.

"It is no very great thing to have written a few books when you have nothing much else to occupy you. In fact, I am writing one now."

"What is it about?"

"I think it may be about me."

Dancing was in full swing, and Jenner knew a moment of panic. "Lacey, I won't be expected to dance, will I?"

"I don't see why not. They are always looking for partners for young ladies."

"But I never did dance much, and I am not sure I could turn those steps around in my head."

"You prefer to go to the card room with me?"

"I prefer not to be here at all," Jenner said rather forcefully.

"So this is the young author?" A tall matron surmounted by an egret headdress accosted them and Lacey abandoned Jenner to the conversation of this and several other women. "I must say the highwayman in your book seems quite authentic. How did you know how he would talk?" her hostess asked.

"I have encountered one, and I have a good ear for that sort of thing."

"You mean you were held up?" an older lady asked in some concern.

"Not exactly. I think perhaps he had just intended to steal my horse, but when he got the idea I was a young gentleman he thought of holding me to ransom." Jenner had her story pat and ready, but did not spill it like a child reciting. She let them pull it out of her a question at a time, all the while looking shyly confused at the attention she was attracting. Why not? This was very close to how she felt.

"How long did he hold you?" a proud-looking woman unbent to ask.

"Three days." Jenner took a sip of champagne and studied her audience. She would not have thought they could suddenly look so motherly in their stiff silks and revealing muslins, jewels glittering on their white breasts.

"Intolerable! Could not your parents free you sooner?"

"They are both dead, and my aunts are used to me arriving or setting off without notice, so no one really knew I was missing. And the note my highwayman delivered did not enlighten them. He could not read, you see."

"Was not that taking a bit of a chance?" a classical beauty asked as she fanned her sweet scent in Jenner's direction.

"I suppose, but he did not seem to want to hurt me. I cannot believe he had ever done anything like that before. He did not even know how to go about it."

"But how did you get away from him?"

"Eventually he just kept my horse and let me go. I think perhaps I talked too much, or else he started to like me and decided he could not kill me."

To Jenner's surprise several ladies nodded understandingly to this most spurious part of her tale.

"Your book is based on his life then?"

"Only very loosely. The towns and villages I describe I have seen myself."

"Are you related to the Pages from Mansfield?"

Jenner looked surprised. "If so it would only be distantly. My father was an American."

"And your mother's people . . . ?" her oldest interrogator asked.

"Disowned her when she married him. They tolerate my visits, but they do not approve of me." Jenner said this with a certain embarrassment, and they all took the hint and did not inquire any further into her heritage.

Lacey flirted with a dozen women that night, always in sight of Jenner, and always looking to draw a jealous response from her. Jenner was too occupied keeping out of trouble to do more than glance appealingly at him from time to time. As for him making up to all those women, she was sure she did not own him, and there was no reason he should not flirt outrageously. When it occurred to her that she was feeling jealous she laughed and relaxed a little. What a mischief maker he was. And what exactly was he trying to do, get her to betray herself? She did feel a little angry with him but, if it came to denying him her bed, she did not think she would do it, for she enjoyed him far too much.

Those few in attendance who had read *The Highwayman* were rather skeptical until they had quizzed her about the book and vowed they could hardly wait for her next piece to be available. Even those ladies who had not read her book thought her so unaffected and shy, not at all like some of the authors they had met, that they were disposed to like her, especially when Jenner admitted that she was afraid to dance. In a world where few people could afford to say what they really meant, her frankness was appealing. And her awkwardness, when they did persuade her to waltz with one of the daughters, made them feel her to be a safe partner, not the sort who would cause them any worry.

Lacey, on the other hand, who was welcome enough to flirt with the married women, was the bane of those with impressionable daughters. It was as though he picked the most disapproving matron he could find and went after her child. He had no real designs on the girl, he just enjoyed creating the fulminating stares and shocked whispers. He needed an introduction, of course, which he procured easily enough from his hostess, who left the nervous girl being deftly courted by him. The child moved uncertainly in his arms at first, casting her eyes down in an effort to remember all her mama had taught her about handling such men. But under Lacey's charming influence she was in a few short minutes chatting happily to him, adoring him with her eyes.

Jenner wondered if it was always so easy for Lacey. She herself had succumbed to the devilish gleam in those eyes. She wondered if he felt anything beyond the physical for her. If he did not, she would be disappointed in him. If he did, then she had served him a backhanded turn to have started a relationship with him knowing that she would so shortly be leaving him. A slight frown marred her boyish face when Lacey returned to her.

"Not jealous, are you?"

"What?"

"You look upset."

"I think I begin to understand the game you play, but what is behind it? What purpose does it serve?"

"None whatsoever. Does that bother you?"

"What a strange world you live in. If these people had any real worries, such as being hungry, they would not play such malicious games." She did not succeed in disguising the contempt in her reply, and when he stiffened, his nostrils flaring, she smiled at him. "I am sorry. I have no right to criticize. You were raised to this life and I was not."

"I introduce you to the cream of London society, the people most likely to pay money for your books, and you turn up your nose at them."

"Does it seem so? I had not meant it to, for I sincerely like some of them. It is only that their lives seem so... limited. I would have thought they would do something more worthwhile with their leisure."

"I suppose next you will be wanting to hear the debates in Parliament."

"Do you think I can get in?"

"I knew it."

In the end it was Lacey who tired of the prattle and came to get Jenner, who was caught up in a discussion with a forbidding-looking, but altogether intelligent, woman who knew all about politics and economics.

"Time for bed, Jenner. I am surprised your head is not aching from all the chatter."

The young woman stiffened, but Lacey only shrugged. "He did not mean that, Miss Sutton," Jenner explained. "I had a bit of a fall last week and kept passing out for awhile."

"Oh, dear. Are you all right now?"

"He had a concussion, and was warned to get plenty of rest, to which end I am dragging him away."

Jenner thanked her hostess sincerely and to Lacey's query replied that she had liked the people fairly well once she got acquainted with them. "But what is the point, Lacey?" she asked as they began the walk home through the lighted streets of Mayfair.

"Does there have to be some purpose? Can't we just have an amusing evening together?"

"I suppose so, but if you intend at one of these affairs to unmask me, I would like some warning."

Lacey stopped in his tracks. "How could you think I would do something like that to you?"

"Don't get upset," Jenner said hastily, feeling guilty at having misjudged him. "I was only joking."

"You must have a very poor opinion of me."

"I suppose I just do not understand you. I mean, I can see how playing this little game could be exciting, but the risks... It cannot be worth it."

"Very well then, you need not come with me any more."

"I did not mean to make you angry." She had to walk at her fastest pace to keep up with him striding along in a passion like he was. After a few minutes of freezing silence, she asked, "Is it much farther?"

"Why?" he snapped, then stopped and looked at her. "Is it your head?"

"No, but I bruised my knee when I fell, and I have been on it more than usual today."

"You never told me that," Lacey accused.

"At the time I was trying to hide as much from the doctor as possible," she said as she caught up with him.

"Yes, even with your leg muscles, I think he would have realized the difference." Lacey laughed. "I will get a hackney."

Jenner feared he would not come to her that night. When he opened the door it must have been after a prolonged struggle with himself. "If you don't feel..." he began.

"Of course I feel like it, you idiot," she interrupted. "No matter how much we may argue, I would never use that against you."

"You are an unusual woman, then."

"I am not a stupid one, at any rate. I enjoy you too much to deprive myself of you. But you will have to get on top."

He laughed and came quickly this time, then held her through the remaining brief hours of darkness. When he awoke she was gone from the room and he knew as always a moment of panic, but her books and things were still laying about. He threw on his dressing gown and stepped into the hall calling for Collins, who informed him Jenner was just going out. Collins had been preparing to follow her

Lacey ran down the stairs as he was, threw open the front door and stopped Jenner getting into a hackney by asking where the devil she was going. As several interested spectators witnessed this scene, Jenner asked the driver to wait and returned to the hall.

"What is it, Lacey? You are acting very strangely."

"I just have the feeling that one of these times you are not coming back."

"I simply did not want to wake you. I am just going to the library and, yes, I am coming back."

"I will take you there myself if you give me half an hour."

Jenner stared hard at Edwards until he vacated the hall. "You would be bored stiff, and ten to one you would want to drag me to one of your clubs again. Well, I do not mind a mixed crowd, but when you take me some place reserved exclusively for men..."

"Did they offend you?" Lacey smiled as he relaxed finally and lounged against the wall.

"Of course not, but it comes under the category of not playing fair, to them, I mean. Doing it once was a joke, but I do not intend to apply for membership."

"You keep making up these rules for your conduct in a game that has no rules."

"There is always good sense to fall back on, Lacey."

"Give me your word—" he came to bar her way, "—that you will not leave without telling me who you are."

"No, but I will promise not to leave town without letting you know. You will have to be satisfied with that."

"Not good enough. I do not want to wake up to find another letter on my pillow some morning. Promise you will not leave without telling me face to face."

"In which case you can certainly stop me—I see." Jenner appeared to consider for a moment. "I will not leave town without telling you in person that I am going."

Lacey moved aside, but Jenner paused in the open door, turning her hat around and around in her hands. "You must still be half asleep, Lacey, to let that get by you." She looked sideways at him, a mischievous twinkle in her dark eyes. "How big is metropolitan London? You see, I can play fair, too."

"What has that got— You little devil. Big enough for you to lose yourself in, if you've a mind." He grabbed her, scratching her face unmercifully with his stubble as he kissed her. "You won't leave this house without telling me face to face that you are going."

"Agreed, now let me go, for my driver has probably given up on me."

Lacey released her reluctantly and watched her stride down the steps. For the first time he felt no fear of her running away from him. Why this was so important to him he was not sure. She was like no one he had ever met before, no woman, anyway. She asked nothing of him and did not attempt to trade her favors for hats or dresses. Why would she? She had a mind and a life of her own. What he felt for her beyond a startled admiration he was not sure. He did know that he did not want to lose her.

Chapter Three

Jenner began to wonder how she could bear to leave Lacey when the time came. Even after a few short weeks she was more attached to him than she had been to Rob. Best to make the break while she still had half her wits about her, but the question was, would he let her go?

She was still pondering how to get away from him when she came back to Grosvenor Street to a strange altercation. There was a post chaise and pair drawn up in front of the house, and a formidable looking woman was arguing with Edwards while a fair, long-nosed girl watched in distress from the carriage and a tall, proud-looking young man stood helplessly by. At least, the girl had the sense to stay in the carriage and not add to the commotion on the steps.

Lacey's house was not pretentious from the outside. It was separated from the street only by an iron railing and a short flight of steps. But there was no way for Jenner to mount the stairs and go inside with Edwards blocking the way, nor did it seem polite to do so. Instead, she introduced herself to the young gentleman, who turned out to be Lacey's nephew, Dennis Langley. Except for the brown hair, he did not resemble Lacey much. He had blue eyes and an open face with a hawklike nose. His sister, Stella, to whom he made Jenner known, was not a dazzling beauty, but when she smiled she was striking, and there was a genuineness about her that impressed Jenner before the girl had uttered a dozen words.

When the formidable dame stopped for breath, Dennis introduced his mother, Lady Caroline Langley. She was solid, tall and rather stately. Just now she was at a disadvantage, in having heightened color and somewhat disarranged locks from her verbal assault on the stolid Edwards.

"A fine thing to open his house to a perfect stranger and not to receive his own closest relatives."

"I am sure he didn't know you were coming," Jenner said truthfully.

"If I had written I was coming, he would have written telling me to stay at Kettering. I know my brother by now."

Jenner was having a little trouble following her logic. "I wish I could help you, but we can hardly expect Edwards to risk his position by disobeying orders. We will just have to wait for Lacey."

"On the street?"

"No, I think you should go to a hotel while I look for your brother. Edwards, where is Lacey?"

Edwards staggered a step and said stiffly, "He is not at home."

Jenner stared hard at the butler. "Which is to say he is at home, but only to certain people. Does he know who is calling?"

Edwards had never seen Jenner anything but docile, so the glittering eyes and set chin rather worried him. "I am to deny him to all company." Edwards skirted the issue.

"Including myself?" Jenner said, climbing toward him.

"No, of course not." Edwards stepped back as though to let Jenner pass.

"Where is he, then?"

"In the book room, sir," Edwards whispered as Jenner reached the top of the steps.

"In the—"

"Perhaps if you were to have a word with him, sir."

"I have only one word for him," she snapped.

Jenner brushed past Edwards, threw open the door to the book room where Lacey was sulking and said, "Coward," quite distinctly, then tramped on up the stairs. When Lacey caught up with her she was loading her books into the bottom of her valise.

"You are not leaving. I won't let you." He gripped her wrist so tightly it hurt.

"I should never have stayed in the first place. And now with your family here . . ."

"They are not staying."

"They have much more right to do so than I," she retorted.

"It is my house. They can have the one in the country. The least they can do is leave me alone in town."

"Are you their sole support?"

"Pretty much." Lacey released her and threw himself down on the bed.

"That must try your sister grievously," Jenner observed.

"I have never deprived them of any reasonable—"

"I meant that she looks to be an independent sort." Jenner paused in her packing. "It must enrage her not to be able to come and go as she pleases."

"How would I know? I keep away from her as much as possible. I purely cannot stand to live with her."

"You should do what my uncle did when Aunt Bette got on his nerves. Pretend to be deaf."

"Perhaps he really was deaf."

"I never thought of that. At any rate, he merely nodded at whatever she said and went about his business as though he had not even heard her. Eventually she gave up whatever it was she was plaguing him about."

"Sounds awful."

"You cannot keep them standing in the street, Lacey."

"Yes, I can. That is what I have a butler for. Jenner, we were getting on so well. This will ruin everything."

"Do you imagine I want to leave you? But I shall have to anyway in another week or so." She sat down beside him. "In the meantime you could come to my hotel."

"I cannot have them here. This is the only place I have ever been safe from Caroline."

"So that's it!" Jenner jumped up and began pulling clothes out of drawers.

"What?"

"Why you have always had a mistress in keeping! To fend off your sister."

Lacey looked confused. "No, that is not why."

"For someone who has risked flaunting me under the noses of the ton, I would have thought running an illicit love affair in the same house as your family would have a great appeal. I can think of nothing more dangerous and doomed to disaster," Jenner flung at him passionately as she went on folding and packing her clothes. "I shall have to mail the rest of my things."

Lacey caught her wrist again, gently this time. His eyes were alight with devilment. "If I let them in, will you stay?"

Jenner's resolve melted under that look, so full of hope. "Only until I find a horse for Aunt Bette."

"I will help you look." Lacey bounded off the bed and yelled for Edwards. Jenner could hear him going down the stairs and saying, "Of course I'm home to my sister, you idiot. Have their trunks brought in." Jenner could imagine Edwards' chagrin and started laughing in spite of herself.

"What did you think of the news that Napoleon has escaped his jailers?" Dennis asked Lacey as they all sat down to dinner.

"He must be mad to attempt such a thing." Lacey laughed. "He won't get far."

"They should have imprisoned him in another country, not treated him like deposed royalty with his own island," Dennis complained.

"They should have shot him!" Caroline said vehemently.

Jenner looked curiously at her.

"They don't execute prisoners of war, Mother," Dennis patiently explained.

"More's the pity."

"Any day now we shall hear he has been captured and returned," Lacey assured them.

Caroline's anger at Napoleon was only slightly greater than her irritation with Lacey for being so irresponsible as to bolt to town without telling them. Jenner could see Lacey sigh and stop listening to her lecture. There was something vaguely familiar about the speech. When it occurred to Jenner what it reminded her of, she laughed in spite of herself. Everyone turned to stare at her. "Sorry, but it has just struck me how much you remind me of Lacey," she said to Caroline.

"What?" Caroline and Lacey asked in unison.

"I was thinking of the drive to Halstead and the lecture you gave me on riding about in the fog."

Lacey shook his head. "Is that what I sounded like?"

"Just where did you and my brother meet, Mr. Page?" Caroline was still suspicious of someone she had never heard of, who had no relations, and who failed to respond to her prying questions with any but the vaguest nonsense.

"We ran into each other on the road to London."

Lacey chuckled. "When Jenner says we ran into each other, he means that quite literally. I ran him down with my carriage and nearly killed him. He had a concussion for a week and is only getting back on his feet now."

"Uncle, how could you?" Stella seemed truly concerned and looked at Jenner as though to make sure she was not going to collapse in front of them.

"Miss Dawson refused my offer. I was having them put along like a madman." Lacey took a large swallow of wine.

"So sorry, Lacey," Dennis said uncertainly.

"I knew it!" Caroline announced. "I knew something must have gone wrong when you did not come back to Kettering as you said you would. And when Hawes came for your riding horses I knew you were in London. It is all the fault of the life you have led. One scandal after another. I was a relief when you went mad and joined the army. At least we did not hear of your excesses, and it gave us the use of the town house for a few years so that I could bring Stella out."

Lacey looked at her from under furrowed eyebrows, his expression stopping Caroline effectively. "I needed to be away for a time."

"Well, as to that, it is all past history. I am sorry your suit with Miss Dawson did not prosper, but she is hardly the only available female in London at this season of the year. I know of at least a dozen who would not rebuff you, especially if they had reason to believe your wild days were at an end."

Lacey was beginning to look hunted and Jenner had nothing but sympathy for him. He was about to speak when she interrupted. "Lacey can hardly offer for someone else so soon in the face of this recent rejection. Aside from his feelings in the matter, think of the appearance it would make. He would seem more fickle than ever."

"That is true," Caroline observed. "You are very wise for one so young, Mr. Page. Perhaps you came to London intending to find a bride."

"No," Jenner said quickly and Lacey smiled with derision at her confusion. "That is to say I shall not be able to afford to marry for years and then only if my career prospers."

"Indeed. I think Stella will marry this season."

"Really? Who is the lucky fellow?" Jenner asked, glad to have attention drawn away from herself.

"I have not decided yet," Caroline said speculatively. Jenner turned to stare at her, openmouthed. Stella blushed and Dennis rolled his eyes. Lacey was looking rather aghast.

"It will involve a few parties, of course, perhaps a small ball."

"Not in this house!" Lacey thumped the table. "And there is no such thing as a small ball."

"Nonsense, you need not worry yourself over these things. It really need not even concern you, Lacey. You do not use the half of this house," Caroline said, looking around the large dining room. "Which reminds me, I must see Edwards about having the salons cleaned." Caroline rose and swept the helpless Stella before her out of the room.

"I am really sorry, Lacey," Dennis said. "I did try to stop her, but you know what she is like once she gets an idea in her head. It's the Dutch tulips all over again."

Lacey nodded, and Jenner, looking from one to the other, finally succumbed to her curiosity. "Tulips, did you say?"

"Yes, Mother took it into her head to replant all the gardens at Kettering in tulips. Drove Lacey's men crazy all one fall digging the beds. And I don't know what all those bulbs cost."

"What happened?"

"It looked fine the first spring, but evidently you are supposed to lift those things out again instead of planting right on top of them. At any rate no one did. Next year they were paltry."

"But we had the plumpest mice coming into the house you ever saw," Lacey reminisced.

"That doesn't sound so tragic. Anyone can make a mistake."

"Yes, but when she wanted to do it all over again that fall, Lacey lost his temper. That's when he moved to town."

"That was eight years ago," Lacey said.

"You have lived apart for eight years because of the tulips?" Jenner asked in amazement.

"Lacey comes for the hunting and the holidays."

"I consider it my annual penance."

"And I sneak up to town from time to time, or meet him at the races. Lacey, whatever happened to Elaina? I mean, I didn't expect to find her here, of course, but I was looking forward to seeing her again."

"She left. I don't know where she is now."

"Sorry. Well, I expect we had better go to the music room."

"What?" Lacey asked.

"Do you mind? That is where Mother asked to spend the evening."

"I suppose not."

Jenner wondered how Lacey's sister would deal with the portrait of Elaina smiling down at them from the wall, but Caroline seemed capable of ignoring the singer's presence in the room.

"Lacey, you have no sheet music here at all. We must find some for Stella. Play this one, dear. You do this so prettily. Dennis, turn for Stella."

Jenner was agreeably surprised by Miss Langley's performance. She played very sweetly and without conceit, and did not seem to expect an effusion of compliments when she was finished.

Inevitably Lacey turned to Jenner with his smug look. "Why don't you play something for us, Jenner?"

Knowing the sort of pieces she favored would overshadow Stella's delicate performance, Jenner remarked, "The piano is not really my forte." Lacey's eyes widened. "I much prefer the violin. You do have one here, I see." Jenner was unpacking the instrument when she glanced up. "Lacey, you cringed."

"I did not."

"Yes, you did. I definitely saw you."

"My brother is not overly fond of the violin, but I'm sure the rest of us would like to hear you play," Caroline said.

Jenner tested the tuning of the instrument and discovered that it had a depth, a sorrow and a joy hers did not possess. No one was more startled and enthralled by her performance than herself. She forgot to even look at Lacey. When the vibrations of the last poignant note died away she stood breathless and stunned. "Thank you."

"We should be thanking you, child," Caroline said. "That was beautiful."

"I had heard that with the violin the quality of the music depends almost as much on the instrument as on the player. I just didn't realize what a difference there could be." She put the instrument away reverently. "Do you mind if I go up now? I am rather tired."

Lacey nodded numbly. Jenner did not wait up for him, and she was sure he had not come to her room in the night. She had wondered if the presence of Caroline in the house would inhibit Lacey to some extent. She felt almost sorry she had insisted on him being kind to them, but it was his duty, even as she had her duty. And if these things drove them apart it was just as well, for there was no future in their relationship.

Jenner came down to breakfast the next morning to discover that Lacey could not face another meal so soon with his sister. Even more depressing than Lacey's shunning of his family was the news Dennis read them from the paper that Napoleon had not been arrested after his escape from Elba, but had reached Lyons, and that all the units sent to intercept him hailed him as their emperor again.

"That is the trouble with the French king welcoming all Napoleon's marshals to him with open arms," Dennis commented. "They are still in charge of the army, and the army is still loyal to Napoleon."

"Will they all go over to him, do you think?" Jenner asked.

"There is no telling. I would hope they could not all be so stupid. They have been roundly defeated, with the better part of the army destroyed in Russia. Whatever they do can only be regarded as a last gasp. Anyone with good sense will realize that," Dennis said confidently as he sipped his coffee.

"But does the French army know it?" Jenner asked.

"That is the problem. Whatever happens it could mean war again. I bet Lacey is wishing he had not sold out."

"He doesn't seem very worried, and I would think he would be a good judge of the situation," Jenner assured him.

"That's the problem. No one is taking it seriously," Dennis insisted.

"Must we have all this talk of war before breakfast?" Caroline demanded. "I think nothing should be read at the table except the society columns."

Dennis cast her a patient look and put the paper by for later.

When Dennis had left and Stella had gone to collect her bonnet, Caroline said pointedly, "Please stay a moment, Jenner. I want to talk to you."

Jenner wondered if some whisper of her and Lacey's relationship had reached his sister, and her mind raced as she tried to think how she would answer the woman. Jenner had felt they could rely on Collins' discretion, but Edwards had always been suspicious of her.

"Why doesn't my brother want us to stay here? Is it because of you? I should think his family had a better claim upon him."

Jenner looked at her empty cup, and something of her discomfiture prompted Caroline to say more kindly, "Lacey does not like me and my interference much. I suppose it is my fault he is estranged from us, but I thought he must have some feelings for Stella and Dennis, if not for me."

"That is exactly what he is thinking of," Jenner blurted out. "He does not consider me an acceptable companion for either your son or your daughter. Yet he is too stubborn to withdraw his invitation to me."

"I see nothing wrong with you, not with your manners, at any rate."

"But I make my living writing."

"What have you written?"

"*The Highwayman,* and another book of stories to come out soon."

"But I have read that. It's a splendid book. Of course, I have not let Stella read it, but I found it rather amusing."

The woman went on in this vein for some time and finally released Jenner, giving the impression that she was thrilled to be the patroness of a promising young artist. Jenner left the room looking rather bleak and numb.

Lacey was just coming down the stairs. "Ready to go look at horses? What the devil is the matter with you?"

"I was just talking to your sister."

Lacey smiled. "She frequently has that effect upon me."

"She thinks my book is wonderful," Jenner said in amazement. "Do you suppose she's got it mixed up with something else?"

Lacey looked a little taken aback but merely shrugged and took Jenner out the back door to the stables. "Do you feel well enough to go for a ride first?"

"Gladly, I have been missing that."

"Not dizzy any more?"

"Only when I listen to Caroline, but I expect there is no cure for that."

"That reminds me, I have a bone to pick with you. I tried not listening to her as you suggested, and she seems to think I have agreed to hold some sort of concert here."

"Sorry. It was just a thought. Let me know when it is and I will arrange to be elsewhere."

"You are not shabbing off. You will stay and suffer like the rest of us."

"But Lacey, in front of all those people, in your own house. It makes me feel queasy."

Lacey only chuckled at her discomfort, but Jenner began to wish she had not been so hasty in her vague promise to stay.

Lacey watched Jenner carefully for the first part of their ride, especially since his town hacks were a little fresh, prancing and fidgeting until they had reached the park where they could be let go for a gallop.

"How comes it that you ride astride so well? You cannot have had much practice at that—unless you pull this kind of stunt all the time."

"Most of the hunters my aunt and I train are for gentlemen, so I ride them astride. I have given up caring what our grooms think of me, or even the neighbors. I have no reputation anyway. And my aunts don't seem to mind that no one calls, so we rub along fairly well together. I heard from them, by the way. Aunt Bette has given me more particulars on the sort of stud she wants."

"How did it happen?"

"What?"

"The child?"

Jenner stiffened, then shrugged. "It was not my fault, if that's what you mean. I was overpowered. Consequently I lead a somewhat looser life than I otherwise would. Since the worst has already happened to me, no one worries about me very much.''

Though she said this lightly enough, Lacey could sense the profound hurt behind her bravado. It had the effect of making him rather thoughtful for the rest of the ride. He lagged slightly behind Jenner, the better to watch her. He tried to think what it would be like for a young girl to suffer that humiliation. Had he himself ever inflicted such a wound? He tried to think only of Jenner's hurt, to keep his mind off her physical presence, but the sight of her muscular thighs gripping the horse filled him with desire. He was on the point of suggesting they return to their adjoining rooms but the thought of Caroline in the same house was enough to discourage the idea.

"What happened to the grass?" Jenner turned to ask Lacey as they were leaving Hyde Park. "It looks like it has been overgrazed or trampled to death."

"It was—last year during the peace celebrations. It was the regent's idea to celebrate in the parks with a fair and fireworks. You can imagine what sort of people that attracted. There were tents everywhere. Whole alehouses moved all their stock-in-trade here. You could find a booth for anything you cared to do."

"Really?" Jenner asked in some amusement. "How would you know?"

"I was not being funny," Lacey said sternly. "It reminded me of a military encampment, but without discipline. And the theatricals and shows were nearly all in bad taste and an embarrassment to the English. I would have thought we could have behaved better in front of foreign dignitaries than using their visit as an excuse to profit. Once entrenched the rabble was not easily dispersed. The whole place was a quagmire this winter. It is only now starting to improve.''

"You think the parks should be reserved for the use of the ton?"

"You will not draw me into an argument on that. I only said things got out of hand."

Most of the horses for sale at Tattersall's were teams or riding hacks. There was nothing suitable for Aunt Bette's purpose, and Jenner was clearly disappointed. To cheer her up, Lacey called her attention to a satiny dark bay colt with black mane and tail. "How do you like him?"

"By his back and face he looks to have Arab blood. He's very young. Do you suppose he's broken to saddle yet?"

Jenner said nothing as Lacey paid rather dearly for the strutting young colt with the white blaze. "He will never replace Tallboy in your heart, but I think you will come to like him nearly as well."

Jenner looked shocked. "You bought him for me? I cannot accept him. Tallboy was not worth nearly so much."

Lacey looked extremely hurt so she said, "I do like him, though. I would like to try him." Lacey immediately brightened and Jenner had a feeling that Lacey had again gotten his own way.

Jenner rode Ebony that afternoon. "He's wonderful. You knew if I tried him I would not be able to turn him down, didn't you?"

"I counted on it."

"Tell me, do you usually give your mistresses such extravagant gifts?" she teased as she cantered along beside him.

"Oh, usually I spend more on them. You have come pretty cheaply, let me tell you." Where another woman would have taken offense Jenner laughed and urged Ebony into a smooth gallop. Lacey kept up with her this time, wishing they were riding through the woods at Kettering

here it would be possible to stop and make love without
eing disturbed.

A great many people watched Lacey laughing as he rode
ith his new protégé and wondered what he found to amuse
im so much in a mere boy.

Once Lacey's friends discovered he had returned to town,
e had little time alone with Jenner except for their morn-
ıg rides. Jenner savored these, for they combined her two
reatest pleasures, Lacey's company and that of a spirited
orse. They often went before breakfast when there was no
ne to be seen in the parks except a few army officers exer-
sing their mounts. Lacey seemed to know them but none
opped to be introduced, each merely sketched a wave that
as half a salute and rode on.

"You introduce me to all sorts of frivolous people, but
ever any of your army friends. Why?"

"Friends? I suppose we were close for a time, but what we
aared is something many of us would rather forget. I do not
ɔ so far as to cross the street to avoid speaking to them, but
can find nothing to say to them that does not seem trivial
ɔ me now."

"Do they feel the same?"

"I don't know. Some of them are more changed than
thers."

"Are you one of those so changed?" Jenner risked ask-
ıg.

Lacey hesitated. "What if I am? At the time I was numb
ɔ the horrors of it. And afterward I tried not to think of the
ɪtchery. You have no idea what happens when you march
ɛsh and blood up against cannon. For a time that was all I
ɔuld think of night or day," Lacey said without looking at
ɛr. "I tried to drink the visions away, but the dreams were
ɔre horrid than anything I had actually seen. I was afraid
ɔ sleep." His voice broke and he turned his eyes toward the

sleek and muscular horse. "I was almost demented. The
the numbness came back, and I stopped caring about any
thing, least of all what became of me."

"What happened then? How did you overcome it?"

"I didn't." Lacey laughed weakly. "I merely got dis
tracted."

"Distracted? By what?"

"A precocious boy who fell under my team's feet an
who has been turning my life inside out ever since."

Jenner tried to smile at this but the admission sent a chi
up her spine. If Lacey had so lately been that fragile, sh
could not predict the effect of her leaving him. She ha
thought her little adventure could have consequences onl
for herself, that it was only her heart she would be breakin
when she left. Now she realized that this was not so.

The men Lacey associated with were mostly older tha
himself, Corinthians and dandies whose bored letharg
covered some remarkable talents. Mr. Gros had a penchar
for landscape gardening. Sir Marlbeck painted portraits an
miniatures, not for pay, of course, but to amuse himsel
Only the most adroit and agreeable ladies could boast c
having been done by him. Lord Curtain was a dead shot, y
had no interest in shooting game, nor had he ever kille
anyone in a duel.

"No one will face me, you see," he explained to Jenne
"There are men who will cross the street to avoid giving m
offense. Damned boring."

"I should think if someone wanted to fight a duel yo
would be the safest opponent," Jenner replied.

Curtain stared at her.

"You could wing a man without even putting his life i
danger. I hardly think you could work up enough genuin
anger to intentionally murder someone."

Jenner had lingered after lunching with Lacey at White's and had just watched upwards of four thousand pounds change hands several times. It made her head spin, and she finally excused herself to go prowl among the shops along Oxford Street.

"What a strange lad," Gros observed after she left. "Young relative of yours?"

"Why, no, but I overrode him with my carriage and nearly killed him. I did kill his horse, in fact. I thought the least I could do was bring him up to town and buy him another."

"You paid pretty dearly for it, I hear," Marlbeck said with his twisted smile. He raised horses himself and kept up with what stock changed hands.

"At least it is not wasted on Jenner," said Lacey, discarding.

Curtain looked at Lacey rather strangely, his snakelike eyes belying the lethargy in his tall frame. Lacey moved uncomfortably under the penetrating gaze.

"Only a monster would have left him lying out of his senses at a common inn," Lacey said.

"I did hear you were compassionate to a fault," said Curtain.

"Has he regained his senses then?" Gros asked.

"Hard to say." Lacey laughed. "I do not know what Jenner was like before."

"He's . . . unusual for a boy his age," judged Marlbeck.

"Cold-blooded young wretch," Curtain insisted. "Does he think it would be a picnic to fight a duel with me?"

"No, he just gets curious about things. It's because he's a writer."

"Doesn't he know how dangerous I am?"

"I must have forgotten to warn him."

"A nobody, but interesting. Why did you take him up?" Gros asked.

"Jenner amuses me, sometimes infuriates me, but neve
bores me," Lacey said truthfully.

"I wonder if I should take offense at that?" Curtai
mused.

"You know you may shoot at me anytime you have
passion for blood," Lacey offered, "but I won't vouchsaf
what Jenner will do if you hit me."

"You have positively frightened me off," Curtain laughe
as he languidly picked up his cards.

Caroline said certainly Jenner would attend her musica
since she had promised several of her cronies the pleasure o
talking to him. Dinner on the eve of the concert was ver
nearly too much for Jenner as she began to realize the mag
nitude of her crime.

To ruin Lacey was bad enough but, if she were found ou
now, it would destroy the reputations of the Langleys a
well. Beyond that was the dread of what Caroline and Stell
would think of her. Even Dennis would be shocked. Wh
she cared so much after knowing them only a few days sh
could not explain. She was so used to being snubbed in he
own village that she had convinced herself she did not car
for anyone's opinion of her. It was startling to discover tha
she did care very much and that she liked the Langleys an
would miss them nearly as much as Lacey when she left.

It was only when Caroline and Stella rose from the tabl
that Lacey thought to ask, "What is the entertainment to b
tonight?"

"Fionello, the Italian pianist. Was I not lucky to get hi
to come?"

Lacey frowned but said nothing. "What is the matter?
Jenner asked when they had gone.

"Just something I heard, that this Fionello comes late,
at all. I wish I had known of this." Lacey shrugged. "But
matters not to me if the evening is a disaster."

"I think perhaps it does matter to you more than you ∎ink. She could not have known."

"Oh, Lord," Dennis said. "I wonder if it's too late for me ⸱ scamper off."

"Not a chance. You'll stick it out with the rest of us," ⸱acey said, rising from the table authoritatively.

Jenner had been curious to see if Caroline would attempt ⸱ remove the portrait of Elaina from the music room. It ardly seemed proper to have the picture of a former mis- ⸱ess presiding over the company. It was still there, but the ghting was so subtly arranged that it was on a dark wall nd drew no one's attention.

Caroline held up bravely for the first hour, busy greeting uests, but finally whispered to Stella, who shook her head nd blushed.

"Jenner, dear," Caroline said, coming across the room, ⸱you play so well. Oblige us for awhile."

"If you like, but they did not come to hear me. They are ke to be very disappointed."

Stella was looking through the music, but Jenner stopped ⸱er. "I looked through all that before, and I don't know any ⸱ it well enough. I will just play from memory, and you had ⸱etter hope I can remember enough to last until this Fionello ⸱ecides to appear."

"You are wonderful, Jenner," Stella said warmly.

Jenner pretended there were not forty odd strangers ⸱earing their throats and coughing as they took seats. She ⸱retended that she was at home playing for her aunts. She ⸱ayed all the Handel she could remember and all the Bach ⸱e dared. There was some whisper of conversation during ⸱r performance, but not enough to distract her. She was ⸱ying to decide if she should venture on to a piece of Mozart ⸱e had just learned but, in the interim, played a march she ⸱d composed, which she called "Home Journey of the ⸱ing." She noticed when she glanced up that the audience

was attentive and silent. There was a puzzled expression on
many faces, which made her smile. Of course they could no
identify it.

From there she moved immediately on to the first thing
she had done, "The Chase," a lively piece, inspired by the
flight of a highwayman. It was not more than seven min
utes long, though, and still no sign of the Italian. There wa
dead silence when she paused. In desperation she began the
series she called "Excursions," which Lacey had caught he
playing.

Once when she looked up she caught sight of Lacey. He
looked transfixed, as though he was seeing her for the firs
time. Half an hour later, as she was mounting the fina
theme, she realized she had no place to go from here. The
clock said nearly eleven, and she could only hope that Car
oline would rescue her after this piece. She finished and tool
her hands from the keys. There was silence for a few sec
onds as she stood shakily, then, to her confusion, ap
plause. While it was not thunderous it was certainly genuine
She almost fell over with relief and nearly forgot to bow
Caroline came toward her smiling and introduced Fionello
Jenner greeted him and humbly left the piano to take a sea
beside Lacey.

"Well done!"

"I thought it was going to be a disaster," she whispered
as she tugged at her cravat.

Fionello played for forty minutes, then rose to tremen
dous applause. Jenner was stunned by the sheer skill of the
man. He was immediately surrounded by appreciativ
ladies. Jenner might have been included in the congratula
tory group had she not slunk away to the refreshment salo
to try to settle her stomach with some champagne. As the
crowd entered the room Fionello came over to her. So muc
for staying out of the way.

"I do not believe I have ever heard those last pieces you played," he said.

"Why, no, how could you?" she blurted out.

His dark mobile eyebrows shot up as did those of the people attending him.

Jenner flushed. "That is to say, they are my own and have never been written down."

"Your own works! How extraordinary! How old are you?"

"Twenty-three," she whispered so low that she might have said twenty.

"Have you thought of studying music?"

"I already know how to play." Even to the nervous Jenner this sounded like an insult. "I mean, what I need to learn is composition."

Fionello chose not to be insulted. He gave her his card and asked her to call on him.

As the last of the company left, Lacey and Dennis found Jenner slumped in an armchair in the corner of the music room. "Here, drink this," Lacey said kindly.

"What is it?"

"A double brandy," Dennis said. "You deserve it."

"I already have a headache," Jenner complained, but accepted the glass. It reminded her of the first time she had given in to Lacey. What would have happened if she had not?

"A triumph, I tell you!" Caroline was saying to Stella as they seated themselves for a postmortem of the evening. "A positive triumph. I think for our next party we should—"

"Please, Caroline," Jenner said, rising and bestowing a kiss on her cheek, "promise you will never put us through this again."

"But you were splendid. Where are you going?"

"To throw up, I think, and then to bed. Good night, all."

Dennis laughed, but Stella looked at Jenner in real sympathy. Lacey followed her upstairs and came to her room after she had gone to bed. He was still dressed and merely sat on the bed looking at her.

"If you were a man, you could be famous," Lacey said, "a writer, a musician, a teller of tales that entrance even the most unromantic of souls."

"If I were a man," she said, pillowing her head on her folded arm, "I would never have known you—not like this, anyway." The brandy and the end to the torturous evening had made her relax.

"Doesn't the unfairness of it make you angry?" he asked after awhile.

"I got tired of being angry about so many things. It's a terrible waste of effort. Besides, I do not want to be famous."

"What do you want?" He was expecting her to say she wanted him.

"I never think about wanting anything," she said slowly. "I never think much at all about myself. When so many possibilities have been taken away from you, the little things become more important. The feel of a strong young horse under you, a few weeks of the maddest life with the most amazing man." She laughed and looked at him. "These become the great things in your life. You will be the last man I will ever love. Of that I am certain."

He snuffed the candle and left her halfway to sleep.

Chapter Four

Jenner came back late from the receiving office with an impressive packet. The discussion when she entered the dining room was all of Napoleon's movements and success in linking up with Marshal Ney, who had been sent out by the king to arrest him.

"And look at what they have done," expostulated Dennis. "Proclaimed Napoleon an outlaw and a disturber of the peace! Does no one take this seriously?"

"I'm sure Wellington will take whatever action is necessary," Lacey assured his nephew.

Caroline changed the subject by asking, "How are your aunts doing without you, Jenner?"

"Aunt Bette says the lads are keeping up with our training schedule. The weather has mostly been fair. They have not lost many days. Tally has foaled finally, another large colt. That's good. Lord Gawl— Well, that would not interest you."

Lacey looked up with a wicked smile at her blunder. "Of course we are interested. What has Lord Gawl done?"

"He's offered eighty pounds for one of Tally's colts. That is a good bit in our—area."

"And where is that, child?" Caroline asked politely.

Jenner was looking slightly lost and said rather stupidly, "In the north."

"You won't get him to talk so easily, Caroline. No one knows where Jenner is from, and he is determined to keep it that way."

Caroline looked up inquiringly and was about to resume the interrogation when Jenner said, "Aunt Milly has enclosed specimens of whatever creature is eating the garden. Oh, that must be this packet."

"Your aunt sent you a packet of dead insects?" Dennis asked.

"I should think they are dead by now," said Jenner in her stride.

"Fortunate you did not open it first," Lacey said, cutting himself another bite of sirloin.

"Yes. She wants me to get them identified and see how to get rid of them. That may take some time. They don't seem to have missed me much yet."

"I'm sure they miss you, Jenner," Stella said, "they just don't want to spoil your holiday by asking you to come home early."

"I'm sure you are right. They will be glad to have me back when it comes time to do the accounts. Neither of them has much of a head for figures."

"Where will you go to find out about your bugs?" Stella asked.

"The library, I suppose, tomorrow. That's where I will start, anyway."

"Why don't you go with Jenner, Stella?" Lacey suggested.

Jenner raised an eyebrow but merely said, "If Stella would not be bored."

Lacey rose early the next day so as to have Jenner to himself after breakfast. There was nothing they could do but ride. This seemed to be enough for him, to watch her, to talk freely with her. They talked of horses mostly, their common love, and only with reluctance returned to the house in Grosvenor Street.

"You know, I could rent a suite at one of the hotels and give a very select dinner party," he suggested.

"Just the two of us, in fact," Jenner agreed. "How would we explain not inviting Dennis?"

"I will pick a night he is busy elsewhere."

Jenner halted Ebony and half turned to face Lacey. In profile she looked almost too feminine to get away with the disguise.

"Lacey, I must go soon," she whispered. "You do know that."

"No, I cannot let you go." He surged forward and laid a compelling hand on her arm. "Not unless there is a way for me to find you again."

The very touch of him unsettled her. "Don't you care what will happen if I am discovered? Your sister will be disgraced and your niece ruined."

"You seem to care."

"Your sister has been very kind to me. I cannot put her through what my aunts suffered—I think I should go before anyone finds out who I really am."

"Including me?"

Jenner glanced at two women watching them and, seeing the direction of her gaze, Lacey let her go.

"What good would it do for you to know where I live?" she pleaded. "We cannot be together there, either." Jenner let Ebony move off from him.

"I see. You mean to walk out of my life just like the others."

"No!— I don't know. How long can we go on like this? I must leave because I do love you. But there is no future for us."

"We could go somewhere else," Lacey said, catching up to her.

"You tempt me. But I have obligations, and so do you." She controlled her voice with an effort. "You are just beginning to realize that."

"Yes, damn you."

She smiled weakly at his frustration. "Caroline is right, you know. You should marry someone respectable and settle down."

"I tried that," he said in a choked voice. "When I overrode you that night in the fog I was fleeing from the most stunning rejection of my life. I had her father's consent to approach her and Miss Dawson herself had given me encouragement when I first came back to England. I was attracted by her spirit—pride, I guess it was. But that was before she knew about me, of course. When I approached her at her home I knew she was angry, but not why. Susan informed me that I was an incurable rake and under no circumstances would she entertain the thought of marrying me."

"What an idiot she is! Why would her father raise your expectations if he knew she was so missish about these things?"

"I rather fancy it was her mother who spiked my guns. She was Lady Amelia Forestor before she married Dawson and is still rather proud."

"Depend upon it, then, she wants a higher title for her daughter and it's nothing to do with you."

"Trying to console me?"

"Only pointing out that it was a fluke, that you could pick from dozens of young women who would make you tolerably happy."

"I do not want to be tolerably happy," Lacey said desperately. "I want you."

"Which is to say you want to be unhappy forever. You would have to give up all your London friends. I could never come here now that my face is known."

"Are they my friends? There is scarcely one I can talk to as I talk to you."

Jenner had no answer for him. She, too, would feel the void in her life when she left him. "I used to think there was some hope for me," she said shakily, on the point of tears. "I always think that I have learned from my mistakes, that I have gotten wiser, and then I blunder into a new disaster and discover I am every bit as stupid as that child who was raped. If only I would listen to my better self."

"Whatever else happens I am glad you did not. If not for you, I would never have known what it is to love someone."

Jenner looked at him helplessly. He had spoken of love often enough in the darkness of the night. Who did not? But here in Hyde Park in broad daylight she finally believed he meant it. "That is the worst of it. I have not hurt just myself this time with my stupid impulse." She dashed a hand impatiently across her eyes. "I have hurt you, and there is nothing I can do."

She rode off from him then in a wild plunge across the park that attracted everyone's attention. Lacey pursued her but with the illusion that she was floating irrevocably away from him, that he could never catch and hold her.

Lacey went sulking to his club in the afternoon and Jenner took Stella with her on a round of bookstores and libraries in quest of the mysterious pest. They found so many likely candidates that they had half a dozen cures for Aunt Milly to try by the end of the afternoon. Jenner was amazed that Stella threw herself into a boring project with such zeal. They returned to the house loaded with books and other parcels. Caroline smiled approvingly at them, and for some reason this worried Jenner.

The next day Caroline suggested Jenner drive Stella in the park, and she began to sense that Caroline considered her more than a convenient escort for Stella. She could not help liking Stella, and she began to wonder what it would have been like to have a sister. Stella chatted happily about her seasons in London, and Jenner drew her out with questions about the people Stella greeted as they drove, since they had some acquaintances in common now. Stella confided that she wanted to marry young and have at least four children. Jenner smiled at this.

"What if your husband does not want so many?"

"Four is not many," Stella said in some amusement. "Two boys and two girls—the perfect family."

"I suppose to an only child it seems like a lot," Jenner said.

"Don't you want to marry and have a family?"

"No— It would be unwise—that is . . . I never liked children much."

"What? Well, I suppose young men are not as interested in babies as girls are."

"I grew up with my aunts and uncle. I never really understood children. They seem almost a different race from adults—not quite human, I mean. This is coming out badly." Jenner laughed at Stella's shocked expression.

"I see, you feel they are not yet civilized." Stella smiled at Jenner's confusion.

"That's it. Also, I cannot remember being a child. I seem to have always thought like an adult."

"How far back do you remember?"

"I can remember helping Aunt Bette train my pony. I must have been eight or nine."

"Nothing before that?"

"Before that my parents died of influenza. I feel awful sometimes that I do not remember them."

"So you have always been like this—responsible?"

"I would not say that. My judgment is often faulty. In fact, I think it gets worse as time goes on," she admitted, thinking of her ill-advised affair with Lacey.

Lacey's older team of grays were showy and solid, but well-mannered enough to give her no trouble. Besides, Hawes was up behind in case anything went amiss. After they had circled the park twice Stella asked if Jenner thought she could learn to drive.

"I'm surprised Lacey has not taught you."

In spite of Hawes pointedly clearing his throat, Jenner positioned the reins in Stella's hands and gave her a concise lesson that would get her around the gentle drives of Hyde Park, where the horses knew pretty much what was expected of them. The third time they passed the gentleman in brown escorting a straight-backed old lady for a walk, he scowled at them so pointedly that Jenner was quite taken aback.

"Do you know who that was?" Jenner asked.

"Where?" Stella asked, turning to Jenner a face too innocent to be true.

"Back there."

"Shall we go around again? Then you can point him out to me."

After circling once more Jenner was so absorbed in watching Stella getting the feel of the horses' mouths that she nearly forgot to look for the odd couple until the brooding blue eyes flew up with almost an accusation. "There. Why does he stare so? Doesn't he like the idea of a woman driving a team?"

"That's Lady Marsh and her son and, if you had to put up with her, you might glare at anyone who looked to be having a good time."

Caroline tended to monopolize Jenner's time, since Jenner did not complain of escorting her and Stella shopping, to concerts or plays. But occasionally Lacey stole her away for an adventure.

"This place is fairly new, but I hear good reports of Roberto. I would like to see how well you fence. Can you take off your coat without embarrassment?"

"Of course. I'm not an idiot."

"Señor Condez, my young friend, Mr. Page, needs a lesson."

Jenner and Rob each hesitated before shaking hands, but not so long that Lacey caught the look of recognition that passed between them. Rob sported a heavy mustache now, and more gray touched his hair, giving him, of all things, a distinguished look. His eyes still crinkled at the corners in a silent laugh, and Jenner felt the warmth of all their remembered closeness.

"I think you will have heavy weather teaching me, *Señor,*" Jenner said to her former lover. "I have not had an opponent to practice with in over a year."

"Let us see what you remember then," Rob said with a wry smile and such a thick accent that Jenner had to look at him again to make sure. They were so used to each other's moves that Jenner realized Rob made her look good. They used the clashing of the rapiers and the general din in the large open apartment to catch up.

"Are you angry with me for not going to America?"

"Why should I be? I only worry that you are safe enough here."

"I have covered my tracks well. I don't think I told you much about my time in Spain . . ."

"No, and I don't want to hear it. The less I know, the safer you are," Jenner replied, blocking a thrust.

"It is true, child. My life is in your hands. Makes me glad we parted so amicably." Rob got under her guard and tapped her with the buttoned tip of his foil.

Jenner laughed. "By the way, I have just sold that book of stories we worked on together. Your half is a hundred and twenty-five pounds."

"Keep it, you may need it to take care of your aunts. Besides, I am doing quite well for myself here. These English always seek a foreigner to teach them fencing." Rob advanced on her in a rush.

"I'm glad to know you are safe, at least," she said as she retreated.

"Speaking of safe, I see you with Raines. He will guess your secret. He has quite a reputation."

"He already has. I beg to inform you that you have been supplanted." They came to grips face to face, blades crossed.

Rob looked surprised, but then smiled. "I beg to inform you that I am married."

"I am happy for you," Jenner said with relief as she disengaged. This was the very thing she had advised Rob to do. She was genuinely glad that he showed no signs of possessiveness toward her and, when she examined her own feelings, she discovered no jealously there for his unknown wife. It was not what she would have expected to feel and she could only think that Lacey was responsible.

"Seriously, child, if you should ever find yourself in need of help, I can best this man Raines," Rob said, making another rush at her.

"Lacey? Perhaps you should rather offer to save him from me." Jenner turned his blade as he had taught her.

"Meaning I should mind my own affairs."

"Never, after all we have been through. I mean he is not nearly as black as he has been painted. He has been ruined one way or another, and the hell of it is when I leave, he will merely feel he has been betrayed again. I wish I could help him."

"Never try to reform a rake, my dear. Waste of time."

"I like him fine the way he is. My problem is I simply cannot keep him."

Lacey nodded when Jenner walked back to him a little out of breath. "Not bad. Now take a turn with me," he suggested, stripping off his coat and donning a padded vest.

"Not fair, *señor,*" Roberto's white teeth grinned under his mustache. "The boy is winded and you are still fresh."

"Yes, but he can give me almost ten years. That should count for something."

Jenner found Lacey as difficult an opponent at fencing as at chess. He was quick and full of surprises, but she had good endurance. Nevertheless they were both panting when Rob called a halt and offered her another lesson on Friday.

"If I am still in town. I must be returning home soon."

"No doubt you are wise. Too much of London can be dangerous for a young man," Rob said with a wink.

"I fear I cannot cry off from this dinner engagement tonight," Lacey announced wearily on their way back to the house. "Do you go to the theater with Caroline and Stella?"

"Yes. I have seen the play, but it is a good one."

Lacey and Jenner returned in midafternoon to a quiet house and the knowledge wrested from Edwards that everyone else was out. Lacey's eyes lit up, making Edwards suspicious, but Lacey merely ordered a bath and told Jenner to lie down for a nap or risk falling asleep during the performance that night.

"Join me?" he invited, stepping into her room in his dressing gown, half an hour later.

"It will be a little crowded, won't it?"

"I don't mind, so long as you scrub my back."

"Collins would do this for you," she said a few minutes later as she did his bidding.

"Yes, but it would not be as much fun."

In the process of bathing between bouts of giggles they splashed a good deal of sudsy water on the oak floor and lost the bar of soap under the bed. After toweling off they crawled between the covers in Lacey's room. The merest touch of his hand aroused her, causing her small nipples to stand up. She knelt on top and slid slowly up and down his shaft while kissing him wetly. The double link completed some kind of spark between them they did not want to end. Each wished they could remain bonded so but Lacey rolled over on top and began a more rhythmic assault. She arched her back as spasms of desire surged through her. He grew large just before he came, then collapsed on top of her.

"If I had known what an hour's fencing practice would do for you, I would have taken you to Roberto's long ago," Lacey said playfully.

"It's you who excites me now, not fencing," she teased as she slid out from under him.

Lacey's smile suddenly faded. "Never leave me!" he half commanded, half pleaded, as he ran his fingers through her damp hair.

"I wish I could stay forever," she whispered, "even as your protégé, but I cannot promise you that."

"You must! We need not live in London. We could go anywhere you like, anywhere in the world."

"Except home, to my aunts." Jenner could not meet his eyes. "Then they would know my trip has not been so innocent as I tell them in my letters."

"You can visit them whenever you like. I would not be so cruel as to—"

Jenner put a finger to his lips. "Don't," she begged, her voice husky with tears. "I owe them so much. They stood by me. They gave up everything for me. I cannot abandon them now that they are old. Indeed, if you knew them, you would not have me do so."

"No, but we will find a way. I know it. This time it is forever."

Jenner sank into his embrace, pretending for the moment that there was a way out of their tangle, tricking herself into believing that Lacey could make everything right.

* * *

When Stella announced Jenner was teaching her to drive, Dennis' eyes flew to Lacey's face, expecting a violent reaction. But Lacey merely asked, "Do you know how to drive yourself, Jenner?"

"I'm not good enough to take chances." Jenner looked at him over her teacup then explained, "Hawes does not clear his throat more than a dozen times as we round the park, so I do not imagine I am that bad."

Lacey laughed. "If he thought you were doing the horses any harm he would say something to me. Just don't let Stella drive on the streets until I have taken her out myself."

Stella's next driving lesson almost proved Jenner's undoing, for there was an unruly team of bays jerking a curricle along in the opposite direction. But Stella did not panic and Lacey's team instinctively gave ground so that they looked like they would pass the other vehicle without so much as grazing a wheel. All the same the elderly gentleman who was a passenger in the curricle had gripped the side and looked apprehensively at Jenner and Stella. It was Lord Gawlton! Jenner's mouth dropped open, then she ducked the brim of her hat over her eyes and marveled at the bad luck which had brought her closest neighbor to town at the same time as her. She glanced over her shoulder and he too was looking back in a puzzled way. Jenner had known him all her life and he had more than once surprised her out riding in breeches and a coat. If he recognized her face he would be sure to know her. She could only hope that they did not frequent the same houses. Better yet, she should take herself off home before she did run slam into him and have him give her away. She would have to seek Aunt Bette's horse elsewhere.

"What is it, Jenner? We passed with feet to spare."

"Nothing," Jenner gasped.

Caroline and Stella had no engagement for the evening but Dennis made it clear he intended to go out. "I have heard of a place called Cato's. They have an E.O. wheel there."

"Some of the play is high," Lacey warned.

"You have been there then?" Dennis asked.

"Yes. What do you say, Jenner? Would you like to see a gaming hell?" Lacy asked playfully.

"I'm not much of a gambler."

Lacey raised an eyebrow at that.

"You can watch if you've not the stomach for it," Dennis said.

Lacey led them unerringly to the side door of a normal-looking house off Jermyn Street. A tap and a quiet word gained them admittance to the red and gold rooms done up in what someone imagined was the Chinese style. Jenner had to admit they had an overstated elegance and certainly the patrons were mostly the nobility, but the smoky atmosphere and the aroma of spirits was almost overpowering. She had trouble believing that such a den existed no more than a long walk from Mayfair.

Lacey showed Dennis the E.O. wheel, and they each laid a bet while Jenner watched. Only Lacey won. He moved his stack to another number and won again. His third guess again doubled his stack and Jenner felt a strange gnawing tension. Dennis' eyes were wide with excitement.

"This is boring," Lacey said suddenly, picked up the money and moved on. There was a collective moan from the observers, especially Dennis.

"How can you just walk away?" his nephew asked.

"Simple."

"But your luck was holding."

"I don't believe in luck. I'm surprised Jenner doesn't like to gamble. Luck is all he believes in."

"Chance," Jenner corrected mechanically as she trailed after them. "It's not quite the same thing."

They had wandered through one card room, with Lacey greeting Curtain and Marlbeck briefly, and were approaching the back room when Jenner caught a flash and the barest glimpse of the muzzle of a pistol. On impulse she grabbed both Lacey and Dennis by the arms and pulled them to the floor in a heap on top of her. A click was followed a split second later by a shot and the splintering of wood.

"Jenner! Are you mad?" Lacey demanded, rising to his feet and inspecting his coat. "You have completely crushed my sleeve."

Dennis and Jenner both looked from him to the splintered door frame behind him and then to the drunken lord who had been firing backward with a mirror to try to break a glass.

"Rugh. I might have known. You always were an abominable shot." Lacey greeted his acquaintance. As he chatted with the man Lacey deftly disassembled the pistol and laid the pieces on the green baize table. In his present state the drunken lord would never be able to put it back together.

The noise had dislodged some of the players in the other rooms, including Curtain, who laughed and shook his head at the near miss. Jenner was still trembling inside as she vowed she would never understand these men. Lacey's life could have ended just now. It was the merest accident that it had not.

Lacey agreed to hold the faro bank just as Dennis' friend, Lord Coyle, came over and asked Dennis and Jenner to join him and Lyme at their card table. The stakes were not as high as Jenner feared and after the first hour she was the most sober of the four, so she tended to win. Her conscience would not let her allow them to up the stakes.

Suddenly, amid the din of the smoky room, Jenner heard a voice that made her choke on her wine. It was her atacker. How could she be so unlucky as to encounter the man in London among so many thousands of people?

As she was winning, she knew a suggestion to withdraw from the game would cause a stir and attract attention. She could only trust to her disguise to prevent him recognizing her. It had happened eight years ago. Most likely he had forgotten all about it. She played on as though oblivious to the predatory eyes that picked her out and seemed to be drawn to the table.

"Sir, do I know you?" the man with the bored, sneering face inevitably asked.

Jenner pretended not to realize he was addressing her, but the beringed hand that was lightly laid on her shoulder could not be ignored and she looked up at him in feigned surprise. Dennis looked inquiringly at both of them.

"Pardon, sir, do you mean me?" Jenner asked as coolly as she could.

"Your face is very familiar. I am Ashton Mowbray."

"Jennerian Page." She shook his hand carelessly, without rising, and committed his name to memory. Her knees would not have borne her weight. And she thought his very breath would suffocate her as it almost had that hot August afternoon. Somehow she prevented herself from shuddering. How silly. She was well able to take care of herself now. What had she to fear from him?

"But I have met you somewhere," he insisted.

The anger she had thought quenched many years hence began to boil in her. He was accepted here as though he had done nothing wrong and, because of him, she was an outcast. The unfairness of it all came back to her as bitterly as ever.

"I have only been in London a few weeks," she observed formally, "but I am quite sure I would remember you."

"No, not London, I think. Perhaps in the north. Such a distinctive face."

Without knowing if he had guessed her secret and wa
baiting her or just stupidly trying to jog his memory, Jen
ner went on the attack. It might be the only way to get rid o
him.

"I have a cousin," she volunteered, "if you are speakin
of family resemblance. Of course she has never left Thet
ford, so I hardly see how you and she could have met." Sh
looked up at him finally with a boldness that surprised her

Mowbray opened his eyes wide at this with a kind o
shock that told Jenner the memory Thetford conjured u
was not a pleasant one for him, either. She wondered wha
possible repercussions there could have been for him. Sinc
he had stopped her to ask directions to the town, her uncl
had made inquiries there, but no one remembered seeing th
man Jenner described to her uncle. It had been their onl
clue.

Mowbray's eyes shifted, veiled inscrutably again. "Ur
likely," Mowbray said critically as he wandered away in hi
previously bored fashion.

"What the devil was that all about?" Dennis asked. "Yo
never told me you had a cousin."

"There is a good reason I do not speak of my relations.
am a bit of an embarrassment to them. I would appreciat
it if you could manage to forget where my cousin lives."

"If that's what you want," Dennis offered.

Lacey awoke with a jerk, the vibration of a cry of an
guish still hanging in the air. He was expecting to be in
tent, and when he realized he was in Grosvenor Street h
blundered into Jenner's room without a candle. "What i
it? Are you ill?"

"It's nothing," she whispered. She was half sitting u
with one hand at her eyes, and he thought she was sobbing

By the time he got the candle lit she had herself more under control. "It's not nothing. Tell me," he demanded gently as he took her in his arms.

"Just a dream, then. I have not had one in such a long time."

"I hope it was not about me. I would hate to think I make you wake up screaming."

"No, silly."

Lacey crawled into bed and held her. He wanted nothing from her, just to comfort her, and she slowly relaxed with his warmth beside her.

"How did it happen?" Lacey asked.

"What?"

"The rape."

"How did you know that's what I was dreaming about?"

"It was either that or being run down by a maniac in the fog."

"I have forgotten all about that." She was silent for a moment then began, "I was very young—fifteen—and very stupid, I suppose. I frequently rode alone. That was safe enough. I am seldom thrown except when I am training the young horses and I don't take them outside the pasture alone. But I also walked alone a good deal or with my uncle's old hound for company. It was one of those blistering hot days we sometimes get in August when the air is so heavy you can barely breath. Even Piper was dragging a bit, but he would still hare off on a scent, then come back to join me.

"There was a gentleman riding sluggishly along the lane toward us. The banks are high just there so I couldn't step off the road. He hailed me and asked directions to—to the town. He was drunk and eyed me in the most odious way as I told him where the turning was. Then he said something about the coppice looking inviting and why didn't we have a lie down in it. I backed away, then turned and ran, but he rode me down and caught me by the hair. Then he fell off the horse on top of me.''

''Didn't you scream?''

''Me?''

''Sorry.''

''I did call for help, but I knew no one would be out in that heat. Then I called for Piper. What a good old dog. He appeared in minutes and lunged at the fellow, but I think he got only a mouthful of coat. The man pulled a pistol from his coat pocket and shot Piper.''

''Killed him?''

''Yes. I was stunned for a second. I fully expected him to kill me, as well. I was too stupid to realize he could not possibly reload and hold me down at the same time. I struck at his leering face, but he hit me on the side of the head, with the pistol, I suppose. That was merciful, anyway—not to remember the worst of it. When I woke up bruised and bleeding as I was, I could think only of Piper. I do not know how, but I managed to carry him the whole way home. I was not thinking clearly. It made no sense. I knew he was dead already. There was nothing even my uncle could do for him.''

''Who was he?'' Lacey asked huskily.

''My uncle never found out. Perhaps no one in the town actually knew him, but he didn't seem the sort to be traveling a long way on horseback. He was a deplorable rider, even allowing for drunkenness. And he used the most suffocating scent. That is what I was dreaming of, that terrible perfume. It was so real.''

''Perhaps you have encountered it again. What is it like?''

''Floral, I suppose—rose, perhaps, but not fresh, like a real flower, more like a dry powder crawling inside your lungs.''

''What happened when you discovered you were with child?''

"They thought of taking me away somewhere, but I was so sick they were afraid. Besides, in a place like that everyone knows what is going on in a few days' time. There was no point in trying to hide it. I must have lost the child in about the fifth month. The surgeon said it would have been too large for me anyway. I had such a fever they cut my hair and I came to like it short." Jenner tried to sound more cheerful.

"That's when you began dressing as a boy."

"Yes. My uncle died later that winter. I suppose I felt safer. A stranger seeing me riding by would never guess I was a girl. That is why I thought I could pose as a man in London."

"You are certainly convincing, but I would like to see you in a dress someday."

"Not possible," she said as she snuggled against him.

"There is one thing that puzzles me," Lacey mused.

"What?"

"How you ever came to let that highwayman—I mean, I would have thought you would be the last woman to..."

"Yes, so would I at fifteen, but at eighteen I was strong and healthy again, more confident, and I was beginning to feel normal desires. I knew, of course, that there was no hope for me to marry respectably. But that is not why I saved Rob's life. At least I did not have it consciously in mind when I nursed him through his chills and fever. He was so pathetically alone, and so was I, in a way. That made a bond between us. When I lay beside him to keep him warm it was a comfortable feeling, that I could be of use to someone, not just a burden. He accepted my help without even asking why I did it. But then I was not the first lady to succumb to his charms. He could be very handsome when his eyes were bright with fever, and he was not at all embarrassed by having to depend on me for everything, even when I had to help him..."

"Are you trying to make me jealous?"

"I'm just trying to explain it. When he was well again he began courting me in his own way."

"What do you mean?"

"He would bring me presents," Jenner said sleepily, "a hare or pheasant left hanging on the gate by the garden, or..."

"He left you dead animals?"

Jenner laughed at Lacey's disgust. "It was sweet of him in its own way. Only someone who's known hunger would think to repay a kindness with food. I met him often after that. I think now he must have waited for me to go riding or walking on my own. Also, he brought Tallboy back to be shod as he had promised."

"What did your aunts think of all this?"

"That I had leased Tallboy to him. Aunt Milly even invited him to dinner one day. That threw him into a panic."

"He seems a shy creature for a highwayman."

"He went slow with me, as you would if you were gentling a spooky horse. You see, he knew who I was—what had happened to me. It was more than a year before we made love. He was very patient—not like you at all," Jenner said, glancing at Lacey.

"I knew you would get around to comparing us."

"There is no comparison, but it is a good thing Rob came into my life first."

"And I am glad he has left it. Do you suppose he is still alive or has he been killed by the Indians?"

"Rob is a survivor."

"Like you."

"I'm sure he is well and happy."

"How can you be? You have never heard from him, have you?"

Jenner was silent, not willing to lie to him.

"How could you?" Lacey mused. "Unless you have seen him— My God! Roberto!"

Jenner flinched. "You are intelligent enough to be dangerous, Lacey."

"So, I have met him. And now I know why he taught you to fence. He discovered how much it excites you."

"You are not worried that I will fall back into his arms?"

"He is handsome still, I grant you, but rather old."

"I told you, he is old enough to have a past."

"No wonder you fence so evenly together."

"He does not surprise me, as you do. And I think however long one might know you, you would not lose that element of unpredictability. It is one of your charms. You won't give him away, will you?"

"Certainly not!"

"In fact, you are delighted to know someone so disreputable." Jenner laughed. "I thought it would appeal to you."

"I think I envy him. What an exciting life."

"I might have known. I will never understand you, but then I do not try to."

She was able to fall asleep with him there and in the morning called him Rob on purpose just to get him excited. He revenged himself on her vigorously before Collins came in to rattle the pitcher and basin in his room. They had not had such a night together since the Langleys had arrived. Jenner felt selfishly glad Lacey had gotten over his scruples, but also fearful at the risk of discovery they were running. She must complete her errand and take herself off before they were found out.

Jenner had so easily become a part of the Langleys' lives that she had gotten over her embarrassment at appearing before them in boys' clothes. She was amazed sometimes that she could carry off the deception with Lacey grinning appreciatively at her. She shuddered at what they would think of her if they discovered the ruse, but if she left now, would Lacey make them leave, as well? She thought not, but Lacey was still a bit of a mystery to her—moody and unpredictable. If he was angry enough . . . But no. Most likely he would leave rather than turn the Langleys out. He would run away like a little boy running away from home. He had the power and the money to run wherever he pleased, but Jenner had a secret suspicion Lacey was fleeing from something inside himself.

Jenner took the opportunity to call on Fionello the next day. She was not sure how serious he had been about teaching her, but as his other company left he began to speak of her music and encouraged her to sit and play for him again.

"You don't actually read music, do you?" he reprimanded.

"No, at least, not quickly enough. I just learn a little at a time and keep adding to it."

He smiled sadly and shook his head as he leafed through his music for a practice piece. "And you compose the same way, building on what you have memorized from before?"

"Yes." Jenner hung her head.

"So, you must learn to read before you can learn to write. Begin with this piece. It is not so fast."

When Jenner left after two hours it was with the realization that she had made some progress. Soon she might be able to write down some of her pieces and not have to rely on storing them in her head. She also realized she would be disastrously late for dinner.

Caroline and Stella thought there was nothing odd about Jenner spending so much time at Fionello's or making the rounds of libraries or bookstores. Lacey did not understand her obsession but he tolerated it with amusement. Dennis merely shrugged. That was why Lacey wandered out of the morning room, looking over his shoulder in a puzzled way.

"What is the matter?" Jenner asked, looking up from an examination of her latest find. She was seated by the window in the small book room looking particularly feminine, and Lacey was so distracted he had trouble answering. "Dennis—he's reading . . ."

"Reading what?"

"A book."

Jenner smiled. "What is so extraordinary about that? He can read."

"If you knew what a time we had getting him through school you wouldn't ask."

"Oh, it must be that book I found on Roman warfare. I told him Napoleon studied Roman tactics."

"That explains it, then. What are all these books you buy, anyway?"

"History, mostly."

"Pardon me for seeming dense, but what is the point?"

"Lacey, you are anything but dense. There isn't one."

Lacey puckered his eyebrows in a way that endeared him to Jenner.

She laughed. "I mean there does not need to be a point. I may study something for it's own sake, or for my amusement or curiosity."

"Without learning anything."

"Oh, I learn all sorts of things in unexpected ways."

"Not just about history, then?"

"About people mostly."

"Are not people history?"

"In an accidental way, yes." Jenner closed her book and walked over to sit beside him on the small sofa. "The amusing thing is that even small acts, sometimes by quite ordinary people, have toppled governments or otherwise changed the course of the world. Forgive me," Jenner said to his puzzled frown. "You probably see the making of human history as some ponderous God-driven vehicle, making use of the peasant or the despot quite against his will."

"Why do you say that?"

"Don't be upset. I was merely trying to project your philosophy on a larger scale."

"My philosophy? The way you describe it makes us seem so helpless."

"Read for helpless—guiltless."

"Then why don't I feel that way? Why do things haunt me so if I am a powerless victim?"

"I cannot answer that for you." Jenner could not understand why Lacey was so upset by what she had said and sought an example to clarify what she meant. "How do you see the revolution that took place in France? As a grand machination or as an avalanche cut loose from a mountain, impossible to stop?"

"Certainly it was planned," Lacey asserted.

"Not by a single person. Who was the mastermind? Not Napoleon. He is merely an opportunist, and a genius at that."

"He is a madman!" Lacey said in horror.

"That, also. Only a madman would have gotten so far. Only one man saw to the end of it, Burke. The way he condemned it one could almost believe he could see into the future. Or perhaps they read his *Reflections*...in France and set out to prove him right."

"It was all for nothing, then? Not by divine or even human design?"

"Not unless God has a sense of humor and engineered the whole thing to discredit Charles Fox." Jenner turned sideways and smiled at him. "It was bad enough the American revolutionaries he praised were so ungracious as to throw off English rule. Imagine his shock when the noble French patriots starting lopping the head off anyone accused of anything. The whole of France was out of control. Twenty years later it still is.''

''I cannot believe it all just happened.''

''Believe what you have to, then.'' She smiled at him. ''I have accepted that there are events beyond the scope of reason, mine, at any rate.'' She got up and began to gather her papers from the desk.

''So one brick tossed through one window might be either the end of a drunken disturbance or the beginning of a bloody riot?'' Lacey asked, and she knew he was talking about England.

''I do wonder why we have not had such a general uprising here. Some of our folk are worse off than the French peasants.''

''Perhaps no one has lit the right spark to ignite events.'' Lacey had relaxed and was toying with her ideas as he watched her stack her books.

''I don't know. Or we have not become hopeless enough to consider the possibility. Perhaps civil disobedience is so lightly taken here that the looting of a few mansions in the West End may be worth the price of keeping the lid on the pot.''

''But rioters were shot and killed only a few weeks ago with the passage of the corn bill. If not for the news of Bonaparte's escape they might still be at it.''

''Strange, is it not? And the next morning everyone gets out and scrubs the blood off the steps and acts as though nothing has happened. I cannot explain it. That is not to say that there is not something that can be done about it.''

''Perhaps it is a good thing you are not a man. If we were to set you loose in the political world no one would sleep at night.''

Chapter Five

Lacey came into the music room late one morning dressed in the most amazing fashion. Jenner looked up from the music she and Stella had been practicing and nearly dropped the violin. She quickly closed her mouth and looked away, biting her lip, since the bold stripes of his waistcoat had not surprised Stella or her mother, or even Dennis, who looked up from the paper he was reading. Lacey noticed her amusement, however, and owned to himself that he didn't much like the rig of the Four-in-Hand Club, since his fashion was normally on the conservative side.

"I have a luncheon engagement today."

"Lacey." Dennis looked admiringly at his uncle's finery. "I don't suppose you could put me up for membership?"

"The way you drive? Not a chance. Do you think you can keep Jenner tolerably amused and out of trouble today?"

"He's coming shopping with us," Stella said.

"Oh, really! You were just dragging him around the shops yesterday," her brother complained. "I know—we'll go to the races. As good a way as any to squander the day."

"Just see that time is all you squander," Lacey warned before he withdrew.

Dennis insisted they set out at once to prevent anyone talking Jenner out of the expedition. He did not like to see the boy always dancing attendance on his sister and mother.

Jenner really needed to get about more. They lunched at an inn on the way where they fell in with Lyme, Lord Coyle and some other rowdy young bucks who seemed to be drinking their way to the racecourse. Jenner laughed at their boasts and tales and hoped none of them would fall disastrously before they reached their destination.

They did not bother her overmuch with their rough talk but they served to put Dennis in a reckless mood. He wagered heavily on the first race and lost. She saw him borrow money to put on a forlorn hope in the second race and tried to dissuade him. She was not betting herself and Dennis' losses were making her too nervous to enjoy even watching the contests. Tearaway seemed to be favored for the third race and Dennis borrowed from her to bet on Lord Coyle's flashy bay. Since Lord Coyle was one of their party they had to put money on his horse, Dennis explained. The young lord came frantically back from the saddling enclosure. His jockey had not shown up and he was desperate to find someone to ride the race for him.

"You could do it, Jenner. You are light enough," Dennis said, "and you have ridden all of Lacey's horses."

"This is not quite the same thing, Dennis. Besides, Lacey would not like it."

"What's he got to say to it? He has no hold over you. Besides, he will never know."

"Would you do it?" Coyle asked her. "We lose everything if he does not run."

Five appealing and slightly drunken stares were too much for Jenner. "Only if you all promise not to tell anyone—and if Dennis stops betting."

"Done," they all said and hustled her off to make the switch. She had no chance to do more than discard her hat and coat and put on Lord Coyle's colors before it was time to mount. She missed most of what the trainer said to her and concentrated on getting control of the headstrong, fidgety beast who was trying to tear her arms out by the sockets.

When the flag went up Tearaway broke clean from the bigger part of the field. If she had only three other horses to keep track of she thought she might have a chance. All she had to do was stay on and give Tearaway whatever encouragement he might need at the end. She let him set his own pace behind the two leaders for most of the course and she was very much in rhythm with him as they came into sight of the finish. That's when she tapped him and asked him for everything.

They moved into the opening between the two leaders but Jenner was almost unseated when the jockey to the right brought his whip around across her face. She swore at him with such vehemence she surprised even herself. It was the sort of language Rob would use if he smashed his thumb. She gave a harsh laugh as she ducked the jockey's next blow. She tapped Tearaway again and he came through with another burst of speed from somewhere. The colt wanted to win even more than she did.

The other jockey merely gave them an angry glance as they pulled away from him. It was not until she had won, had slowed the galloping horse and worked him into a calmer state, that she realized what a stupid chance she had taken. But the faces turned to her were so overjoyed she could not help but smile at them. They were still boys, all of them, Dennis especially. He helped her down and solicitously daubed at the cut under her eyebrow.

"We should lodge a complaint against that man. I saw him hit you. It was on purpose."

"What would you complain of? We won, didn't we?"

"Yes, but we might not have, and you would have been trampled if he had knocked you off."

"It's a rough game, Dennis. I admit I didn't know how rough. But I suppose I would be mad, too, if a novice stole a race from me like that. Ready to go?"

"And miss the last race?"

"You promised no more betting."

"Oh, right. Might as well leave, then. Hate to miss the celebration, though."

"Dennis, I can't half see. And I have to get this eye fixed up before I face Lacey."

"Of course, what am I thinking of? Besides I'm money ahead this way, even after I repay you and Coyle."

It was typical for both Jenner and Dennis to consider their horses first and take them back to the stable before seeking out a doctor. Jenner slipped into the house to wash her face and blot the blood off her shirt while Dennis went off to find a hack. She was caught by Edwards in the hall and she turned her right side away from him.

"Lord Raines is in the book room and wants to see you and Mr. Langley directly."

"Don't tell him we're home yet. We have to go out again."

Edwards stiffened but was saved from making an obvious refusal by Lacey calling out. "Jenner, I'm in the book room. How did it go?"

"Damn," Jenner whispered and walked over to open the door. She looked at Edwards menacingly until he took himself off with a sniff. She poked her head in, but showed Lacey only her left profile. "Fine, Lord Coyle's horse won, which made it a profitable outing for all Dennis' friends."

"Did Dennis back it?" Lacey asked in amusement.

"Why, yes, I believe he came out ahead today."

"That's a switch. Dennis has incredibly bad judgment where horses are concerned. What about you?"

"I'm not much of a gambler."

"Not much of a gambler? That's rich. With the chances you take." Lacey looked at her, clearly expecting her to come in.

"I have been trying to get out of this mess," she said in her own defense.

"Jenner, I've got the hack." Dennis bounded into the hall. "Where the devil— Oh, Lacey, you're home," he said as he came to the book room door. Dennis was so obviously embarrassed that Lacey got suspicious.

"Where are you two off to again? You'll be late for dinner."

"Just a quick errand," Jenner retreated. "We'll be back in under an hour."

"No," Lacey said rather severely. "There is something you are not telling me. Get in here, both of you." Dennis dragged into the room in defeat with Jenner following. "What have you been up to?" Lacey asked Dennis.

"It was my fault, really. I said Jenner could ride Tearaway. I never thought—"

Lacey whirled to face Jenner. "My God!" He strode to her and pried away the handkerchief she was blotting her eye with. "Dennis, go fetch a doctor here at once. Move!"

Dennis blinked and took himself out of the room, glad to get off so lightly and somewhat surprised by Lacey's concern. Lacey usually laughed off cuts and bruises, his own or anyone else's.

"Let me see," Lacey demanded.

"It's just a cut. It doesn't even hurt much," she insisted.

"Sit down," he said, pushing her into a chair. Jenner noticed that the hand that poured the brandy was not quite steady. Jenner was much less shaken by the injury than by Lacey's reaction. It unnerved her to think that his normal cool composure was such a thin veneer. Surely he must have encountered far worse wounds during his career as a soldier. Perhaps it was not just the sight of blood, but the fact that it was hers.

"Say it." She broke the silence.

"What?" he croaked, as he folded his handkerchief into a pad and pressed it in place.

"It was a dammed fool thing to do. It could have ruined all of you."

"I don't care about that. You could have lost an eye, or been killed. Don't you ever think about what could happen to you?"

"Hardly ever, or, at least, not ahead of time," she tried to say lightly.

"Who are you? Tell me," he pleaded, his hand gripping her shoulder. "I can't bear the thought I won't be able to look after you."

"Oh, I think I will be safe enough away from Dennis and his friends," she said shakily.

"Do you think I have forgotten you do this sort of thing for a living?"

"I'm sorry if I gave you a turn, Lacey. I did not mean to walk in on you all covered with blood."

"I thought you had better sense."

Jenner was glad to see anger taking over now that Lacey's initial shock had past.

"Wait until I get my hands on Dennis," he vowed.

"I hope you are not going to read him one of your lectures. It was Lord Coyle who asked me to ride his horse. I could have refused. Dennis had little to do with it, except to say I could do it." Lacey stared at her in exasperation. "It would have been terribly unsporting to have refused," Jenner continued brightly.

Lacey opened his mouth but was interrupted by Caroline, who poked her head in to ask what all the shouting was about.

"Just a cut, ma'am. Nothing to worry about," Jenner assured her.

Caroline sailed in and inspected the wound dispassionately. "You would be better off with a cold cloth on it.

Lacey, I'm surprised at you, keeping the boy down here drinking when he should be lying on his bed." Caroline dragged Jenner off in a motherly way that was endearing and guaranteed Jenner would not have to listen to any recriminations from Lacey for a time.

Several copies of *Bridle Lay* arrived in Grosvenor Street the next day and they were commandeered by Lacey and Caroline as soon as Jenner opened the package at the breakfast table. "I think Jenner should get first chance at one," Stella said. "It's his book."

"I'm tired of reading it," Jenner said, squinting at her. "And if there is an error in it I don't want to know it."

"You cannot read anyway with that eye," Lacey remarked acidly, "and I won't let you ride until you can see properly, so do not badger me about that again."

"I suppose I could ask Dennis to exercise Ebony..."

"I will ride Ebony myself. He is too hot for Dennis."

Dennis looked up from the paper in a brooding way but did not protest for fear of getting another tongue-lashing about leading Jenner into mischief.

"I cannot believe it," Dennis burst out suddenly. "They have yet to move against Napoleon. Do they mean to let Boney raise all the armies again?" he asked them earnestly.

"We must assume Wellington knows what he is about," Lacey said confidently as he buttered his toast.

Dennis dove back into the paper and could not be roused again during the meal.

After much prodding Lacey agreed to take Jenner to watch Parliament, especially now that there was likely to be debate on war issues. The proceedings there always bored Lacey, but he thought it might take Jenner's mind off being restricted. A few coins gained them admittance to the gallery in the Commons. Lacey was puzzled when Jenner looked uncomfortable almost as soon as they were seated.

He could not know that she had almost walked slam into Lord Gawlton in the anteroom and was sweating out whether he would follow her or not. That he had recognized her in spite of the bandaged eye she could not doubt, for he had opened his mouth to call her name. If she were alone she would simply leave, but if Lacey suspected she was avoiding someone it would be too good a clue for him.

Jenner could spare only half her concentration to listen to the speeches. The rest was spent listening for anyone entering the gallery, for she refused to let herself look around. She tried to compose in her mind what she would say to her neighbor if he confronted her in this state but she could think of nothing. He had often chided her for walking or riding alone after the attack. Perhaps that's why she now dreaded his shock at discovering her here. If Lacey knew of her predicament he would think it the height of adventure, and he would probably flaunt her before Lord Gawlton. It was certainly the most uncomfortable hour she had spent, but she was very nearly getting used to the danger. At least her heartbeat had resumed its normal pace.

"Had enough?" Lacey finally asked.

She nodded and followed him out, afraid even to look behind her until they had walked several blocks.

"Well, what do you think?" Lacey finally asked.

"I think I had better not say. You are in no very good mood to begin with."

"You find us just as trivial and stupid in there as elsewhere."

"I think I am surprised we won the war."

"Ha, that was on the strength of the army. The politicians did all they could to hinder us by not allowing supplies or pay. I'm surprised they passed a renewal of the income tax."

"What does that mean, that they would pass a war bill?"

"Possibly it means that they would get around to it eventually. Most likely they simply see no reason to drop the tax."

"I see. They are not all of them without sense, of course, but even the best of them are woefully out of touch with the real problems."

"I feel sure you are going to tell me what those are."

"Lacey, it doesn't matter whose fault it is that markets are depressed, that food is expensive and that wages are low. It only matters that there are people starving, in the country as well as in the cities. All the laws they can pass won't help that situation unless those that can do something about it see that they are responsible."

"Meaning me. I suppose you would simply feed all the hungry."

"It's not that easy, but I have done what I can in my corner of the world and in such a way that it is not resented as charity so often is. I pay those who work for us a fair wage. When food goes up I pay them more. It means the world to them if they don't have to take parish relief. At least the exorbitant price these people pay for my books gets put to good use, rather than being frittered away on gambling or silly hats. There, are you angry at me yet?"

"Never. At least not over that. I suppose you will expect me to make sure none of my tenants have to fall back on the parish."

"I am sure none of them do."

"How would you know?" He laughed.

"I asked Dennis." Jenner glanced sideways at Lacey's set face and compressed lips. "Now you are angry with me."

"Just how does Dennis know this?"

"You may think him still a boy, and I suppose, in many ways, he is, but he has worked hard to make sure all goes well at Kettering, not from any selfish motive, you understand. He wants you to be well-liked."

"You mean if I cannot be respected."

"Lacey, you are making me say the most awful things about you. And none of this is your fault."

"Whose fault is it, then?"

"I think it was the enclosures that started it."

"The enclosures are a necessity. Forest land cannot regenerate with cattle and sheep eating the young trees, let alone the damage done by those gathering firewood. The cutting of peat has to be stopped. The soil is simply being stolen away."

"So, you do know something." Jenner smiled at him with satisfaction.

"I can show you a young forest at Kettering that used to be a wasteland. Enclosure is necessary to save the land."

"I have not said some such measures are not necessary, but those most affected by it have no say in the matter and you cannot deny that it is unfairly applied. Even laborers that get a share of the land are so overburdened with the cost of fencing it that they have to sell."

"If they want the land badly enough, they will do what is necessary to keep it."

"You may be right, but what it comes down to is that a cottager who used to keep a milk cow and some meat animals has no pasture now and must buy fuel for cooking and heating when he can scarcely afford food. His children will grow up colder, hungrier and smaller than before. And they will grow up without hope."

Lacey had no reply for this but said after a time, "It's really too bad you are not a man. If you were, I have no doubt you would have been elected to Parliament by now."

"You don't mean that."

"Well, not the part about you being a man."

"What are you, anyway?"

"You know what I am, child."

"I mean in the nobility."

"A mere baron, my dear. Lovelace Raines, Baron Kettering."

"Lovelace?" Jenner gasped and shot him a mischievous glance.

"Yes, Jennerian, a person of practically no influence, less even than your friend Lord Coyle, who is a viscount. Do you want to run for Commons?" Lacey asked with a wicked light in his eye.

"No! I was wondering if you ever spoke."

"I do not even show up unless someone particularly asks me to vote for a bill."

"I see. As a personal favor."

"My dear child, respectability is not a cloak one can put on at will. No one would take anything I said seriously."

"If you said something serious, they might."

"What are you trying to do to me?" he asked in exasperation.

"Me? Why, nothing. I have no right to try to influence you."

"Don't play the innocent. If you ever become a nag like Caroline we shall fall out."

"Whatever else you may be accused of, Lacey, hypocrisy is not one of your sins."

"No, everyone knows exactly what I am."

"If being a rake could be considered a vocation, you have worked hard at it, except for that woeful lapse when you joined the army and fought quite creditably for three years."

He eyed her suspiciously.

"It does make me wonder," she continued with a sigh.

"What?"

"If being a rogue is just a cloak you have put on."

"I tell you I am every bit as bad as they say I am."

"Now I've hurt your pride." Jenner smiled sympathetically.

"You tease," he grabbed her by the nape of the neck and shook her gently. "You would believe me if I cast you aside for another woman."

"Not even then, but if you mean to do so, find one with skirts."

They often joked about their relationship, for it was too painful to discuss it seriously. Any reference she made to leaving started a scene that ended with them clinging ever closer together. It was easy for Jenner to let herself be swept along and let Lacey take care of everything in his overbearing way. No one had ever taken care of Jenner in the way Lacey did, and she could not deny that she liked it or that she was deeply in love for the first time.

The night of Caroline's ball Jenner tried to shab off but was informed by Caroline that even an indifferent dancer was needed to supply enough partners for all the young ladies she had invited. Lacey had been drinking steadily through dinner and he scowled at Caroline. Jenner supposed the aforementioned young ladies were being trotted out for his benefit.

Lacey was pointing out some of the notables to Jenner and making her chuckle against her will with his spicy tidbits of gossip. "That fair damsel who glanced at me and blushed furiously is Miss Dawson."

"Rather cold-looking," Jenner said objectively. "I would not have thought her your type."

"And just what is my type?"

"A rogue like yourself, I suppose. But you can hardly marry such a one. Over there, in the blue dress. Who is that?"

"Sarah Kirkpatrick. Normally a lively girl, but I frighten her to death."

"Who is the pretty brunette? She is short for you but she looks to have a sense of humor."

"That is Templeton's young wife. He guards her close. He won't let me near her for fear I will contaminate her. And just a year ago he was wilder than I am."

"So it is possible," Jenner mused, looking at Lacey speculatively.

"What?"

"For a rake to change."

"Reformed by a virtuous woman? I give them a year before he is making the rounds of the bawdy houses. Look how he is glaring at me already." Lacey whispered close to Jenner's ear, "Shall I make him really jealous?"

"No," Jenner said, sensing that Lacey was falling into a dangerous mood. "I have seen the way you look at some of the men who dance with Stella. You look like you could cut their hearts out."

"That is because I know them. You are the only one I trust her with."

"By the by, thrusting her on me so much is not a good idea. Not that I do not enjoy her company. But I treat her with more consideration than her brother, being sympathetic to the way women are hedged about, and I fear she begins to—I mean, it is difficult to. . ."

"Are you afraid she will find you out?"

"Yes, there is always that. But I fear Stella has come to regard me..." Jenner hesitated and flushed slightly, a thing she rarely did.

"I know you are safe when you are with her rather than Dennis. Who knows what danger he may lead you into?"

"I would be much safer out of London altogether."

"No!" Lacey said so loudly several heads turned toward them. Jenner cringed, but Lacey disregarded all stares.

"I did not set out to make you angry tonight. I know we shall always disagree on that. What I was going to say is that I think Stella grows too. . . attached to me."

"What? Seducing my niece?" He shot her the look of a satyr from under his eyebrows. "What next will you be up to?"

"Will you keep your voice down?" Jenner pleaded, glancing around her.

"Why? I have just done your reputation a world of good."

"I fear my presence in the same house with her may have already given rise to gossip. I wish these people had something else to employ them besides conjuring up such nonsense."

Several people looked up at the laugh Lacey gave and Jenner looked vengefully at him.

"Never tell me she's in love with you."

"Not yet—Lacey, this is not funny," Jenner said desperately. "Do you imagine I want to hurt her?"

"I wonder how Caroline will take this," Lacey teased.

"With interest, as a matter of fact. She is trying to discover what my prospects are, other than from my writing."

This set Lacey off again, and Jenner made as if to leave him, but he caught her arm and walked with her toward the card room. "Tell her you mean to make your living gambling. That should put her off."

"I will save that if I need to be completely disgraced. Oh, over there, the pretty blonde by the door..."

"I am not certain. Why are you asking about all these women?"

"We may as well have a look at them as long as they are here."

"Stop it, Jenner," Lacey burst out. "This is impossible. My mistress helping me to choose a wife." He laughed harshly and dragged Jenner after him.

"Well, someone had better make a push to help out. Is there no one who has ever impressed you?"

"There was a girl some years ago, an audacious brat like you. She was not afraid of me at all. She said she liked me because I was dangerous."

"That sounds hopeful. Where is she now?"

"Married. I found out later she was using me to make the man she loved jealous." He took a glass of champagne from a tray and downed it. "It must have worked."

Jenner shook her head. "Just because you are a rake, they think you cannot be hurt. Have you never met a woman who did not betray you?"

"Not yet, except for you and Stella."

Jenner looked at him in some concern but there was nothing she could say. Sooner or later she would have to hurt him also.

"Why don't you go dance with her?" Lacey suggested. "She is looking a little lost."

"Me? It makes me too nervous. You dance with her. I want to see what I am missing." Jenner watched as Lacey and Stella laughingly took the floor. He was an elegant dancer and seemed scarcely to think about it, so deep in conversation he was with his young niece. Jenner knew a moment's jealousy, not of Stella, but of all the women who had danced in Lacey's arms, and a deep regret that she never would. Then she remembered that if it had not been for her very peculiar life she would not even have met Lacey.

Jenner shifted her focus to take in all the dancers, the gentlemen mostly in black or dark blue or uniforms of scarlet and white standing out starkly against the pastel silks and muslins of the ladies. She had only two or three nice gowns herself. What would be the point of wasting time or money on such fripperies? She spent most of her days in one of her drab riding habits.

In a vague way, she envied the empty-headed gaiety of women who must array themselves in a new outfit for every occasion. If her parents had lived, if she had not been ruined, she might be one of these spoiled, blushing misses twirling about the floor. Somehow she could not see herself there and she wondered momentarily if Lacey was right, if it was her destiny to lead a unique life. The fact that she believed it all a matter of accident and not design made it even harder to convince herself she was better off with her strange freedom, and she could not suppress a shudder of regret.

Lacey brought Stella up to her. "Your turn. It's just a country dance. You can handle it."

They had passed down the floor only twice when Jenner said, "There is that fellow glaring at us again."

"George Marsh," Stella supplied.

"How did you know who I meant? You didn't even look."

"George always glares when he's not dancing with me."

"Why doesn't he dance with you then?"

"He will, but I promised him only two dances, so the rest of the time he just broods."

"Sounds serious."

"George is very serious."

When Jenner sought refuge from the dancing in the refreshment salon she was cornered by several middle-aged ladies who tried to pump her for more details about the stories in *Bridle Lay*. She was amazed at how quickly her book had been taken up and read in London and embarrassed to find herself something of a celebrity. It was not the kind of notoriety she wished for and she supposed she had Lacey to thank for it, although the women, many of them Caroline's cronies, attributed the discovery of Jenner to Caroline. That would make it doubly embarrassing for Lacey's sister if Jenner was ever found out.

Jenner was just sweating over this realization when she was disconcerted to discover that these women guessed close to the truth on many items in the book. If all the stories were so transparent she could cause a good deal of embarrassment to some of the ton. But gossip seemed to be the meat on which many of them sustained themselves. She could do no more than dance around the truth in her refusal to add any specifics. Lying was something she avoided except in the context of storytelling. It bothered her too much, but she was uncomfortable with the skill she was acquiring in parrying such questions.

Dennis was commandeered for the whole evening and, to do him credit, he did not spend all his time gossiping with the young officers. He tried to appear polite and cheerful as he danced with the young women and teased their mothers. There was a point at which Jenner caught him staring at Lacey in a puzzled way, not resentful or brooding, but actually worried. She had been talking to a group about her book and Lacey, she now realized, could have been seen to be hanging on her words. That was what Dennis was watching—Lacey watching her. It was a dangerous triangle of glances and made Jenner start to sweat. If Dennis suspected something extra in that look of Lacey's, then the more avid gossips would surely read the worst possible meaning into it.

It was a wearing night one way or another, but Caroline and Stella both seemed pleased with themselves as they went tiredly off to bed. Dennis had stuck it out faithfully to the end, and even Lacey had a rather contented smile on his face as he bade the last of the guests good-night. Jenner thought he wore the cloak of a family man quite benignly but had the good sense not to mention it to him.

The London thoroughfares were wide but artificial, except where they were broken by broad grassy squares with hopeful rows of young trees. If it were not for the vast parks, Jenner would have gone mad in a place so naked of greenery, and the whole aspect of the place was that it was too open to scrutiny. And now that she was acquainted with

Dennis' friends she had to steel herself to being hailed from across the street or even accosted from behind. She was in no way as voluble as they were, but they seemed to like her in spite of that, and she found to her surprise that she enjoyed being with them, for they always made her laugh.

Jenner had read history in the library all morning and had promised to meet Lacey at White's for lunch. She did not mind invading the dining room there so much as the card rooms and lounges. The porter had admitted her and she sat idly reading a book she was carrying until she realized she was being scrutinized. Someone had entered and abruptly stopped talking at sight of her. The man's voice finally penetrated her fog and she realized it was Mowbray. She schooled her features to an abstracted pleasantness she did not feel and looked up at him.

"I did not know you were a member here," he sneered.

"I'm not, just an occasional guest."

"Do you expect to join?"

Jenner suppressed her annoyance. "Lacey offered to put me up, but it hardly seems worthwhile. I am only in town a few weeks."

Mowbray frowned even more severely at her. "Then you go back to...Thetford, was it?"

"Yes, you have a remarkable memory, sir."

Mowbray looked at her sharply.

The nearness of his scent, so sickeningly sweet, brought back that sweltering day in August that had spelled her ruin. She remembered his drunken kisses, as disgusting and horrifying as the rape itself. A slight shudder went through her as she revived all the hatred she thought had died out of her. She had been weak then. She was not the same person now. Whether he guessed her secret or not, she was not afraid for herself. The look she turned on him must have held disgust and contempt. It scorched him and his eyes bulged.

"You live there?"

"Only when I stay with my cousin," she taunted.

"And who is that?"

"You would not know her. After all, you say you have never been there."

He turned a shade more saturnine and passed on to the other chambers. She sat puzzling over what she should do about him as she waited for Lacey.

Lacey did not disturb her at first. He amused himself by watching Jenner imitate Dennis and his cronies. When she lounged in a chair, her booted legs crossed at the ankle, no one would suspect there was any difference between Jenner and any other young blood, except her youth. She rode with as much skill and a great deal more care than many of them. And she took their gibes and hazing in such good part that she was popular with all of them. Just now she wore such a serious scowl that Lacey himself had trouble seeing anything feminine about her.

"You are very thoughtful today."

"Just pondering what to do about a certain pest. Which looks most like Aunt Milly's?" She held up the book for him. "This one or this one?"

"Ugh. Please, after we eat."

When they left the dining room an hour later Lacey put his hand on her shoulder in a possessive way. Jenner thought nothing of it until she caught sight of Mowbray regarding them fixedly. He met her eyes, gave a contemptuous snort and turned on his heel. Jenner had an uneasy feeling he meant to make trouble and that whatever mischief he intended would include Lacey.

Lacey had a dinner that night outside London for which he left in midafternoon. Jenner had tired of her musical and literary pursuits for the day so she went to see Rob. She was in the habit of taking a lesson from him in the morning on Fridays. But at this hour of the day there was no one else about so they could talk of old times and laugh over their exploits. Jenner was rather surprised when he invited her to take an early dinner with his new family, but she was curious to see Merilee.

The woman was nothing like herself. She was fair, very feminine and surprisingly young. She kept the sleeping baby in the room in his cradle, and when they had finished their meal asked Jenner if she would like to hold him.

"I'm afraid all my experience has been with lambs and foals. I might hurt it."

"Nonsense." Meri laid the sleeping child in Jenner's arms and Jenner froze for fear of not supporting it right. She had never held a child before. If mothering was supposed to be instinctive, there must have been something wrong with her for the baby made her uncomfortable. She would have known what to do for an animal, would have even talked to it. The child must have sensed something of this for it awoke and began to fuss and cry. Jenner cast a panic-stricken look at Rob, who was laughing at her. It was he who came and took the baby. She looked on in amazement as he cooed and bounced his son back into a better humor.

Meri came and took the babe to feed it and laughed at Jenner's embarrassment. "Are you an only child?"

"Yes, I've never been around a baby before."

"You will be more comfortable with them when you are older and you start a family of your own."

Jenner only grimaced at the young woman's words.

"You were with him again tonight, weren't you?" Lacey said as he slid into bed with her and she responded to his merest touch with a heavy sigh and erect nipples.

"Lacey, you are incredibly drunk." She laughed as she inhaled the fumes from his breath. Yet the smell of drink on him did not repel her and she brushed the hair from his forehead to look into his hazy eyes.

"Answer me. The fencing master. He's old enough to be your father. What do you see in him?" Lacey demanded.

"I see an old friend. That is all there is between us now. Lacey, I have never lied to you," she said as she turned in his arms.

"Perhaps not, but you are sometimes reluctant to part with the truth, and that amounts to the same thing."

"Anything I keep from you is for your own good. Besides, I could not go back to Rob even if I wanted to. He is married, and happily. I was shocked at how domestic he has become. Now that I think of it he may have taken me home with him for that very reason—to show me that we are still friends, but that he is no longer available."

Lacey turned her toward him and looked at her searchingly. "I do not know what I would do if you betrayed me, too." He pulled her tighter to him.

"Does it bother you that there is someone else who knows about me? It should excite you, or it would have a few weeks ago."

"Are you sure this Rob won't talk?"

"Do you forget his freedom hangs in the balance? But we do not hold a knife to each other's throat. It is not possible that either of us would betray the other. I know this just as surely as I know his secret is safe with you."

Chapter Six

Lacey was rising from one card table and being hailed to join another game when Jenner interrupted him ruthlessly. "Lacey, have you seen Stella?"

"In here? Not likely. I thought you were going to keep an eye on her."

"That is difficult to do when I am trapped in conversation with someone," Jenner complained, following him into the Tauntons' ballroom.

"Simply walk away."

"I know you would."

Neither of them could spot Stella among the dancers forming the next set.

"You check the other salons and the balcony. I will look in the garden," Lacey commanded and strode off.

"Lord Marsh, have you seen Stella?" Jenner asked of Stella's frowning admirer as she passed him.

"She's out there with Poulton," George said, nodding grimly toward the balcony doors.

"You let her go with him?"

"How could I stop her without creating a scene?"

"Not by staring at her, that's for certain," Jenner said directly.

"You mean to go to her?" Marsh rose and followed in Jenner's wake.

"Of course. She may need help. Stella?" Jenner called as she opened the door and stepped onto the narrow balcony.

"You aren't wanted here, boy," the tall man said with more menace than seemed to be justified by the occasion.

"What does Stella say?"

"Oh, very well, Jenner. What do you want?" Stella seemed more annoyed than anything.

"Nothing, if you are content to remain here."

"James, I may as well go with him. Otherwise he will set Lacey onto me."

"Don't let this little cockerel scare you away. I fancy he would be easy enough to get rid of."

Jenner instinctively backed a pace and came up against the balustrade. When she glanced at it Poulton rushed her and got her by the throat, bending her backward over the low wall. Jenner had one hand on his arm and the other holding the rail.

"James! Stop it!" Stella said as to an overzealous hound.

Jenner restrained herself from striking at him. He could easily choke her or tip her over the railing onto whatever lay below. She concentrated on getting an arm hooked round the stone railing in case she lost her balance.

The door opened. "What is happening?" Lord Marsh finally burst out in frustration.

"George! Thank God! Make him let Jenner go." Stella rather impeded this suggestion, for she rushed to George and grasped his arm.

"How can I? Stella, you must come away from here."

"No!" she said angrily, lunging at Poulton herself and pounding him ineffectively on the back.

"Have you seen the rose garden yet?" Poulton asked Jenner wickedly. "I hear it is not to be missed at this season."

"Lacey!" Jenner gasped as loudly as she could.

"He's not here to save you, pup," Poulton sneered.

There was the rapid scrape of feet on the steps to belie this statement and Poulton was wrenched away. He got in one hit at Lacey before he was felled by successive punches to the face and midriff.

"Jenner, are you all right?" Lacey asked breathlessly.

"Yes, I fancy this neckcloth is ruined, though," Jenner gasped.

"Your neckcloth?" Stella asked in amazement. "When you have almost been choked to death. If I had any idea—"

"Didn't I once tell you how dangerous balconies are?" Lacey spit at his niece. "Are you sure you are all right?" Lacey asked Jenner. The change in tone was dramatic.

"Really, I'm fine, Lacey."

"I want to leave now," Stella said defiantly. "George, will you take me?"

"I am taking you home," Lacey said.

"Neither of you is fit to be seen inside," Stella stated. "I have to leave the balcony, at least, with George."

"I'm afraid she is right, Lacey," said Jenner, as she dabbed at Lacey's bleeding mouth with her handkerchief. "We'll have to sneak out through the garden."

"Oh, very well. Marsh, will you oblige me by seeing my niece and sister home?"

"Of course, only too happy to be of service."

"What the devil brought that on?" Lacey asked as he finished mopping at his lip. They descended the stairs without a thought to the unconscious man above.

"I don't know. You can be sure I was careful not to say anything offensive."

"Most likely the fellow was drunk."

Jenner was about to say she didn't think so, but merely asked if Lacey thought they could beat the others home.

Lacey came to her room after Collins had doctored his face. He held the candle to look at her. "He has bruised your throat," Lacey said tragically.

''Never mind. Come to bed.''

Something about defending her had stimulated his desire for her. He kissed her passionately then thrust his eager member inside her. She luxuriated in the spasms his robust attack caused deep inside her. Then she contracted her inner muscles and he moaned with relief as he came. He collapsed on top of her, too weak for a moment to move. The sound of voices from belowstairs finally roused him. Caroline still had something of an inhibiting effect on Lacey if he heard her voice. He crept guiltily out of bed toward his room, shushing Jenner's giggles when he stumbled over a chair.

Jenner continued to work on her new story when Lacey was not entertaining her. It was about her, and was more an attempt to analyze what had happened to her from another point of view than something she seriously meant to sell. She had not thought about the attack and the stillborn child that resulted for years now. Time had robbed the incident of its sharp edge of terror, but her hatred, she found, was as strong as ever.

Now that she knew her long-ago assailant's identity there were two men who would gladly kill him for her, but at what cost to themselves? There was also something in her that made her want to settle accounts with Mowbray herself. How she could possibly do this was not something that she spent a great deal of time thinking about, but she would not run from him. Another reason to stay, or was it just an excuse to remain with Lacey a little longer? She had never had her inclinations so at odds with her good sense before.

Dennis had persuaded Lacey to take them to Cato's again. He and Jenner spent most of an hour watching Lacey, Gros, Curtain and Marlbeck win and lose large amounts with equal coolness before Coyle enlisted them to play in another room. It was with a start that Jenner realized she had won more at cards since she had come to town than she had made in a whole year writing. She could just as easily have lost it all if gambling had been in her blood, but she set herself a limit beyond which she would not lose.

As Coyle looked about for a fourth, Mowbray lounged over to the table and Jenner felt herself sicken a little. Mowbray must have seen the disgust in her face, but she quickly masked it with an unconcerned expression as Coyle welcomed Mowbray to the game. She had not, after all, opened hostilities with him. The worst that could happen was she would spend an uncomfortable evening. She was rather surprised at how easily she could control her hatred after the initial rush of anger left her heart pounding.

Jenner had noted the presence of Poulton when they sat down to play. He stood behind her now and for some reason that made her want to guard her hand, leaving the cards face down on the table when she was not actually playing. It was something Rob had taught her. She struggled to remember if Poulton had been about that first night she had met Mowbray. She could not be certain, but it was plain that he was one of Mowbray's cronies.

She had leisure during the rest of the game to speculate on the chances of Poulton really being interested in Stella. Certainly he would never be permitted to marry her. Mowbray could have been trying to get at Jenner through Stella, but more likely they had just used Stella as bait to lead Jenner into a quarrel. If she had died falling off the balcony, it would probably have been put down as an accident. But why was Mowbray so desperately afraid of her? He was not even sure she knew his guilty secret.

Jenner grew suspicious when Mowbray suggested raising the stakes after the first hour. By then Dennis and Coyle had imbibed rather freely, and so, too, had Mowbray, she thought. Yet the cultured drawl might have less to do with being drunk than with pretending to be. She had seen him misdeal twice or do something extra with the cards. She almost opened her mouth to speak but she had been in London long enough to realize that such an accusation could be answered by Mowbray in only one way. It did occur to her that Mowbray might be trying to bait her into a fight by being deliberately clumsy with his tricks, but it went against the grain to let him get away with it.

On impulse Jenner laughed. "Ha, what a joke smith!" She feigned a drunken lurch as she grabbed Mowbray's arm and produced a spare card from his cuff. "But you can leave off with the sleight-of-hand tricks, Mowbray. It may impress the ladies, but you will need skill to win tonight."

Mowbray fumed impotently as Dennis and Lord Coyle looked at him in stunned silence. The game eventually resumed when Jenner took up the deal, but the constant scrutiny made Mowbray fidget in his seat. Unaccustomed to playing fair, Mowbray did not play well, but then he dared not win now even if he could, after being caught out like that.

In the meantime Lacey had grown bored and extricated himself in the middle of a winning streak. Since Coyle's game looked to be breaking up also, Lacey leaned against the wall to watch Poulton watching Jenner. He was about to accost Poulton but the lean hanger-on slipped from the room. The game continued dispiritedly for another half hour. As soon as he settled his losses Mowbray also escaped.

"Mowbray's face when you caught him cheating!" Dennis said. "I thought surely he would call you out."

"How could he," asked Jenner, rising from her chair, "since I treated it as a joke?" She was rather proud of how adroitly she had handled Mowbray. "Never leave a man with nothing to lose," she whispered to Dennis. "It makes him very dangerous." Dennis nodded. "Besides," said

Jenner, almost to herself, "if I ever have to meet Mowbray it will be on my own terms and it won't be over a card game." Dennis shrugged.

Just then Jenner turned and saw Lacey looking at her from under furrowed brows. She had been indiscreet, but she could not be sure how much he had heard. "You have missed all the fun," she said lightly. "Between us we have taken Mowbray for close on to four hundred pounds."

Lord Coyle moved to another game. In spite of the lateness of the hour the other three decided to walk home. Jenner had stowed her winnings in her boot. She almost resented how easy it was to make money if you were a sober and a careful card player—but not enough to quit playing. She could put the money to much better use than it would find in London since it would go to hardworking laborers. How would she get used to dealing in pence and shillings again instead of pounds?

Fortunately Jenner was walking between Dennis and Lacey. The attack when it came was a surprise to all of them. Four ruffians with clubs sprang out of an alley, and they meant business. Dennis took a blow on the arm in the initial onslaught. Without Lacey they would have been finished. He brought one man down while another struck at him. Jenner kicked her opponent in the knee before he could hit her and spun backward into him, thrusting her elbow into his stomach and finally managing to wrest the club he carried away from him. She did what damage she could with it while dancing out of reach of the man's clumsy lunges. The attackers made off after a last round of blows.

"I guess we showed them," Dennis panted. Jenner looked around at Lacey, who took one step and crumpled to the street.

"What is it? Where are you hurt?"

"Just my leg," Lacey mumbled as she held up his head. "It's so numb."

"Dennis, can you find a hackney?"

"Not at this hour, and I won't leave you in any case Lacey, can you walk at all, at least to a safer street?"

"Give me a minute."

Between them they got Lacey back to Cato's and Lord Coyle took them home in his carriage. The doctor, when he could be persuaded to attend Lacey, pronounced that the leg was not broken, but Lacey would have to stay off it for awhile. "That's not to say don't use it. Keep it propped up but work it a bit to help get the swelling down," the doctor advised.

By the time the doctor left Collins was still grumbling about it not being safe to walk the streets.

"They did not get my winnings," Dennis said with a yawn as he took himself off to bed.

Lacey dismissed Collins, as well.

"I don't think that's what they were after," Jenner said when both men had left.

"What are you talking about?" Lacey asked. "Why else would we be attacked in the street?"

"Lacey, I have nearly gotten you killed," Jenner said passionately, the tears starting to her eyes as she came to sit beside the bed and take his hand. "I'm so sorry."

"Nonsense." Lacey laughed through his pain. "The same thing might have happened even if we had never... You're not telling me something. What is it?"

Jenner rose and paced to the window. For his own protection she should tell Lacey what she suspected, that Mowbray was trying to silence her or, at least, drive her from London. But she knew Lacey well enough to predict what he would do, bad leg or not. "I meant," she said shakily, "if I had not stayed..."

"Don't lie to me. You don't in the least believe that would have affected what happened tonight. I know that much about you by now. You suspect that attack was directed against you." Lacey half rose in spite of his pain, and Jenner came over to ease him back onto his pillows.

"Don't. You will only make it worse. Rest for now."

"Who is after you? I have caught Lord Marsh looking daggers at you more than once."

"That is because he thinks I am cutting him out with Stella. Why doesn't he just ask her to marry him instead of languishing over her?" Jenner asked in an effort to redirect Lacey's thoughts.

"Is she interested in him?"

"It is hard to say what's in her mind."

"I don't think he has the backbone to face me, if you want to know the truth."

"Have you any particular objection to him?"

"I don't like the fellow, but I have no say in the matter." Lacey looked thoughtful and returned to the problem of the recent attack. "I suppose it could be Poulton, but I am the one he should come after. I don't suppose your highwayman is afraid enough of you exposing him to risk having you put away." Lacey glanced up at her but Jenner had regained her composure and smiled sadly at him.

"I would as soon suspect you as Rob." Jenner chuckled.

This seemed to disturb Lacey who moved restlessly and cursed his aching leg. "You see him quite often, don't you?"

"Is that so unusual? We were friends a long time."

"You were a damn sight more than friendly, if you are to be believed. You told me once you don't love him any more."

"I told you I still care about him." She moved from the chair to the edge of the bed to humor him. "I also told you that you are the last man I will ever love."

He reached for her with a smile of relief and then choked on the flash of pain that pulled him down. "Damn, why did it have to be my leg?" Lacey tried to shift to a comfortable position but failed to find one. "Had the attack come late I would have guessed that Mowbray might be responsible But he left Cato's only a few minutes before we did. H would not have had time."

"That is true," Jenner mused as she struggled to remem ber if Poulton had left earlier. She had the impression h had.

Lacey's brow was furrowed with thought and perhap pain. "Why did you come with us tonight? You don't en joy gambling in the least."

"You will laugh," she said, glad to distract him fron thoughts of Mowbray. "To try to keep Dennis out of trou ble. He moves with a fast and rather reckless set. When I an with them, I can sometimes curb Dennis' rashest impulses He seems to listen to me, Lord knows why. I'm a sort o walking conscience, I suppose."

"Caroline says it is my fault Dennis is suddenly so wild and I begin to think there is some justice in what she says," Lacey admitted. "I have not set much of an example fo him."

"Do you want to know what I think?"

"Always, love."

"Dennis is trying to cut loose from a dominating mother He still loves her, but she has always been the driving forc in his life. Unless he is in a position to buy himself a com mission soon, or otherwise gain his independence, I fear hi attempts at rebellion will continue just as your attempts t escape continue. And with another war brewing he is evel more restless than before."

Lacey looked startled. "I don't think it will come to a wa precisely. And that's not what sent me into the army, but suppose I do try to keep away from Caroline."

"Is she very like your mother?"

"Yes. She doesn't cry as much." He stared at Jenner fo a moment. "You are like no other woman I have evel known."

"I'm not sure I want to know what brought that on."

"I mean it. You never resort to tears or tantrums to get your way. My mother did. That is what drove my father away. And you never deny yourself to me no matter how badly I've behaved."

"Did they all treat you like that?"

"Every other woman I have known."

"How many has that been in your vast experience?"

"I have kept three mistresses in this house," he said with mock pride. "Not at the same time, of course."

"I should hope not." Jenner laughed. "Does that three include me?"

"I don't count you as one of them. I don't keep you. You choose to stay."

She bent over to kiss him. "I can see why you have been soured on women. But you must see that most of them have little power or means to fight back without resorting to such tactics."

"And that is why you are so different? You have some control over your life."

"Yes, and I have been very much alone most of my life. If I cried in the night, there was no one to hear me, so it seemed a singularly useless thing to do."

"Whereas I had an overabundance of attention."

"Strange that two such different people should get along so well."

"You mean to let go of me and leave, but I don't want you to."

"If I tried to hang on to you I would be no better than the others, and you would come to hate me, as well."

"It is I who wish to hang on to you. Tell me your real name."

"If you promise to go to sleep I will tell you my initials."

"A game? All right. What are they?"

"J and P."

"You vixen!" He caught her arm and pulled her down to kiss her again. "You will keep your promise? You won't leave without telling me?"

"Do you imagine I would abandon you while you are laid up like this?"

Jenner would have stayed by Lacey's side until he was fully recovered if he had let her, but he would not permit her to haunt his sickroom. He did not like being coddled and resented even more the need to stay in bed. Jenner thought it might be better if she did go about as usual, but she had no taste for any of the pleasures of London when all she could think of was Lacey lying there in pain.

Dennis presented himself in Lacey's room late the next morning.

"Collins said you wanted to see me."

"Yes, Dennis. I want you to keep an eye on Jenner for me."

"What do you mean, spy on him?"

"No, of course not. Just see that he stays out of trouble. He doesn't know his way about yet. So when he is not with Caroline and Stella, I would just like you to look out for him."

"Jenner? He can take care of himself."

"I know, it's just that after last night, I realized what a dangerous place London can be. At least make sure he doesn't go wandering the streets at night."

"I will ride with him or take him about at night, but I will be damned if I let him drag me off to his libraries and museums. You know he just barely escapes being bookish."

Lacey laughed. "He would be glad to hear you have such a high opinion of him."

"But I do like him, and if he is overprudent sometimes, it's not from cowardice."

"I admire Jenner, too—so young to be so responsible."

"What is that supposed to mean?" Dennis asked suspiciously.

"I was comparing Jenner to myself, not you. I have foisted far too many of my duties onto you as it is. You are entitled to your fun."

"If you are not satisfied with the way I managed Kettering in your absence you have only to say so."

"For God's sake, Dennis. You must have a terrible head from last night. I didn't call you in to pick a quarrel with you. Go back to bed."

"Bed is where I would still be, but Jenner says we must ride at least twice a day to keep all the horses exercised. But I ask you, before breakfast?"

"I expect you will be hard-pressed to keep pace with Jenner. I know I am."

"Enjoy your rest, then. And I will keep an eye on him, but I think you are worrying over nothing."

Dennis tended to keep to the more populated paths on these rides so that he could greet acquaintances. Riding with him was much more formal than going with Lacey, who would tear off on a gallop first to limber up the horses. Dennis and Jenner usually rode in Hyde Park in the morning when it was less crowded, then in Saint James Park in the afternoon.

Three days after the attack they were cantering home from Saint James by cutting through the leafy triangle of Green Park when a large horse with rider sprang out of the bushes almost on top of them. Both their mounts reared. Jenner's horse whirled and carried her into a tree limb that scraped her off. The mysterious rider disappeared as quickly as he had appeared, and Dennis caught the bridle before the horse could collect himself to bolt.

"Jenner, are you all right?"

"Yes," said Jenner picking herself up resignedly and recovering her hat. She remounted the sweating horse and cooed to him to calm him down. "It was not your fault, boy." She stroked his neck. "For God's sake, Dennis, don't tell Lacey I fell off Lancer. He might not let me ride him again."

Lacey was asleep when Jenner came in so she lay down on her bed for awhile. The fall had meant nothing but a few bruises, but she was tired from too many late nights and fell asleep. She awoke to see Lacey sitting on the edge of the bed and smiled at him. "Lacey. Should you be up?"

"Let me take you to Kettering. We can do as we please there."

"Something tells me I would get into more trouble there than in London."

Thereafter Jenner made her rides with Dennis more random, sometimes changing her mind about where they would ride at the last moment. She broke up their daily routines as much as possible. She told Dennis the horses got bored if they did not do so. Dennis grew a little impatient with this nonsense, but Jenner was, after all, Lacey's guest, so he said nothing.

Jenner packed her next letter to her aunts with news of her music lessons, the plays and concerts she had attended and the buildings she had seen. Even to her it sounded too frantically gay. The truth was Jenner felt herself growing more and more entrapped. Each day she felt closer to Lacey and less inclined to give him up. The frightening thing was that she knew his feelings for her went beyond possessiveness. And now she feared she had placed him in danger—and Dennis, as well. The thought that Stella might also be victimized by Mowbray was even more unsettling. As soon as Lacey was well enough she would have to leave before anything else happened.

* * *

With Lacey laid up, Jenner had almost sole responsibility for escorting Stella and Caroline about at night. This was no real burden to Jenner and not even dangerous since they went in the carriage. But Jenner worried that Stella's dependence on her would turn into something more.

After the encounter with Poulton, Jenner never willingly let Stella out of her sight, not that she would be any use against someone like Poulton. "Please, no more balconies," Jenner begged. Stella reluctantly agreed and, for the most part, behaved herself. It seemed that it was only when the possessive gaze of George Marsh was upon her that Stella evaded Jenner. This sent Jenner searching through the crowded salons with a hunted look upon her face until she discovered what a good pointer George was. If she could but locate him he was sure to be staring doggedly in the direction Stella had taken. Why George did not pursue Stella or at least wander nonchalantly into the room where she was closeted, Jenner could not fathom. Finding Stella tête-à-tête on a sofa somewhere had become such an ordinary thing for Jenner that she was not even surprised by it. Fortunately, it was usually the callow youth with Stella who blushed and stammered. Occasionally Jenner encountered her with an amused soldier, seldom with an impatient rake. Stella was popular and lovely in her own way, but not such a stunner as to attract the more competitive males. Her expectations from Lacey were not accounted to be great enough to put her in danger from seasoned fortune hunters.

Jenner came upon George pacing the hall at the Averys' ball.

"All right, where is she?" Jenner asked tiredly.

"Does her mother have no control over her at all? Someone must tell her it is not the thing to be closeting herself with strange men like this."

"I have tried, George. Why don't you speak to her?"

"It's not my place."

"I suppose you are right. In here?"

Jenner had a rather bored expression on her face, expecting to confront another younger son or half-pay officer, when she came up against Mowbray. A tremor went through her, and he saw it. For once, Stella had nearly lost her self-possession and seemed glad to see Jenner rather than disappointed.

"Ready to go in to supper, Stella?"

"Stella is going to dine with me tonight." Mowbray looked at Jenner with a fulminating challenge.

"I see." Jenner walked toward them, putting her hand in her pocket. "Stella...your vinaigrette," Jenner said, extending her hand.

Stella managed to extricate her hand from Mowbray's to take the article, then prepared to follow her, but Mowbray took her arm. Jenner had no doubt that Mowbray would follow her. If Mowbray intended to pick a quarrel with her, or even just torture her, he most certainly would.

Caroline was not aware of anything particularly unsavory about Mowbray, so she had no qualms sharing a table with him. She even found him amusing. In spite of what she knew about him, Jenner had also to admit he could be quite charming.

"And you," Mowbray broke into her thoughts. "I thought you said you were soon leaving."

"Yes, I have just one more errand to perform," Jenner said, pushing away her untouched plate and reaching for her wine. The look Mowbray cast upon her almost made her choke. What on earth could he think she meant that he would look at her so, as though he would gladly kill her? That look frightened her but it also gave her a strange sense of power. There was a way for her to hurt him. It was her misfortune that she did not know what it was. How to get him to tell her was the problem. Perhaps she had more than one task, then. Her heart gave a little leap and her blood pounded with the thought of revenge. She had not realized how close her hatred was to the surface until that moment. She pushed it down with an effort. "So many stories to tell," she sighed as she turned from the gay, chattering throng of guests to look into Mowbray's menacing eyes.

"Have a care your stories do not land you in trouble one of these days."

"They may already have done so," Jenner assured him.

His hand was arrested in the act of taking snuff but he said nothing.

"Have you read Jenner's latest book?" Caroline asked.

"Oh, yes, I have made a study of it," Mowbray assured her in a tone that boded ill for Jenner. She thought frantically over her books, but no. She had been over them dozens of times to assure herself that she could not give Rob away by so much as the description of an inn or a tree. Mowbray would find nothing useful there.

"I wonder that the runners have not been to visit you. You may hold the key to more than one unsolved crime."

Jenner swallowed hard. "There's very little I could tell them," she said.

"How was it?" Mowbray continued. "You were kidnapped and that is how you and your captor passed the time, trading stories. That is the weakest of all your tales. Why did he let you go?"

"Perhaps he tired of my company."

"Yes, I can believe that. But why not just kill you?"

"For a highwayman he had a clean conscience. He had never done murder, at any rate."

"There are those who could do murder with a clean conscience."

"Yes, I am just beginning to see that."

"I didn't know you were kidnapped, Jenner. How terrible for you," Stella said.

"Did your aunts ransom you, then?" asked Caroline.

"If they had known they might have done something. But the note I wrote was utter nonsense. You see I took a gamble that the highwayman could not read. I wrote them that I had been called away for a few days."

"You do take chances." Mowbray almost looked like he was beginning to believe her, and she enjoyed leading him on with one of her stories.

"It was sweet of you not to worry your aunts," Caroline insisted.

"Oh, they were worried enough when you consider the fellow delivered the note tied to a brickbat thrown through the sitting room window."

Even Mowbray gave a snort of laughter.

Stella suppressed her giggles. "It was not funny at the time, I am sure."

"How did you explain their lack of response?" Mowbray asked.

"I implied that he would be doing them a favor, that they would be well rid of me."

"Yes, I quite see that...but your cousin," Mowbray drawled. "Surely she could have helped you."

Jenner flinched and looked sharply at him. "How could she? Scarcely more than a child herself and ill into the bargain. They never told her."

"I did not know you have a cousin, Jenner," Caroline said.

"What is she like?" Stella asked.

"Very like me," Jenner said, regaining her composure.

"But you must bring her to town and your aunts as well," Caroline invited.

"No. They never go anywhere." Jenner was beginning to worry that Mowbray might reveal where her cousin lived.

"But why not?" Stella asked.

"They used to go to Bath for a month in the winter but when people there found out about my cousin, there was no joy in that any more. If they are to be shunned anyway they may as well suffer it at home."

"Why, Jenner, what is wrong with your cousin?"

Jenner had to tread a fine line between shocking them and giving a dig at Mowbray. She stared at the table as she began. "She was ruined very early in life by an attack unworthy of a man, let alone a gentleman."

Mowbray stiffened. Caroline and Stella looked all sympathy.

"How terrible. Did they catch him?" Caroline asked.

"No." Jenner took a gulp of wine and plunged ahead. "Mercifully, she lost the child."

Mowbray's head came up, not in shock, but in anger. Jenner forced herself to be objective about his reaction. She decided he looked ill-used, as though it was her fault he had gotten her pregnant.

"Surely she would be better off where people don't know her then," suggested Stella.

"She does not lie to herself. She will not deceive anyone else."

"But how will she ever meet anyone?"

"She will not." Jenner looked levelly at Mowbray. "When my aunts are gone she will be quite alone."

"At least she has you," said Stella.

"I am very nearly useless to her."

"You must bring them to Kettering for the holidays, at least," Caroline invited.

"They will be touched by your kindness, but they will not come. So you see, Stella, why I trail after you so boorishly when you wander off." Jenner turned to look at Mowbray. "A reputation is such an easy thing to lose."

"I won't do it again," Stella promised.

If Jenner had detected the slightest hint of regret in Mowbray, she might have gone home and forgotten him. But in his face she read only discomfort, hatred and perhaps fear. No, it was puzzlement. He wondered why she did not expose him. He could not know that it was the last thing Jenner wanted. If it became necessary to save Stella, then she would have to tell them and risk Lacey finding out. But Lacey was in no shape right now to deal with the likes of Mowbray, not that a bad leg would have stopped him trying. The remembrance of Lacey choking back the pain these past four nights made Jenner's eyes glitter. There had to be a safe way to get rid of Mowbray.

Suddenly she realized how close she had come to setting foot in his trap. Her heart set up that awful thudding again. Had she accused him of the crime he would have called her out. Whether they fought with pistols or swords Jenner felt it would have meant the end of her. Not only was Mowbray ruthless, he was clever. If she let her hate get in the way again she could destroy them all. She was a fine one to be lecturing Stella on prudence when she herself presented the greatest danger of all to the girl.

"Jenner, are you quite well?" Caroline asked.

"Red wine never agrees with me."

"We are ready to leave anyway."

"I will send for the carriage then." Jenner swayed a little as she stood, and it was not a ruse. She was feeling giddy after such a close brush with disaster. How many other ways would Mowbray find to provoke her?

Jenner and Dennis had exercised two of Lacey's hacks after breakfast. Then Dennis had rushed off to his clubs to discuss the latest war news. Jenner came back from the stables hoping to get in a few hours of work before lunch but she heard voices in the morning room, George's low murmur and his mother's querulous complaining. In good conscience she could not leave Caroline and Stella to bear the brunt of Lady Marsh's tongue. To her surprise Caroline was alone with them, suffering an interrogation into her daughter's conduct the previous night. Jenner found this confusing since she assumed Lady Marsh did not approve of Stella, anyway. Why then would she bother to come here and complain of her conduct? There was some commotion in the hall and Edwards finally intruded to ask for Jenner.

"It's Miss Langley's maid, sir. The foolish girl has come back without her."

"What happened, Molly?"

"A gentleman stopped us in the park and invited her to drive with him, but it was so long ago and they never came back."

"Who was it? Did he say?"

"She called him Ashton."

"Mowbray! I must find her. Where did they leave you?"

"Near Green Park."

Jenner poked her head in the door. "George, a word with you."

"What is going on?" Lady Marsh demanded.

Jenner was so frantic she blurted out, "I need him to help me look for Stella. George, you can take my horse."

"George is not dressed for riding," his mother asserted.

George looked resentfully at his mother but said nothing.

Jenner opened her mouth and was about to offer him Lacey's team but stopped herself. She had no time for vacillation. "I will go myself, then."

She dashed out the back door and was cantering out of the stable by the time Caroline had wrung the whole story out of the maid. She was having trouble understanding Jenner's concern, or Molly's.

Jenner was racking her brains to remember what Stella had been wearing that morning since she had no idea what

Mowbray drove. She went no slower than a canter and cut through the open spaces at full gallop, causing disapproving stares and raised eyebrows as Ebony's thudding hooves threw up chunks of sod and generally disturbed the well-ordered pace of the day. She covered Green Park in a very few minutes and rode on toward Hyde Park. Lord Coyle hailed her and she thundered up to his team of blacks, just barely stopping in time. "Have you seen Stella?"

"Yes, with old Mowbray. What is the world coming to...?"

"Where? I must find her."

Coyle pointed toward the North Ride and Jenner tore off disregarding all stares. Ebony seemed to sense her excitement and threw himself into the mad gamble with a passion. Jenner had never ridden him flat out before and ordinarily would have enjoyed an excuse to test him to the limit. But her fears for Stella pushed all else from her mind. Finally she saw a curricle being jerked along by a rackety bay team. The curricle's occupants were obviously disputing over something, which was not making it any easier for Mowbray to control the disorderly horses. Jenner thought now that she had seen the bays before but she could not really remember when. She thundered up to them and doffed her hat.

"Nice day for a drive." Jenner saw bloody froth dripping from the bits. "Having a problem?"

"No! And what do you think you are doing here?"

"Why, looking for Stella, of course. Caroline wants you, Stella."

Stella opened her mouth to speak but was cut off by Mowbray.

"I will bring her home when I am good and ready."

"I will ride with you then."

"We don't want your company, boy."

Mowbray cut at Ebony with his whip and caught the valiant horse on the nose. Ebony staggered sideways and nearly fell over on Jenner. So much for the light approach.

"I said I must take Stella home. Caroline is not well. Are you going to bring her or not?"

"In my own time."

Jenner caught the near horse's rein and pulled it up, causing the curricle to turn slowly toward her. Mowbray started cutting at her with the whip but Stella struggled for possession of it.

With an effort Jenner yanked the rein out of Mowbray's hand. The team danced in place and looked ready to bolt. Jenner played the rein out and kept the team circling slowly as she edged Ebony to Stella. She kicked her foot out of her left stirrup and held one hand out to Stella. "Don't be afraid, Stella. It's only a step." A careful girl would have been frightened of trying to step from a moving curricle onto an excited horse. But Stella did not hesitate. She put her foot in the iron, grabbed a handful of mane and swung herself around to sit sidesaddle fashion on Ebony's withers. Jenner dropped the team's rein, took a good hold on Stella and cantered off with Mowbray's curses ringing in her ears.

"I shall call you out for this!"

"What did you say?" Jenner shouted over her shoulder at him.

She saw Coyle's team coming toward them and brought the tired Ebony to a walk.

"Coyle, I must get Stella home," Jenner said breathlessly. "Would you . . . ?"

"Of course. You know I have read about carrying a fair damsel off over your saddlebow," Coyle said as Jenner helped Stella off the horse and into his phaeton, "but I have never actually seen anyone do it."

"I do not recommend it," Jenner said grimly as she mounted the tired Ebony. "It is a miracle we both stayed on—and stop laughing at me Coyle! Stella, if you want to get me shot you are taking the quickest way to it. Mowbray will not soon forget my interference today." Jenner had been cool enough during the rescue but now she was feeling shaky, her leg muscles twitching with fatigue.

"I had no idea what he was really like."

"But you have been on the town for three years. You should know better than I what is proper behavior. Oh, don't look at me so. You make me feel like a monster after you had the courage to trust me with your life."

Coyle joked with Stella until her fright had left her and he had even talked her out of the sulks by the time they reached the house. The groom who came out to take the lathered Ebony raked Jenner with a look of reproof. Just when she thought nothing more could go wrong Stella tumbled out of the phaeton into her arms with a passionate kiss. Jenner staggered under her weight and the shock, for Stella had never before offered her more than a sisterly peck on the cheek. Coyle was laughing at her again, and to make matters worse Jenner spied George Marsh's angry face at the window as Stella tripped into the house. All in all she decided she would rather face Hawes' wrath than George and his mother, so she turned her steps in the direction of the stable.

Lacey limped downstairs for dinner that night. Dennis came in late and no more sat down than he attacked Jenner with mock anger. "What is this I have been hearing about you riding around the park with Stella up before you and kissing her in the street?"

"Oh, you were talking to Coyle," Jenner surmised, flushing slightly.

"Yes, but he was not the only one who saw you." Dennis nodded at Lacey's look of amused surprise. "Now they are laying bets at White's as to whether the Ice Maiden will fall to you or not.''

''The what?'' Jenner blurted out.

''Oh, that's what they call her.''

''What does it mean?'' asked Stella, entranced.

Dennis thought for a moment and said, ''That no one has touched your heart.''

''I rather like it,'' Stella mused.

''I do not,'' Caroline said coldly. ''It is not the thing for a young lady to be the subject of wagers at a gentlemen's club.''

''How is the betting running?'' Lacey asked, suppressing a smile.

''Two to one for Jenner, even though I told them Stella would probably break him like a stick.''

Jenner cringed at Dennis' remark.

Lacey chuckled. ''And how did you bet?''

''I would not waste my money on such a trifle. I did wager twenty guineas Napoleon would reach Paris without being arrested, and I'm sorry to say I won.''

Lacey ignored this. ''As I recall Stella is not the first one to bear the title of Ice Maiden.''

Caroline flushed.

''Mother!'' Stella gasped.

''In her day Caroline broke far more hearts than you and then chose quiet Henry Langley. Don't you mean to have any of them, child?''

''Well, of course I do. I know what I am about,'' Stella said.

Jenner winced as Stella smiled kindly on her.

As Jenner prepared to work in the book room that evening Lacey said, ''I thought you were going to the theater tonight.''

''Dennis is filling in for me.''

"I see. Lying low for awhile."

"In a manner of speaking. You realize I am a very dangerous person for Stella to be associating with. It is time I should be thinking about—"

"No! You promised you would not leave me while I am laid up like this," Lacey said with an almost childish petulance.

"Of course I will not leave you now. But what if Stella really does develop an attachment for me?"

"I would not worry. Most likely she is just making use of you. Women do that, you know."

"All of them?" Jenner asked in amazement.

"With perhaps one exception."

Jenner looked away, then asked, "Shall I read to you?"

"I can do that myself. You go on about your work."

They read and worked in companionable silence for a few hours, Jenner at the desk and Lacey propped up in one of the armchairs. Jenner was very nearly oblivious to Lacey's presence, and he liked that. It left him free to observe her, how the dying sun picked out red highlights in her hair, how the newly lit candles made her dark eyes sparkle when she came upon an idea. The scratch of her pen relentlessly across the paper was a comforting domestic sound to Lacey. He would give anything to spend all his evenings thus, reading a bit, dozing a little and waking to find her always there.

Edwards and the tea tray finally roused Jenner and she took a deep breath, coming back into Lacey's world with a sigh. Where she had been or what she had been doing he would not know unless he got to read what she had been writing. The wonder must have shown in his face.

"Why do you look at me so? Oh, I have been ignoring you. I'm sorry," she said, bringing him his cup.

"But I like to watch you work."

"What are you talking about?"

"Occasionally you say little things like, 'Of course,' or, 'Why not?' or you hum part of some music."

"Do I? How annoying of me. I didn't realize it. My mind is so cluttered it gets things all mixed together."

"When will I get to read that?"

"Not until it is printed, if it ever is. I should not be keeping you up. Shall I help Collins put you to bed?"

"No, he is used to helping me when I am laid up."

When they had finished their tea Jenner trailed after Lacey as he hobbled up the stairs. He had excluded her from any intimacy with him since the injury. When she thought about how horrified he was over a bruise or a cut on her, she began to understand why he did not want her to see what must be a horribly dented and bruised thigh muscle. If he was that upset by disfigurement, the war must have wreaked havoc with his sensibilities.

Chapter Seven

"How did the shooting go at Manton's?" Lacey called from the book room when he heard Dennis come into the house.

Dennis pushed the door open and raised his eyebrows at Lacey's propped-up leg. "Should you be up?"

"The doctor told me to use it," Lacey said resentfully. "Where's Jenner?"

"I left him at the library." Dennis lounged tiredly into a chair. "And it did not go well. How can someone who rides like a demon, and even fences passably, be such a terrible shot?"

Lacey chuckled as he polished one of his antique pistols. "When I am on my feet again, I will see what I can do with him."

"How will you cure him of flinching?"

Lacey looked at Dennis and knit his brows. "There is a reason for that," Lacey defended his protégé.

"What?"

Lacey hesitated, thinking frantically. "When I first met Jenner—crashed into him—his horse was hurt so badly it had to be destroyed. Hawes shot it. Jenner was extremely attached to that horse."

"I see. That's why you gave him Ebony."

"Yes. Not jealous, are you?"

"The only thing I want from you is the one thing you will never buy me."

"A commission."

"Yes."

"What for? This little flare-up will all be over before you could get into it."

"That's the thing. It may be my last chance," Dennis said passionately then subsided as he read the answer in his uncle's eyes.

"What are you up to tonight?" Lacey asked.

"I thought I would take Jenner to the show at Vauxhall. Not quite his style, but he may enjoy it."

"Good. That should be safe enough."

Jenner laughed through the operettas and pantomimes and confessed to Dennis that she did find the gardens more enjoyable than an evening at Cato's. "But I can see why Caroline won't let Stella come here. I have never seen so many unchaperoned girls in my life."

"Yes, it should be easy to set up a flirt. I fancy that little blond chit over there."

"Don't let me hold you back. I can amuse myself."

Jenner left Dennis leaning over one of the boxes chatting up the pretty girl and strolled for a time around the lighted paths, ignoring the giggling and lovemaking going on at the tables and secluded benches. She returned to the main pavilion in time to see Dennis ousted by the appearance of a dragon of a mother. Jenner turned away so that Dennis would not catch her smirking and ran smash into Mowbray. Her apology died on her lips when she saw the child he had hold of. Mowbray cursed her. It wrenched Jenner's stomach to watch his hand tighten on the girl's white arm. Whatever it cost her Jenner knew she had to make a push to free the child. She could not take her eyes off the young woman's face, since the look of terror was one well known to her.

"I think you are not looking well, child," she said to the trembling girl. "Shall I help you find your mother?"

"Oh, yes, please." The young woman was desperate enough to accept help even from a stranger.

"Who asked you to interfere?" Mowbray snarled.

"The young lady, of course. I think you are too drunk to entertain her properly."

Mowbray lunged at her, but since Jenner picked that moment to stand on his left foot, he fell quite ungracefully on his face. He could not have been so drunk as Jenner supposed for he was on his feet in a moment and made a grab for her, but Dennis, who had been more than a casual observer, spun him about and knocked him out as expertly as Lacey would have. Dennis then took the other arm of the girl now clinging to Jenner and strolled off with them as casually as though he had just changed partners at a dance.

"Who are you here with, child?" Jenner asked.

"My aunt, but she went to talk to someone, and when Trudy and Ben left the box to dance, this man came. I don't even know him."

"If it comes to that, you don't know us. But that can soon be mended. I am Dennis Langley. This is Jenner Page."

"I'm Emaline Barnstaple. I didn't know what it would be like."

"I advise you not to come here again without a male escort that will take his job seriously," Jenner advised. "Your reputation could easily be ruined."

Emaline's light brown eyes gazed up into Jenner's dark ones as though Jenner was some kind of heroic savior. "I shall never come here again. Oh, there is my aunt."

The girl introduced her new acquaintances and the old woman seemed vaguely pleased to meet them.

"Good night, Emaline. You will be careful from now on."

"Oh, yes, and thank you."

"Too bad her aunt showed up," Dennis confided. "You were doing all right for yourself."

"I'm not sure where I would have been if you had not intervened."

Dennis laughed. "I don't know where you get your cheek from, taking the chit right out of Mowbray's arms."

"I couldn't leave such a child in Mowbray's clutches. You don't know what he is capable of. You would have done the same."

"Why? You interest yourself a great deal in a tradesman's daughter."

"I would not have cared who she was. I would have tried to help any girl trapped by him against her will."

"She is a taking little piece."

"Is that an accusation or merely an observation?" Jenner looked suddenly scornful.

"I simply meant I can scarcely blame Mowbray for—"

"Are you saying that you would have taken advantage of her, as well?" Jenner asked pointedly.

"No, I suppose not."

"But you see her very ignorance as a fault that justifies his behavior. A strange world where innocence is a sin punished by the likes of Mowbray."

"You have something against the man, don't you?"

"Yes, I had almost reconciled myself to it, but now, knowing that he continues on the same path..."

"What do you mean to do?"

"I don't know. Don't say anything about this to Lacey."

"As you wish, but you know how he worries about you."

"Yes, I know. He is determined to restore me unscathed to my aunts."

* * *

"You are very thoughtful tonight," Lacey commented when Jenner came to say good night and fuss with his pillows.

"It was something Dennis said."

"What?"

"I just hope Dennis knows you well enough to model himself after you, not after your reputation."

"Why should he model himself after me at all?" Lacey asked, propping himself up on one elbow.

"He worships you, Lacey. You must know that."

Lacey frowned, his eyebrows knit.

"It's not just you. It's all the men he associates with. How old was he when his father died?"

"Just fifteen."

"When he needed him most. Is it any wonder he looks to you?"

"I don't want him to."

"No, you would not. But he cannot help admiring you any more than I can. He, for what he thinks you are—I, for what I know you to be."

"What do you mean?"

"Perfect people are so boring. That is why people enjoy Chad Bostwick's story so much. And I love you more for your flaws than your virtues."

"Fortunate for me." Lacey smirked.

"It means you are human. But when Dennis tries to emulate you . . ."

"What brought all this on?"

"We rescued a young girl tonight from a drunken gentlemen—never mind who. Dennis seemed more in sympathy with him than with the girl. He even suggested that since she is not a lady—whatever that means—she is fair game for such advances."

"In such a place, I suppose she is," Lacey said darkly.

"Would you seduce an innocent child who finds herself alone in the wrong place?" She expected some flip remark. Instead, the light died out of Lacey's eyes and the hunted look came. "I might have done. I have done so."

"What are you saying? You forced a woman against her will?"

"If it was not rape it was something very close to it. She refused me and I took her anyway."

"Who was it? Do you know?"

"It was Elaina."

"Oh. Here?" Jenner asked in some relief.

"Yes."

"Is that why she left you?"

"I think so. She was the only one who showed the least spark of independence, and I tried to crush it. I could not, of course."

"You loved her." Jenner walked to the window to look out at nothing.

"Yes, or what passed for love with me in those days. You have taught me better."

"And you felt you had to tell me," Jenner mused.

"Knowing what you have been through, I had to tell you. If it had been me riding down that lane instead of the other man, it might be me you hate now instead of him."

"I do not think it would have happened that way," she said as she turned to sit on the windowsill, her arms folded.

"If I were drunk enough..."

"You have a certain compassion for the helpless that would have prevented such an act."

"Do you know me so well?" he growled. "Are you never afraid of me?"

"Never," she said softly.

"Well, I am afraid," he whispered. "I do not know what I am about sometimes...how I should act. Everything should not be a whim."

"Your first impulse is the truest I have found."

"My first impulse when I saw you naked was to have you there and then," he admitted.

"Do you imagine things would have turned out differently if you had?" She walked to the bed and sat beside him.

"I don't know. It frightens me to think of it."

"Your first impulse when you saw me fallen in the fog was to rescue me."

"But I didn't know who you were then."

"Oh, if you had guessed I was a girl, you would not have saved me. I see."

"You cannot turn this into a jest."

"I will concede you the blackest villain I have ever encountered, if it will make you happy. But I know better. If only Dennis . . ."

"I will speak to him, but a lecture on morals coming from me is not likely to meet with any very serious reception."

Jenner did not think Lacey had succeeded in talking to his nephew, for the next night Dennis, Coyle and Lyme took her to Lady Simms' gaming salon. There was one significant difference between Cato's and this place—it abounded in ladies, young and otherwise. They ran the E.O. wheel, dealt faro, played piquet individually with customers and joked and laughed with everyone. The games were fair so far as Jenner could make out, and the wine was passable and free. Therein lay the downfall of most of the young bloods, but perhaps it was so pleasant to lose to a pretty face they did not mind it.

Jenner could not help but notice the procession of couples up and down the stairs. She had seen Lord Coyle slip away and assumed her other two companions had done the same. The place had such a well-bred air to it that Jenner did not feel in the least uncomfortable being left to her own devices. That is, until a self-possessed beauty walked up and introduced herself.

"Mr. Page? I am Louisa. Lord Coyle recommended you to me."

Jenner looked vaguely at the finely chiseled face and the magnificent black curls. The woman was in her thirties, but attractive and refined.

"What?" Jenner asked.

"If you should like to go upstairs, I'm sure I could give you satisfaction."

"Oh! Yes." Jenner gulped. "I'm sure you could, too, but I doubt that you would be satisfied with me." She found herself flushing as the older woman smiled at her. "I'm afraid I have had far to much wine to contemplate that to-night, but—what is your usual fee?"

"Fee? A gift of twenty would be appropriate, but there is no need . . ."

"I would like to talk to you. Could we have supper to-gether?"

"Yes, I think they have laid it out in the gold salon."

Jenner was impressed by the fare, delicate cakes and fresh salmon, green peas from the country, champagne and all manner of other delicacies. It puzzled her that they could afford to lay out such a feast every night.

"What did you want to talk about?" Louisa asked as Jenner seated her.

"London. I am a writer of sorts and not very familiar with the town yet."

"You want me to tell you about the sights?" Louisa laughed. "I do not get out much myself. Stay north of the river and do not walk about alone at night. That's all I can tell you."

"This house is not exactly what I expected. It's rather . . . pleasant. What is it like to work here?"

The woman's eyes narrowed.

"You needn't answer me, but I promise I am only curious. I suppose I had pictured that you might be victimized, but I do not think that is so."

"Why no, I have chosen my life. I'm not saying I would not prefer another if I were rich, but I had choices to make and this seemed the most pleasant."

"But isn't it . . . demanding?" Jenner finally got out.

"Not particularly. In fact, you would be surprised how many men want just to talk. There are a few strange ones, but we do not have to entertain anyone whom we particularly dislike. We have some quite famous guests, you know," Louisa said with pride.

"I can imagine," Jenner said, but encouraged no confidences about these. "Have you—I would not ask you to mention names, but I was wondering if a man named Mowbray ever comes."

"Oh, him. Not often. Not unless we have someone new. He only likes the young ones. But I don't think Lady Simms invites him any more. He frightened one girl into leaving. A friend of yours?"

"Hardly." Jenner stared into space for a moment. "What would happen to you if you got with child?"

"Nothing very bad. I would go into the country until it's born. I have two children already, two girls. I see them every Sunday. They are in a good place."

"I'm happy for you."

Louisa seemed inclined to talk about her children and Jenner was interested. It was a different world from that of the ton, or even from that of a ruined woman in a small town in the north. It struck her that Louisa had not fared badly and that she had a great deal more freedom than many others. Jenner also suspected that the woman had been fortunate.

"Ready to go?" Coyle walked up to Jenner adjusting his neck cloth.

"Yes, thank you very much, Louisa." Jenner slipped her gift discreetly into the woman's hand as she took her leave of her, but this did not escape Lord Coyle's notice. Dennis and Lyme wandered in and nudged each other.

"Dennis!" Louisa said in pleasant surprise. "Where is Lacey keeping himself? I haven't seen him in months."

Jenner staggered a little but regained her composure almost immediately.

"He's laid up right now with a bad leg."

"Came off one of his horses, I'll wager."

"Actually, we were attacked in Jermyn Street," Dennis replied.

"These footpads grow more bold every day. I was just warning Jenner about them."

"No use in doing that. He consorts with them." Dennis was as drunk as Jenner had yet seen him.

"I have never met a person I could not learn something from, if only to mind my own business," Jenner said with a chuckle. "Are you going to be able to walk home, Dennis? For I cannot carry you."

Dennis was as good as his word in not divulging any of the scrapes Jenner fell into. Whether from loyalty or a reluctance to provoke Lacey, Jenner could not be sure. But she was glad all the same. Jenner might have been better off if Lacey had not asked Dennis to keep an eye on her, for Dennis' idea of taking care of his young friend was to take her along on all the reckless enterprises he and his cronies got into.

"Where away tonight?" Lacey asked Dennis.

"Coyle has invited us to dinner."

"And cards afterward, I imagine," Lacey suggested.

"I have been holding my own," Dennis defended.

"Would you rather I stayed home and played cards with you?" Jenner asked Lacey.

Lacey only tossed this over in his mind once before shaking his head. He would not be satisfied with cards, and he was not up to anything else yet.

"Where is this dinner that we need the horses to get there?" Jenner asked as they rode southwest out of London.

"One of Coyle's father's estates near Woking. I have been there twice before, so do not worry about me losing the way, and we will arrive before dark."

"It's not getting there that worries me."

They had been cantering over open country for some time but came now to a small dark wood. Jenner was just thinking it would be a perfect place for an ambush when a horseman cut them off and aimed a pistol at her.

"Throw me your purses, both of you." The voice was unknown to Jenner, and she breathed a sigh of relief and made as if to comply. "I'll have that horse you be riding as well, lad."

"Don't be a fool. You couldn't keep him in feed," Jenner replied calmly.

"Off, I say."

"No, you will just have to shoot me. But remember, once you fire, even if you kill me, you can't get the horse. And unless you have another loaded pistol, Dennis will very likely overcome you."

The robber's horse was dancing nervously under a tight rein and the man appeared to be considering. But if Jenner's reasoning had undermined the man's confidence, it had bolstered Dennis'. He spurred his horse forward and grappled with the fellow's pistol arm until they both fell under the trampling hooves. The pistol discharged harmlessly into the ground and Dennis rolled on top and knocked the man out with one blow.

Jenner had managed to catch the reins of the loose horses and dismounted to look at the man. He was old, nearly sixty, she thought, or looked it.

"Give me your handkerchief?" demanded Dennis.

"What are you going to do?"

"Tie him up."

"No."

The would-be highwayman had come to and sat listening dispiritedly to their debate.

"What the devil do you mean? He could have killed you."

"But he didn't," said Jenner, giving the man her hand and pulling him to his feet. "A foolish risk for a few guineas, grandfather, but I expect you are hungry." She gave him most of the money she carried, close to twenty-five pounds.

"Are you mad?" asked Dennis. "We must turn him over to the authorities."

"What for? He's harmless enough. Besides, if we go by your moral code we deserved to be robbed for riding this track at dusk. Think of it as paying a toll, Dennis." Jenner put the reins of the bony cob back in the old man's hands. "I wish it were enough to buy you a new way of life."

"Not at my age, lad," he said, pocketing the money and recovering his pistol. He remounted wearily.

"I can't believe you mean to let him go."

"Well, I suppose we could take him with us to Lord Coyle's dinner." She looked an invitation at the ragged highwayman and Dennis' mouth dropped open.

"Ah, no, thankee, lad. I can dine better at an inn I know of."

"Have a care you don't hurt anyone. I should hate to see you hang," Jenner called out to him.

"Oh, I never puts a ball in." The old man chuckled as he cantered off, touching the pistol to the brim of his hat.

"Are you not at least going to lay evidence against him?"

"We should look a pair of fools, when you still have your money and I gave mine freely to an old man with an unloaded pistol."

"I shall never understand you."

"Probably not."

Dennis lost no time in describing their adventure to the assembled crowd at Coyle's well-laden table. Most of them, coltish lads like Dennis, were surprised. That Jenner would not surrender her horse they took for granted, but they could not understand why she let the man go.

"Another story?" Coyle asked.

"Perhaps. I would rather think of him lightening purses along the road or robbing ladies' trinkets than rotting in prison."

She refused the loan of stakes to gamble with and instead offered to play music for them while they were at their cards. She knew a good many ballads from Rob and sang the words in her low, rich voice. It was into the early hours before she realized how late it was, and by then Dennis was drunk past staying on a horse. She let him rest where he fell asleep in a chair, not envying the head he would have in the morning. Even Lord Coyle had not gone to bed, but lay sprawled forward on the card table still holding a wineglass.

She found a book, a tolerably comfortable chair and a candle that had not burned itself out. She was well contented until nearly dawn when she took herself for a walk about the grounds. Dawn was too tempting to miss. There was something magical about watching the light creep into the shadowed woods and the sun break over the horizon with great streaks of red, lighting first the tops of the trees before washing the rest of the landscape with gold.

She informed the sole stable boy who was up and about that they would need their horses by eight o'clock and slipped him half a crown to see they were fed well before that time.

Lack of sleep had made her a bit giddy, but once she had splashed some cold water on her face from the small stream that fed the ornamental pond, she tackled her walk with more vigor. She had not realized how much she missed the country, but instead of thinking about home, she found herself wondering if Kettering was so well placed and laid out. Best not to think of it, for she would never see it.

She had made a broad circuit of the gardens and woods and was approaching the house again from the front and feeling rather refreshed when she saw Lord Coyle pacing the circular drive and smoking. He was looking rather strained for one so young. Jenner was amazed at how much she liked Coyle and the others. Part of it was the way they treated her, like one of them. She couldn't help enjoying the novelty of having friends for the first time in her life. She wondered how Lacey would have treated her if he had not discovered her identity. Probably the same she thought. Even so, she would still be trapped. She would not have been able to keep in touch with him. It would have been too risky.

She shook off her brooding and walked up to Coyle. "I was just admiring your grounds."

"You must have a hard head, Jenner—up all night drinking and you look as fresh as the morning dew."

"Just the opposite. I can scarcely drink at all."

"You keep pace with us."

"I may raise my glass as often, but only to take a sip. Have you not noticed that I drop the stakes when you are all in your cups? Else I would be guilty of fleecing you."

Coyle laughed. "I just thought you were running short of funds."

"No, I am pretty well fixed."

"Have I ever told you how much I envy you?"

"Me, a humble teller of tales?"

"Whatever you are you have made yourself. You could be left penniless in a foreign country and earn your keep, whereas I would most likely starve."

"Not if there were any pretty women about."

Coyle crushed out his cigar, laughed and started toward the house. "I think they are laying out some breakfast for us."

"I could do with some coffee, but I think it would be unwise for Dennis to look at food."

"I should have left orders to have them put to bed."

"Hardly worth the effort."

The sound of a carriage and horses coming up the drive made them turn to see a curricle being pulled by a familiar pair of blood-red chestnuts.

"Is that Lacey's team?"

"Lord, yes, and he looks as mad as fire. I was hoping we would be home before he got up."

Only Jenner had noticed Lacey's face change, at sight of her, from anxiety to a momentary joy before it became wrathful.

Hawes pulled the team up at Lacey's command. "So you are not lying dead on the road."

"No, did you expect me to be?"

"When you did not return."

"Dennis was in no condition to ride, so I thought it best to wait for daylight."

"Why?" Lacey demanded as he gingerly descended from the curricle.

"I have heard that there are highwaymen about." She winked at Coyle and the young man burst out laughing.

"I would have thought that would have delighted you," Lacey said tartly, leaning on his walking stick and looking in a puzzled way at Coyle.

"It did," said Coyle, chuckling as he helped Lacey up the steps and into the house."

"What is that supposed to mean?" Lacey asked as he limped into the breakfast room.

"They were held up," Coyle explained.

Lacey jerked to a stop and scrutinized Jenner to make sure she was not hurt. "Anyone you know?" he asked casually.

This set Coyle off again, and Lacey found it difficult to maintain his anger at the same table with the giddy young lord and the substantial breakfast being served up to him. By the time Dennis made a disheveled appearance he got no more that a stern look from his uncle.

Dennis looked none too pleased to see Lacey, but caught the end of the highwayman story and renewed his complaints that Jenner had let the man go. "I can't understand it."

"That's because you have never been hungry," Jenner said, munching on her toast.

"Have you?"

"No, but I have seen what it can do to people."

"Speaking of being hungry," Lacey said, "try this ham, Dennis. It is excellent."

Jenner thought Dennis went a shade paler, if that was possible, and she watched with concern as he excused himself and bolted from the room.

"Well, you are revenged on Dennis. I wonder how you will punish me for worrying you."

"I will think of something. If he is going to be sick, he had best get it over with before we start for home."

In a few minutes Lacey himself looked as though he was going to be sick, for Lyme had thoughtlessly mentioned their visit to Lady Simms' establishment. Coyle noted Lacey's difficulty in swallowing and could not but be amused by the older man's discomfort.

"Louisa asked after you," Jenner said impishly, and Lacey nearly did choke.

"Louisa?" he asked in a strangled voice.

"Yes, she entertained Jenner last night," Coyle supplied. "You had a good time, didn't you Jenner?"

"It was...enlightening."

When they reached town midway through the morning, Lacey sent the miscreants off to bed, but appeared in Jenner's room before she could even undress. "You little wretch! Why didn't you tell me Dennis took you to such a place?"

"I didn't think it would do your peace of mind any good to find out, but when you did, you looked so funny I could not resist baiting you just a little." She sat on the bed and he sank down beside her.

"But how did you manage? You didn't tell her?"

"I did not go upstairs, Lacey. I said I had too much to drink. But I enjoyed talking to Louisa. I quite like her. I had wondered what you did all this past year."

"The thought doesn't bother you?" Lacey stared at her rather numbly.

"I like it better than the thought of you brooding in an empty house."

"And after you are gone?"

Jenner was silent and could not meet his eyes.

"Tell me where you live," he begged. "I can see you often." He tried to take her hands.

"No. My aunts were worried enough when Rob was about." She got up and paced to the window. "They are not stupid. I will not put them through that again."

"That's why you sent Rob away!"

"That was part of it. I will not run such a rig again. It worries them too much and I have already brought enough disgrace upon them."

"Then visit me at Kettering." Lacey came up behind her. "Say you are coming to look over my horses. You have not found one yet."

"Aunt Bette would come with me." Jenner turned to face him, her arms folded.

"We could still..."

"No. You may be able to handle it with Caroline in the house, but I could never manage it under the same roof with Aunt Bette. The shame of it is she would like you. They both would. I know it."

"Somewhere else then," Lacey offered desperately, taking her shoulders.

"If only I did not know your family so well I could stay always in the country and say I hated town. But I can never meet them as myself now." Jenner walked out of his embrace. "I have covered all this ground before. There is no way out or I would have found it by now."

"What am I thinking of?" Lacey said. "You must be dropping from lack of rest. You sleep now. I will think of something. And I will speak to Dennis."

Lacey was surprised to see Jenner dressed to go out in the early afternoon.

"Where to now—more books?"

"No, I'm going to accompany Lord Coyle on his ride with his fiancée, though what he needs with me I cannot imagine. I do seem to be getting embroiled in such a lot of things. So much for a quiet visit to town."

"You like Coyle."

"Yes."

"But you don't..."

"May I not like someone without being thought to fall in love with him?"

"Very well. But you did spend the night with him."

"With him and six other drunken snoring young men, several of whom mumbled and moaned the whole time. Not exactly a romantic evening. I am sorry I worried you, though."

"Worry is one of the hazards of knowing you, I think. What is it?"

"I was just thinking how many of these people I have come to like. I know as a class I don't have much use for them, but individually many of them are quite charming. If they are ignorant of the real world, then that is something I should try to put to rights."

"You will bore them if you try to talk to them of such things."

Jenner looked at Lacey and smiled at his unconscious separation of himself from his fellows, but she only said, "I can write about it, though, and subtly enough that they won't know I am changing them."

"You mean to go on writing then?"

"Yes, what else is there for me?"

"How can you ask that?" He turned suddenly serious. "I would give you everything."

"It's not possible, Lacey. Talking of it again will not change that."

"What did you think, that you could just walk out of my life one day?"

"Yes," Jenner gasped. "Else I would never have let this happen. I never thought you could be hurt by me. That is the only reason I stayed. Now I see that you are more vulnerable than I am."

"Why do you say that?"

"Because I am used to being alone. I expect nothing else. I never planned for this to last."

The look of hurt and anger on Lacey's face was too much for her and she turned away. "I know that sounds cold-blooded of me. Indeed it was. You are not at all what I thought you were. I should never have stayed and now I must leave you."

"Go then!"

She caught her breath at the finality in his command and turned to leave without facing him when his voice, gentle again, stopped her. "And please, at least, try to stay out of trouble."

"How much damage can I do in a public park?" she asked in relief. It had cut her to the heart to think he was rejecting her and made her spirits soar to realize she had been mistaken. But sooner or later she would have to contrive to leave him. If it meant deliberately turning him against her, then she would have to do that. For now, it did not bear thinking of.

Jenner returned from a concert with Caroline and Stella to encounter Dennis on his way out. "Coming to watch the cock fights tonight?"

"I don't think so." Jenner laughed tiredly. "I need to sleep sometime."

"Too bad. Coyle is fighting a brace of his cocks and he particularly asked if you were coming."

"You don't bet on these things do you?"

"Yes, of course." Dennis turned on her suspiciously. "Don't you start on me as well. Are you coming or not?"

"Perhaps I will come along if Coyle wants to see me."

The proceedings were already in full swing and it took some effort for Dennis to make a path for them to get a look at the birds being set on each other. The next match started slowly, with the two cocks circling warily as they eyed each other. Jenner was surprised at the size of the bets being laid on the tiny animals. It was not as though it was as interesting as a horse race. She had no appreciation for the excitement that even so small an amount of blood could arouse, spattered as it was over the raised platform, the handlers, the cocks themselves and the closest spectators. The birds were locked by the spurs, flapping and frantically gouging at one another. It looked to her as though at least one of the combatants, possibly both, would pay with its life.

As one of the birds lost an eye, Coyle turned to observe Jenner staring passively at the gore. ''Is this the first cock-fight you have seen?''

''Why, no, but I was always trying to separate the birds, not set them on one another. I did have to destroy Aunt Milly's old rooster when a young cock cut him up too badly.''

''How did you do it?'' Dennis asked, trying to picture Jenner shooting anything.

''What do you mean?'' Jenner asked in some surprise. ''I simply wrung his neck, of course. I suppose you have never had to kill a chicken for dinner.''

''No,'' Dennis denied, regarding Jenner with fascination. Coyle laughed.

Both Coyle and Dennis had wagered successfully and left Jenner to go collect their winnings. It was while they were gone that the fight in the audience broke out beside her. She backed away from the combatants with some difficulty because of the crowd. In the process she backed into a tall ruffian who grabbed her coat collar and pressed something sharp into her ribs.

''Make for the door slow like, or I'll skewer you where you stand. Don't turn round.'' He emphasized his words with a jab.

Jenner stiffened at the hoarse whisper and the knife digging into her back. It was not Mowbray, nor did she think it could be Poulton. She glanced desperately around with her eyes, but neither Dennis nor Coyle would be able to hear her above the din of the brawl. Even if they did, she would be dead by the time they got to her. Strangely enough, what she dreaded most as she walked slowly through the low-framed door into the dark night was not her own death but the embarrassment she would bring on Lacey and his family.

Once outside, the man wrenched her around to face the dark end of the street and forced her to walk away from the scant light of the doorway.

"Might as well have your purse now. No tricks. Toss it off to the side."

Jenner used both hands to unbutton her coat and tossed her bill case backward to the left. When she imagined his eyes following it she spun and plunged her elbow into his stomach. The knife raked across her back. He went down on one knee but still did not loosen his grip on her collar. She was almost out of her coat, cursing the tightness of the fit, and still expecting any moment to feel the cold steel inside her, when she heard a crashing blow and the man slumped behind her, pulling her down.

"You are an easy mark, lad."

"I know your voice. You are the old highwayman from Woking!"

"I'm not old. Well, p'haps I am, but I'm still able to account for the likes of a cutpurse."

"Somehow I do not think that is his only calling," Jenner said as she rose to her feet and shrugged her coat on. She winced a little at the fabric pulling over the cut on her back. "And it looks as if I owe you another dinner." She took the case he handed her and opened it.

"No. Fair is fair, lad. You saved my neck once. Now we are square."

"I wonder... Would you consider working for me?" Jenner asked on impulse.

"Work? I haven't worked in years."

"It would not be work exactly. And it would be dangerous."

This seemed to punch up his interest. "What would I have to do?"

"The same sort of thing you did tonight. Save my neck. It would only be for a few more weeks. Of course, we would have to pretend you are my groom or footman—my groom, I think."

"Work!" he said again, shaking his head in disgust. "I dunno."

"You would only have to pretend to work. I would pay you in advance by the week."

"Best pay me after, in case I don't make a good job of it."

"You'll need some different clothes," she said, handing him some bills. "Not a fancy livery, mind you, and not new if you can help it. Come to Lord Raines' house in Grosvenor Street at eight o'clock tomorrow."

"In the morning?" he protested.

"Nine then."

"Ten if you expect me to shave."

"Fair enough."

"We'd better scarper off from here. The watch will be coming to break up that mob," he advised, nodding toward the growing din in the cockpit.

Just then a dozen stout fellows rounded the corner. Two came after them, the rest plunged into the cockpit. It was not Jenner's first instinct to run, but the old man dragged her after him and she sprinted along in good earnest when she realized that neither she nor her companion could afford to be taken up for questioning. He suddenly pulled her sideways into the gap between two houses and clapped a hand over her mouth until their pursuers had overshot them.

"Ouch," she said when he released her. He dragged her into the cross street and set off at a trot, which did not let up until Jenner was hopelessly lost in the maze of irregular streets on the South Bank. She was beginning to feel winded by the time he showed her into a small gin house and led her past the few curious sets of eyes in the smoky taproom to the dim kitchen.

"Horace, who's the child?" the stout cook demanded.

"Never you mind. Just fetch us some bandages. The lad's been knifed."

"Really, it's just a scratch," Jenner protested.

But the old man ruthlessly stripped off her coat and pulled up her shirt in back.

"Lean on the table. What the devil? What are all these bandages?"

"Cracked ribs," Jenner said glibly of the linen that bound her upper chest.

"Ha! You had better slow down, lad, if you want to get much older."

"You are too skinny, boy," was the cook's verdict. "It's gone down to the bone over this rib."

The linen she produced to bind the wound was clean, so Jenner did not protest and was soon sharing a meat pie of unknown composition with her new groom.

"Shall I call you Horace or will you choose a different name?"

"A different name, what for?" the old man inquired between bites.

Jenner looked at him in some amusement, but merely said, "Jenner Page is not my real name. I never miss a chance to make up a new name."

"You make one for me then."

"How about Nathan?"

"Pshaw."

"George Trent."

"Too prissy."

"Roland Emmet."

"That has a ring to it."

"Or Emmet Roland."

"There you are. I like that. Eat up, lad, if I'm to start work I'd best see you home."

They walked through Southwark, since there were no hackneys to be found there at that time of night. Once they had crossed over the bridge into the city proper they were able to hire one to take them to Grosvenor Street.

"What do I do tomorrow?"

"Ride with me in the morning."

"Shall I bring my horse with me?"

"If it's more convenient for you. Otherwise you can ride one of Lacey's. I will have to ask him, of course."

"What else?"

"Hang about the stables and get as much sleep as you can during the day. I'm going driving in the afternoon, but I won't need you then. Come with me if I go out tomorrow night."

Jenner jumped down from the hackney and paid the driver to take Roland where he asked. Roland sat back in some state and shouted after her, "Mind you see a doctor, now."

"Yes, sir."

Jenner was rather surprised to see the lights on in Lacey's book room so late, or rather, so early. Another night's sleep gone begging, but she could not have gone upstairs without seeing him. As it happened there were voices being raised in the small room, Lacey's in accusation, Dennis' in meek defense, and Coyle's, as well.

"Who's lying dead somewhere?" she asked lightly as she pushed open the door.

"Jenner, my God! You are all right." Lacey's look of relief was vastly greater than Lord Coyle's, and she was sure Dennis noticed this. Dennis cast her a rather resentful glare out of a swelling eye. Coyle's hand was bandaged but his face was unmarked.

"Sorry I funked on you two, but I saw no point in all of us being arrested."

"I suppose I can take myself off home," Coyle said as he pushed himself up from the desk where he had been half sitting.

Lacey got up tiredly. "If I were not lame, I would take this walking stick and beat you."

"If you were not lame, you would not have the walking stick," Jenner said flippantly.

"May I go to bed now?" Dennis asked wearily.

After Dennis had left Lacey came and hugged Jenner. "What is it?" he asked at her sharp intake of breath.

"I seem to have backed into a knife during the melee. I have already had it tended to."

"You have too many accidents!" Lacey said desperately. "There is something you are not telling me. Don't give me that innocent look. Someone is trying to harm you, not just frighten you. Do you know who it is?"

Jenner shrugged and regretted it. "It is possible that one of the stories in *Bridle Lay* has set someone's back up. Did you find anything in there that could provoke these attacks?" she asked by way of distracting him.

"No, but most of those things happened before my time. I could ask Caroline."

"Perhaps I had better ask her, if you mean to put it to her that way."

"Well, if it comes to that, she would not remember most of the things, either, but she has heard all the gossip for years and remembers it better than I do."

"Time enough for that tomorrow. Do you want Collins to help you upstairs or will you lean on me?"

"I am quite capable of negotiating the stairs myself. And I want a look at that knife wound before you go to bed."

"You must be on the mend to be wanting my clothes off."

Next day Dennis gave the man Jenner presented as her groom only a cursory glance. Roland was clean-shaven with a black military-looking coat. It looked in fact like a uniform with the ornament removed, the kind of thing a groom might inherit from his master. Suddenly Dennis turned to stare in amazement at the highwayman saluting him from the back of one of Lacey's hacks.

"Have you lost your mind?" Dennis seriously asked Jenner.

"Not recently. But Lacey says I have been demented since before he met me."

"I can well believe it. Does he know about this?"

"That I hired a groom, yes."

"I fully intend to tell him who the fellow is."

"Be my guest. Ten to one he will only think it a famous joke."

"I hope he can keep laughing when we are all murdered in our beds."

"Now you sound like Caroline."

Jenner asked Dennis to stop at Tattersall's that morning. She had been checking there once a week, but no horse seemed to satisfy all Aunt Bette's requirements. Jenner was beginning to wonder if this was really so or if she was simply reluctant to complete her last errand. It was enough for Lacey's grooms to keep Ebony, who was still a colt, away from Lacey's mares. Once Jenner acquired a fully mature stallion she would have to leave for home with it immediately. Dennis gave it as his opinion that with war imminent all the likely stock had been bought up by the cavalry and other officers and was on its way to Belgium. This robbed Jenner of her only real reason for staying.

Her errand done, she went home and penned a long letter to her aunts full of all the small concerns that a homesick person thinks on to try to feel closer. She had planned to be in London no longer than two weeks. It was closer to two months since she had set off on her ill-fated ride. She had let her aunts assume she was taking the mailcoach and that Rob would have Tallboy while she was gone. She thought Aunt Bette had looked at her suspiciously, but her stern guardian had pointedly not inquired into her travel arrangements. And Aunt Milly never thought to do so. Jenner felt guilty deceiving them, especially since she would have to go back and tell them of Tallboy's death.

Aunt Bette had asked casually in her last letter when she meant to return and had filled the rest of the sheet with descriptions of the young foals, how the yearlings were taking to the lead line and the two-year-olds to ground driving.

Before she left Jenner had seen to it that Bette hired an extra lad to help with the stable work, but who would stay up if there was a hard foaling, and who would help Aunt Milly if there was another crisis in the garden? She remembered their painstaking extermination of cabbage worms the previous spring. It was a good fight and they had won it. By the time she got home the trees would be in full leaf and most of the spring flowers over.

Stacked against all the things calling her home were a few more precious days with Lacey. Jenner had never been confronted by such a choice before and felt the need to take a long solitary walk or to hoe weeds for a few hours to think the problem through. But there were no rows of peas or carrots in Grosvenor Street and she had a feeling no amount of thought could solve her dilemma.

Even if there was some magical way to make it acceptable for her and Lacey to live together, it was obvious that she was a country person and he was, for whatever reason, more comfortable in town. When he was not with her, he was so much in the company of any number of friends she suspected he was afraid to be alone with his thoughts. After the season he would normally attend a round of country house parties, ending the year with an obligatory stay at Kettering for the holidays and the hunting season.

How he made it through the winter months she could not imagine, for whatever devil drove him would never allow him the sort of peace and contentment that overtook one on long winter evenings by the fire. Perhaps only she knew how desperately hunted he felt at times.

The ink had dried on her pen without inspiring her with a way of ending her letter. Resolutely she suggested that she might have to give up looking in London for Bette's new stud. As she sealed the letter it was with the intention of following it a week later with notice that she was returning. Once committed she would have to leave.

After their adventure at the cockpit, Dennis had slept most of the day, so at dinner Lacey asked him to take Stella and Caroline to the Evans' party so that Jenner could sleep. Jenner tried to look innocently tired, but she must have been unconvincing, since Dennis looked at her suspiciously. Dennis finally agreed and resigned himself to a dull evening as he went off to change. Lacey threw Jenner a conspiratorial look as he informed Edwards they would not want tea later.

They went to Lacey's room and by getting on top Jenner contrived to make love to him without wreaking havoc with his injury. They talked then, as they lay cuddled in the aftermath of passion, of horses and racing, hunting and the different sorts of country Lacey had seen, for he had visited all parts of England. He spoke also of Spain and Portugal and the tamer regions of France, but only of the good times he had there—nothing of the war.

"When the fighting was over we rode across France at our leisure toward Boulogne. That part of the country was untouched by the war and, with wine only a few sous a bottle, you can imagine our expedition was far from sober. But of all the places I have been I like the country around Kettering the best. I have not spent a spring there in years. I wonder if the bluebells still bloom in the woods."

"I am afraid you may have missed them again this year."

"I should like to show you Radnor and my mares. Perhaps you would like one of his colts for Aunt Bette."

"Tempting, but it would be unwise for me to go there."

He looked an inquiry.

"I might like it too well."

"That is what I am hoping. The house itself is not so large, but the stable yard has two bays with twenty stalls each and fifty acres in pastures and paddocks."

"That is bigger than our whole farm. I had no idea you ran such an operation. How can you bear to be away from it?"

"I suppose I lost interest in it during the war."

"What happened? Were you wounded?"

"No more than a scratch or two."

Jenner could picture what he might mean by that and waited for him to finish.

"And I did not get killed," he said in some amazement, "like so many others—boys younger than Dennis—torn to pieces by the cannon. I did not die and I meant to—I mean I was ready for it. It would not have mattered to me. Thank God I did not let Dennis go into that."

"Did he mean to enlist?"

"Yes, but he couldn't very well, since I did."

"I see."

"Do not look at me like that."

"Like what?"

"With admiration. I am not noble, so do not think it of me. I went for my own reasons."

"How do you know why I look on you with admiration? It may have nothing to do with the war. But what selfish reason could you have for enlisting?"

"I cannot explain it."

He said this with such finality Jenner let the subject drop, but she wondered if Lacey really knew why he had become a soldier.

"Tell me more about Kettering," she finally begged.

"There are two lakes, one for use and one for pleasure. The cattle and horses drink at the lower one. The upper one has a small dock for fishing and a boat. The woods come down so close to the shore there is scarcely room for a footpath."

"How big are these lakes?"

"It takes a full hour to walk around both of these them, but you can cut across the breast between them. We skate on the upper one in winter, or we did when I was a boy."

"I wish I had been there when you were growing up. You have so many happy memories."

"Only from being outside. The gamekeeper and kennel master practically raised me. I was either with them or in the stables.

"The house was different. The best Caroline and I could do was stay out of the way. I never remember my mother and father looking happy together, not even when we had company. It always made me nervous. I could never enjoy anything very much in their presence because I was always afraid of laughing when they were not in the mood and starting a quarrel."

"I suppose that is where you got the reputation for being spoiled and hard to please."

"Who told you that?"

"I just got that feeling from some things Caroline said."

"I'm not spoiled."

"Well, at least you are not hard to please. I should know."

"I want you to come to Kettering with me. I want to see you in a dress."

"And have people forever wondering, as they did of the Chevalier d'Eon, if I am a man or a woman? We live in a different age, Lacey. People do not tolerate such nonsense any more. And what about Caroline? How could you serve her such a backhanded turn?''

"We were like two conspirators growing up," he reminisced. "She was always cleaning the mud off me before I got caught, or binding up my wounds to hide them from Mother."

"Considering the way you were raised I'm surprised you turned out so well."

"You agree I am not spoiled, then."

"Perhaps a bit imperious sometimes."

"And you ignore me."

"Never."

If sleep had been their object they failed to pursue it except halfheartedly, being too content with their intermittent lovemaking and the long embraces between times. They slept toward dawn and only awoke when they heard Collins bringing hot water to Jenner's room.

Jenner felt she had been selfish not to tell Lacey of her decision, but as he rose and threw on a dressing gown she said, "I will have to be leaving soon."

"Collins will await our convenience. Do you fancy to breakfast in bed?"

"I meant your house, not your room," she said grimly as she rose and pulled on her nightclothes.

"No!" he said at his most imperious, but Jenner overlooked this.

"You knew I would have to leave eventually."

"I will go with you, then."

"I don't want that kind of life, even if I had not my aunts to consider. Neither of us would be where we belong or where we want to be."

"I won't let you go."

"How will you keep me?" she asked tiredly.

Lacey turned eyes full of pain on her and she relented, her resolve melting under that suffering look.

"I cannot stay forever, Lacey."

"Awhile yet. I need time to think—to plan. Do you never think of the future? What it will be like for you when your aunts are gone and you are alone?"

"I never think that far ahead. It is too...dangerous, besides being a waste of time. So much can happen to change things."

"It's not fair."

"That is the one thing I try to keep out of my mind. I will simply work with what I have and try to make a life of it. You must do the same."

He paced away from her. "Up until now I have always been able to run away from my problems, my father when he was angry, my mother and Caroline when their nagging demands got unbearable, even from other women when their weeping and accusations killed whatever I managed to feel for them. Now you—the one woman I would stay with forever—you flee from me. I suppose there is some justice in that."

"Never think that—that you are being punished for something! You make it sound as though I do it deliberately to torture you. I will be unhappy, too, but better that than come to hate one another."

"I cannot even imagine that," he said, turning to her.

"Neither can I," she whispered. They fell into each other's arms, and Jenner lost whatever ground she had gained as further discussion became impossible. She was astounded at her own weakness.

Chapter Eight

Jenner had not expected Roland to guard her back except at night, when he would be fairly anonymous, but Roland seemed to take his new position quite seriously. Next to putting Dennis out of countenance, he particularly liked accompanying Stella and Jenner for their drives. It gave Jenner's stomach a turn to think of him sitting proudly erect on his perch behind the curricle staring down his nose at some of the people he must have robbed in his long career. If even one of them recognized his voice he would be arrested.

Perhaps some men never lost that craving for challenge and danger. Certainly Rob had not. And Lacey—he was perhaps the maddest of them all. How had she let him talk her into such an adventure with so much at stake? As for herself, she could face disaster coolly enough if there was no alternative, but she did not purposely run on it. All the same, it was useful to have Roland with her on her book-hunting expeditions, for he never caviled at carrying stacks of volumes to the hackney, and actually enjoyed abusing the drivers.

They found themselves in the main part of the city at noon one day waiting for a shopkeeper to open after his lunch. Roland took her to a coffeehouse to eat. He was not particularly known there, but he had a presence that demanded the attention of serving maids. Jenner finally decided it was, of all things, dignity. As they waited for the food, Jenner watched workmen rubbing shoulders with literary types and followed a pithy discussion between a clerk and a carter on the economic situation when it struck her that they made more sense than many of the speeches she had heard from the members of the aristocracy. She was rather amazed and delighted that such places existed in London where men could meet as equals and abuse the government without repercussions. She might have worked up to joining in the general talk, but Roland claimed her attention.

"Will you listen to me?" he growled at last.

"Sorry, what is it?"

"I was saying, if you're willing to spread some blunt about I think I can find out who's trying to do you in."

"I already know who's trying to kill me," she said as coolly as she could.

Roland stopped chewing and stared at her for a frozen moment. "Well, who is it then?" he demanded.

"Ashton Mowbray, and don't tell Lord Raines about him." Jenner applied herself to her food and Roland stared at her as he masticated another mouthful and washed it down.

"For a bit more money I could see he was done away with. Not my line of work, you understand, but I could get it done for you."

"What a resourceful fellow you are." Jenner chuckled. "No, if I decide he has to be killed, I will take care of it myself."

The matter of fact way Jenner said this as she sipped her coffee caused Roland to pause again in his meal. "What a hell-born babe!"

"What I cannot make out is why he wants me dead. I know something against him, but I have not spoken of it the whole time I have been in town. Even if I had, I do not think most of these people would consider it a serious offense."

"P'haps he fears what you might say in future."

"I suppose, but I deliberately told him I was leaving town. And when I do, he'll be quite safe."

"Until you decide to come back again. P'haps it's the waiting that's chewing at him."

"Well, I shall be gone in a few weeks, anyway." Jenner looked at Roland speculatively. "I don't suppose you would be willing to travel north with me. I'll be needing help if I find another horse."

"You never give up, do you?"

"What?" Jenner was all innocence.

"Trying to reform me."

"Well, I can't help liking you."

"You shouldn't like me, or trust me, for that matter. What if I took off with that shiny horse of yours? What then?"

"I would follow you and take it back, of course. I have done so before, you know," Jenner said boldly.

"You are a strange one." Roland shook his head.

Jenner wished she really felt the confidence she displayed when with Roland. He was as solid and dependable as a brick wall. She could rely on him to keep her safe, but she could not expect him to solve her problems. Not only had she to disengage herself from Lacey, but she must keep any more accidents from befalling her friends until she could get away.

It was one of those rare nights when there were no entertainments that required Lacey's or the Langleys' attendance. Dennis had gone off with his friends. Lacey requested the story of Garth Griffen for his niece and sister. Jenner told it willingly, but differently somehow. Perhaps she had left out some of the gore. Did she tell it differently depending on who was listening or just change it without realizing it, Lacey wondered.

"What do you think?" Lacey asked Stella.

"I did like it, but I thought the girl was a bit stupid."

"Ah, I see. You would prefer a more active heroine," Jenner noted.

After the tea tray was brought Stella begged for another story, not unlike she used to as a child, Lacey thought. He had spent little time with her while she was growing up, even after her father died. It was just as well. She probably did better without his influence.

Jenner took her cup and saucer from Caroline and sat facing the fire again. "You might like the story I have been working on lately. In fact, I need a little help with it. I cannot think of an ending."

"Tell us," Stella encouraged, "and we will help you think of one."

"It's called 'The Remembrancer' and it's about a scribe to the king. What the king does not know is that his scribe is a girl disguised—" Jenner paused since Lacey had inhaled a crumb and was desperately trying to regain his breath.

"Are you all right, dear?" Caroline asked in concern.

Lacey nodded as he regained his composure.

"As I was saying, the scribe is really a girl, but she has a rather boyish face so no one realizes the imposture. The king is only glad to find someone to write letters and contracts for him. He can read, of course, but he finds writing or transcribing all his documents a labor so he dictates to his remembrancer. Together they also begin writing a history of the realm."

"But how did she get to be a scribe?" Stella prompted.

"She was originally of good family. She was an only child and was taught by her father, more to amuse himself than for any other reason. There were not so very many books to read then.

"Strangers were a rarity in the valley where she lived, where peasants still believed the hills were haunted by dragons when the thunder rumbled, and where no one went any farther than the market town, or if they did, they never returned. So when she saw a strange knight, she was not so much afraid as surprised and curious. He came riding across the field on a charger, a great sweating black brute that looked dangerous to Filon. She stepped back as the man rode up and demanded the way to the village. She gave the directions meekly and answered with her name when he asked it of her. He got down and pulled off the plumed helmet he wore. His face was hard and savage and the way he said, 'Don't be afraid,' made her blood run cold.

"She called her old dog to her, the only protection she had, and it growled and snapped at him. He drew his great sword and lopped off the creature's head with a laugh. Filon was so stunned she did not run. She scarcely even breathed, for she thought at any moment her head would be laying on the ground, as well."

Stella and Caroline were spellbound. The story held a particular horror for Lacey because he knew how close to the truth it ran.

"But he grabbed her instead, and although she struggled bravely she was no match for him. One blow to her face and she was unconscious. He did as he pleased with her and left her.

"Filon awoke near dark, aching and bleeding. She dragged herself to a stream and washed, but knew she could not wash away the bitter memory of that day. She went to her father crying and shaking and told him what had happened. There was nothing her father could do for her except hide her away, for the knight was the new procurer of taxes for the king and he collected these with great diligence from rich and poor alike.

"Filon was sent to a cottager's family in the deep woods where she discovered she was with child. The babe was stillborn, and when Filon was strong enough she returned to her father's house only to find that he had died and another tenant had taken his place. She could scarcely go to the black knight and demand the house back. She decided the safest course was to move to a different shire and, since it was unheard of for a woman to travel alone, she dressed herself as a boy.

"She traded her work for food and shelter, but discovered the greatest skill she possessed was her learning. She would write letters for farmers on animal skins and even carry them to the other towns and villages. She traveled about like this for seven years and in her wanderings saw much that was good in the land, but much misery as well. Some areas were worse than others, the taxes were more unfair or more ruthlessly exacted. Nowhere were conditions worse than in her old village.

"One of the procurers paid her to write and carry a letter to the king. That is how she was admitted to the court. The king was curious about the boy and talked with her not as a king would, but like the lonely man he was, hedged about on all sides by those wanting to shield him from the realities of life. She spoke the truth to him in all things, told him who were his just governors and which ones were cruel and greedy.

"She had written down the worst of the injustices, and once she had the ear of the king, was able to suggest certain changes as though they were the king's ideas. This is one of the things that prompted her to take the position of remembrancer to the king, the possibility that she could encourage change for the better. Once she had charge of his accounts, she was also in a position to point out discrepancies in the taxes that had been collected in some shires with what had actually come into the treasury. The king came to trust Filon's judgment and planned to call to account those procurers who might be guilty of misusing power.''

Stella was frowning so blatantly that Jenner felt compelled to break the spell by asking, ''What is the matter?''

''Where is the handsome prince?'' Stella demanded.

''There is no prince in the story.''

''But there has to be a hero of some sort or the story will not be complete.''

''Do you expect every story to be a love story?''

''No, I suppose not, but it won't be nearly as interesting without a prince.''

''No prince,'' Jenner said firmly. ''Where was I? Oh, did I mention that the king is very young and handsome?''

Caroline chuckled.

''No, you did not,'' Stella said. ''You have been teasing us. Now I am satisfied. You may continue.''

''By accident the king discovers that Filon is a girl, but he has become so attached to her he cannot bear to part with her. In fact he is rather amused by the situation.''

Lacey coughed, but Jenner continued.

''Does he fall in love with her?'' Stella prompted.

''Do you really think he should? It would be very unwise, for he can never marry a commoner.''

''Yes, but unrequited love is better than none at all.''

''I had not thought of that,'' Jenner said, glancing at Lacey. ''Very well, they fall in love, and are happy just being together for a few short months.''

''Then what?'' asked Stella.

''The black knight reappears, of course, to defend himself against the accusations hinted at by the king. He sees Filon and looks at her suspiciously, but she has changed in all this time. She is stronger now, and when she looks at him it is not with fear in her eyes, but contempt.'' The room was rather dim, since the candles were guttering, but Jenner could see that Lacey looked bothered.

"Filon's reports put the black knight out of favor with the king, and the man is hard-pressed to excuse his misdeeds. But the king is inclined to give him another chance, hoping that he will behave more honestly if he knows he is being watched. Filon does not tell the king the one thing that would pit him against the black knight in combat."

"Why not?"

"In this realm, whoever makes such an accusation must face the accused in combat. If Filon does so, she will be sure to lose. The king can probably defeat the knight, but there is always the chance he will be wounded or die. Filon will not take that chance."

"But the king must fight the black knight." Caroline was getting involved. "That is the way it always is. You can be sure the king will not die. You are writing the story."

"But Filon cannot be sure, so she does not reveal the crime."

Lacey stirred uneasily.

"The knight has made inquiries about the remembrancer, and when he finds that Filon comes from his own shire he assumes the lad is the brother of the girl he ravished. In desperation he attempts to do away with Filon by poison, even if it means the death of the king, as well. But Filon tastes the bitterness in the wine at the first sip and instinctively dashes the king's cup from his hands."

Jenner paused to take a sip of her tea, and such was Stella's involvement in the story she almost blurted out, "Don't drink that." Instead she prompted, "What happens then?"

"Filon decides to leave. She must do so anyway. She can never be more than the king's remembrancer. And if she leaves, she will take the danger away from the one she loves."

"What about the black knight?" Caroline asked.

"I don't know. That is where I am stuck."

"But he must be punished," Stella commanded firmly.

"By Filon? How?"

"She must find another way to expose him."

"The crime you find so heinous was rather lightly regarded at the time. In fact, it is not taken much more seriously now."

"Yes, I know," Stella seethed. "But this is a mythical place, is it not?"

"Yes."

"The king makes the laws. He can change them as well."

"Oh, I had forgotten the advantage of being omnipotent. And what should the punishment be for such a crime?"

"Death, of course," Stella demanded.

"I can see that it would be dangerous to be a man in this realm. One might lose one's head over a misunderstanding or an unjust accusation."

"Banishment, then. That, at least, is like what happened to Filon."

Jenner was about to agree when Caroline said flatly, "It is not enough."

"You are a bloodthirsty lot." Jenner tried to keep her laughter light. "I do not think I want to know how you would punish him."

"I agree it is not enough," Lacey said gravely. "He must be stopped."

Jenner looked at him seriously. "Why?"

"Because he won't stop until he kills Filon."

"That does not make any sense."

"We are not talking about sense. He hates her and fears her. For whatever reason, she is a threat to him as long as she is alive."

"I agree," Stella said.

"They are right, you know," Caroline said sagely. "Death to the black knight." The sight of Caroline raising her teacup in a mock toast jolted Jenner, and she laughed nervously.

"If I cannot finish the story, it will not be for lack of material."

"Who is he?" Lacey asked helplessly as he held her that night. "And don't give me that innocent look. You know who I mean."

"What good would it do you to know? Would you call him out for something that happened such a long time ago, before you even knew me?"

"I could, at least, protect you from him."

"That is why I hired Roland."

"You admit then that there is a danger?"

"Yes, and I cannot make out why. That is the only thing that worries me. If I leave, will the attacks stop or will all of you still be in danger?"

"Don't go. Let me fight this black knight for you. I will find a way."

"I'm sure you would. That's why I'm not telling you."

"I will find out who he is."

"You said that about me."

"You have never lied to me. Is it Poulton?"

"Lacey, this is not a game. And I do not want you in the middle of it."

"Is he the one?"

"I will not answer that question about every man we meet. Now may we please go to sleep?"

Lacey appeared at Roberto's fencing salon, more mobile, but still leaning on his heavy walking stick. Rob's look went from the limp to the haunted, strained look in Lacey's eyes.

"Surely you do not want a lesson, *señor.*"

"I want to know where Jenner lives," Lacey said flatly when they were alone.

"She told you about me," Rob said, dropping his accent.

"She thought you had gone to America. I guessed who you are from the name."

"You are a quick one—very dangerous." Rob laid down the pair of foils and sighed.

"No need to go packing your trunks. I have no interest in revealing your identity, only Jenner's. Who is she?"

"If she wanted you to know she would have told you."

"I am glad to see she has such a loyal friend. If that's all you are."

"I think that is all I ever was to her, a good friend."

"Is that why you left?"

"I would have married her if it had been possible," the older man said with a spark of anger. "I had nothing to offer her except worry. I think it was our loneliness that drew us together. Merilee is so different. She is totally mine, dependent on me. I want to treasure her. I know I will never go back to that kind of life now."

"That is how I feel about Jenner."

Rob turned to look at Lacey. "Jenner is very...complicated. I never understood her. I am not sure she fully understands herself. One thing I do know—she is stubborn. Once she has decided something, she cannot be swayed."

"Yes, I know," Lacey agreed.

"Also, for a woman, she thinks too much for my taste. You never know what idea she will come up with next."

"Yes, I find that is one of the charms of knowing her. I have never met a woman before who caused me more worry than I gave her. Can you think of anyone who would want Jenner dead?" Lacey asked abruptly.

Rob looked up at that, his black brows furrowed. "No, what are you talking about?"

"Someone has been trying to kill her. I am convinced of it now."

"Who on earth would want to harm Jenner?"

"I think it is the man who raped her. She has seen him again in London. Who is he?"

"She never said. Truly, I do not know. She never wished to speak of it. I heard the story, of course. I do not believe she knew his name."

"She knows it now and she won't tell me!" Lacey clenched his fist.

"Jenner is not one to burden others."

"She has hired a groom, a man called Roland."

"I have seen him in the street. That is not his name, but he is harmless enough."

"Will you talk to him?"

"You think he knows?"

"If she hired him to protect her she would have to tell him from whom."

"I will see what I can do," Rob promised as he saw Lacey out.

Jenner came into her room to change and found Lacey seated on the bed reading part of the manuscript that lay on her desk.

"I had no idea what you had suffered. Who is he?"

"You should not have read that," Jenner said angrily as she shoved the pages into the desk drawer. "In some ways I am better off now to have a name for the face that I see in my nightmares."

"Tell me."

"No, I'm not afraid of him any more."

"How will it end?"

"The story? Or my life?"

"Both."

"I'm not sure if I will have my revenge or not," she said calmly. "He is in some ways too pathetic to bother with. As for me, I suppose in the end I will do the right thing."

"What is that?"

"Leave."

"No!" Lacey cried like one wounded. "Is that why you stay then, because of him, not me? Once you have decided his fate, you will be gone?"

"There is no future for us."

"My life is ruined anyway. Tell me his name and I will kill him for you. Then we can fly to the continent."

"You tempt me, but we are not alone in the world. And we are not children to hurt others so selfishly by running off."

"How can you take this so calmly?" He rose and took her in his arms.

"I suppose I am used to being disappointed, and I have other things to occupy me, my writing and music, and my horses."

"Whereas my life is empty."

"You know I would trade all of it to be with you. But I cannot ask you to bury yourself in the country and never see your family and friends again. Certainly you could never bring me to London."

"London is not the world."

"It is your world."

"Not any more."

"We would not be able to live at your home, not when Caroline is there. I would not hurt your reputation so, anyway. It is important what your people think of you. It is also out of the question for you to visit me in—visit my home. I will not put my aunts through such a thing again."

"At least tell me where I can find you again."

"Don't you see? That would be more cruel than leaving you. Then you would not even attempt to make a life for yourself."

She freed herself from his embrace and turned away. "I am not unique in the world, Lacey. You could be happy with someone else."

"And for you, no one?"

"I have accepted that. I have been alone all my life. Until I came to London, I had no friends. I will have to get used to being alone again."

"I cannot imagine it, what you must have endured."

"Oh, no one ever says anything to my face. How could they? I see them only at church. But there is always that undercurrent of talk that you suspect is about you even if it is not. It sets you apart. You don't dare approach anyone for fear of a rebuff. After a time you get used to it. You pretend not to hear or care. Eventually you truly do not care."

"You cannot go back to that."

"I have to. It is my place. And any life with you would mean the same sort of isolation, but for both of us."

Lacey clutched her to him with that desperate passion that was giving him a more than usually hunted look of late. Jenner feared he would give them away just by the hungry way his eyes followed her sometimes. He was more guarded in company, but mealtime especially was getting to be a strain for her.

All the fun had gone out of the deception now, even for Lacey. He felt more trapped than Jenner, since he could do nothing about it. If he had let her go that day his sister had arrived, her face would not be so well known to them that he could not have introduced her as a woman later. But there was no more chance of her revealing her identity now than then. All his inquiries, based on the few clues he had, led no further than Halstead.

* * *

The next night, Lacey entered his book room to see the hangings still swaying with no hint of breeze at the window. He calmly went to the desk and loaded the pistol he had left lying out, then pointed it at the heavy draperies. "I cannot possibly miss at this range, so you may as well come out."

Rob slipped from behind the curtain with a chuckle and lounged into a chair. He was dressed all in black and looked a sinister figure to anyone who did not know him. Lacey shook his head as he put up the pistol and poured brandy for them.

"Did it never occur to you to use the door?"

"Old habits..." Rob observed as he swallowed the potent drink.

"What have you found out?"

"Precious little. You can have a go at the fellow yourself if you like, but it strikes me that he would cut his tongue out sooner than betray her. And he does not even know she is a woman. Of that I am certain."

"Did you offer him money?"

"Yes, quite a bit, in fact. Yours, of course, not mine."

Lacey laughed tiredly. "I tell you, she is aging me."

"You think I was always gray like this? I am glad you are taking care of her now."

"The hell of it is she won't let me."

"I told you she is stubborn. What will you do now?"

"Wring the truth out of Dennis. My nephew has been taking her about of late. She may have let something slip in front of him."

"Good luck. If there is anything else I can do, call on me."

Lacey's interrogation of Dennis was followed so closely by a request from Jenner to be taken to Manton's shooting gallery that Dennis suspected his young friend to be in serious trouble. After watching her practice for half an hour with little or no improvement he asked her flat out, "Have you got a meeting I don't know about?"

"What? Oh, no, nothing like that. But I now realize there is a sad gap in my education. If it should come up, it would be damned embarrassing to have to say, 'Sorry I can't fight you. I don't know one end of a gun from the other.'"

Dennis laughed at her in spite of his worry. "I think this is too heavy for you. Try the feel of this one."

"It's much lighter."

"Yes, you won't be so likely to drop the barrel."

After another hour Jenner had succeeded in hitting only two wafers, but she was becoming proficient at loading the weapon. "I rather like this pistol. I may have to get one for myself."

"I can show you where you can buy one, but I do hope you are not planning on defending anything important with a pistol."

"It does seem rather hopeless, doesn't it?" Jenner coughed from the powder smoke.

"You just need practice. Didn't your father ever take you shooting?"

"I don't remember him at all. And my uncle was not in good enough health to go tramping around the countryside."

"It's a miracle you turned out as well as you did."

"How close would someone have to be for me to be sure of hitting him?" Jenner asked as she squinted at the target.

"Close enough for the average fellow to kill you outright."

"Thank you so much, Dennis."

"If it should come to that, insist on twenty paces, at least. Your small size will work in your favor. Even a crack shot might still miss you, and you, of course, would never be able to hit the other fellow, but that's not entirely bad. You don't want to go killing someone."

"I thought that was the whole idea."

"Not always. Then you would have to flee the country."

"That's no problem," Jenner observed, almost to herself.

Dennis stared at her. "If you want my advice don't go picking any quarrels you cannot settle with a sword. There you will at least have a fighting chance."

"That is easy advice to give."

Lacey had been wearing himself out making the rounds of the clubs and hells trying to run Poulton to earth. He called in at Cato's and asked Curtain if he had seen him. "At the faro table, three parts drunk. What do you want with him?"

"I've a little score to settle."

"Lacey, you are in no frame to fight anyone. Want me to shoot him for you?"

"Kill him, you mean?"

"Well, if you like, but I would just as soon shoot off something unnecessary."

"I will let you know," Lacey said noncommittally. After all the years he had known Curtain, he could still not tell if the man was serious or not.

Poulton glanced at Lacey's walking stick and took in the knotted eyebrows and guessed at the pain behind them. He smiled smugly and picked up his winnings. He did not sidle from the room but walked boldly past Lacey.

"A word with you." Lacey stopped him with the cane and Poulton glanced at it with an ugly smile.

"Have an accident?"

"No accident. Someone has knifed a friend of mine, and as it happened in a dark alley, I immediately thought of you."

Poulton looked daggers at him. "If you want to keep your little pup safe, keep him home. It's nothing to me if he gets mauled."

"How did you know I was talking about Jenner?" Lacey asked triumphantly.

Poulton looked surprised for only a second before Lacey's fist crashed into his face. He staggered, blood spurting from his nose. There was a collective murmur of surprise as two of the gamers he staggered into grabbed him by the arms and tried to right him.

"What the devil did he say to you?" Curtain asked as Lacey advanced on the semiconscious man. "I say, Lacey, you can't. The man cannot even stand on his own." Curtain followed this up by physically restraining Lacey with surprising effectiveness.

"I'll kill him!" Lacey said, but Cato himself was between them by now mopping up the blood with towels, although he seemed more concerned about his carpet than Poulton's face.

"Lacey, let it rest until later." Curtain tugged him a few strides away. "But if you want to avoid drawing insult on yourself, stop flaunting that boy all over town."

Lacey wrenched his arm from Curtain's grasp as though his longtime friend had stuck a knife in him. He stared at him in disbelief, then looked at Poulton, who was now propped up in a chair and did not seem any closer to regaining consciousness. Lacey limped alone the whole distance to Grosvenor Street in the hope that someone would waylay him so he could take his anger out on them. Never before had one of his pranks gone so utterly awry.

He could never confess to what he had really done, for it was much worse than what all of them supposed. He convinced himself that he did not care, that keeping Jenner safe was all that mattered. He spent the rest of the night cleaning and polishing his three sets of dueling pistols, his greatest concern being which he would prefer to kill Poulton with.

Collins finally took him forcibly to bed and could not answer Jenner when she asked what was wrong. Lacey slept through the better part of the morning, slightly feverish again from the strain he had put on his leg. Dennis returned home at noon, looking ravaged but with news of his uncle's doings. "A row with Poulton at Cato's. They are taking bets on whether Poulton will challenge Lacey or not."

"Must they bet on everything?" Caroline inquired with irritation.

"So it seems, Mother." Dennis stared pointedly at his plate, careful not to look at Jenner. This made her suspicious as to the cause of the quarrel.

"What was it about?" asked Stella.

"Who knows?"

"We will find out anyway," his mother reminded him.

"It was about me, was it not?" Jenner asked hoarsely, without meeting his eyes.

"Poulton claims he made some harmless joke . . . There's nothing you can do about it."

"Yes, there is. I can go home, a departure that is long overdue. The thing is, I hate to leave all of you to face the talk alone. But it will only get worse if I stay."

Dennis flung up his hands helplessly and Caroline looked on in concern as Jenner excused herself to start packing. Jenner decided she would keep to the house until Lacey was recovered again, but leave she must, especially now that Caroline knew what the gossip was about.

"Well, I fancy I have mended matters with Miss Dawson for you," Caroline announced after they sat down to dinner that night.

Thus interrupted in one of his thoughtful moods, Lacey dropped his spoon in his soup and spattered his white neck cloth with brown spots. Dennis murmured his condolences. Jenner looked at Lacey wide-eyed, waiting for the inevitable explosion.

"What do you mean?" Lacey asked with menace.

"Well, actually I didn't talk to the girl, but her mother. I told her how disappointed you were, how distraught. She had no idea it had gone so deep with you."

If anything, Lacey was looking distraught now. "How dare you meddle in my affairs?"

"Someone had to do something. Of course, it didn't hurt to mention how well you came out of the war. What a lucky accident that you didn't leave Dennis or me a power of attorney. We would surely have sold you out of the funds when they were so erratic. Now they are worth more than ever."

"It was no accident," Lacey growled.

Dennis' chin came up and he looked offended.

Caroline blundered on, "Yesterday when I saw Amelia she said they would be glad to receive you. I take it to mean that Miss Dawson's answer will be yes this time. What is the matter? Why are you looking so blackly at me?"

"I have no intention of asking Miss Dawson or any other insipid girl to marry me."

"Need I remind you—" Caroline began to get on her high ropes "—that it is your duty to marry. It is not fair to leave Dennis in the expectation of inheriting Kettering when you may at any time cut him out."

"Mother, that's enough!" Dennis exploded.

"Has Dennis expectations?" Lacey asked pointedly.

"From you, none whatsoever." Dennis threw down his napkin and left the room.

"Lacey, I don't understand you. I thought you wanted to marry the Dawson girl. Last fall you spoke of it as a certainty."

"I never wanted her!" Lacey flung himself back from the table.

"But then why did you ask her to marry you?"

"I don't know. I must have been mad." Lacey exited, tearing at his stained neck cloth.

"This is too much. After all the trouble I have been to. He has no gratitude. He never has appreciated anything I have done for him." Caroline began to weep gustily, then excused herself from the table. The butler returned to remove the soup and was somewhat startled to note the dwindling of the dinner party. He raised an inquiring eyebrow at Stella, who bit her lower lip and said, "I fancy Mother has the headache and would like to have a tray in her room."

"And m'lord?"

"I believe he means to dine at his club after all," Jenner supplied gamely.

Edwards stared hard at Dennis' empty seat.

"Gone out," Jenner said sweetly as she received the next course from him.

The butler grunted and left the room in chilly silence.

"I don't think he approves of us," Stella confided. "He was extremely stiff to us the three seasons we were here."

"I don't think Edwards likes anyone very much, but that's not required of him."

"I suppose I should go up to Mother."

"Please don't, dear, brave Stella," Jenner said laughing. "I think they each deserve to be left to pout alone. How comes it about that you are the only one in the family who is not spoiled, argumentative and hot-tempered?"

"I suppose I saw so much of that all my life I have a real disgust for making a scene."

"And you are always trying to smooth things over between them."

"Yes, not very successfully. No one pays much attention to me."

"Did I mention they also lack good sense? How will they manage when you are married and gone?"

"I don't know. I'm afraid to think what might become of them. I can't recall that we have ever had a peaceful meal. Mother has a silly talent for setting everyone's back up except yours. I think she could say anything to you and you would just smile."

"And I think she would be offended if she knew how much amusement I get out of her."

"If only Lacey and Dennis merely thought her silly. She has no hold over either of them, really. I don't know why they pay any attention to her."

"She is pretty hard to ignore. And I think, since deep down she does have their interests at heart, they feel a little guilty when they run counter to her, no matter how mad her schemes are."

"Like coming here uninvited. If it had not been for you, I don't think Uncle Lacey would have let us in. He seems to have gotten worse since the war."

"What do you mean?"

"He was always wild, from what we heard, but he used to at least go through the motions of taking care of Kettering. Now he doesn't seem to care for anything."

Jenner brooded over this for awhile.

"I'm glad you are here. Your writing has given him an interest, but it's odd."

"What is?"

"I would not have thought you and he would have gotten along so well. He doesn't like . . . that is, I mean . . ."

"No, I'm not exactly in his style, am I? We have very little in common except an appreciation for fine horses. I suppose when I have gone he will forget all about me."

"I never will."

Jenner stared in a troubled way at the wine still high in her glass. "It would be very much better if you did."

They practiced music together that evening, Stella on the piano and Jenner playing the violin. Stella was helping Jenner write down the "Excursions" piece and she knew it nearly as well as its creator now. They were not disturbed until Edwards brought the tea tray.

Jenner came to expect it now, that sudden hush when she entered a room, even from people who had not been talking about her. She almost understood what Lacey got out of it, having everyone think you were so much worse than you actually were. She might have enjoyed being infamous had she been alone in the thing.

Though Lacey still laughed at the rumors flying all over town, she feared they would permanently damage him. He said they were just idle talk. She knew the source and the purpose. Mowbray intended to drive her from town. So far Mowbray had done his damage with anonymity. There was no way she could counter the accusations. For Lacey to have entertained a mistress at the same time as he did his family was certainly a worse crime than a little playful sodomy.

Jenner was working in the music room late the next morning. Everyone was out of the house on various errands. She heard the door open and looked up, smiling, expecting to see Lacey, but it was a woman, and a familiar one. Jenner turned involuntarily to look at the portrait. It was the same Elaina, in a green morning dress instead of the elegant ivory evening gown. She looked as young and beautiful as ever. Edwards announced Miss Claridge, then made an embarrassed retreat. The man who had kept Caroline at bay had been conquered by a pair of green eyes. Jenner looked at the visitor with a sort of wonder.

"Edwards says Lacey is out, but that Mr. Page is home. Who are you, Mr. Page?"

"A visitor. Caroline and Stella are out shopping. They will be . . . sorry they missed you."

She laughed. "No, they won't. In fact, you will be quite glad if they miss me."

"Well, Dennis, at least, will be sorry he missed you," Jenner said with a laugh.

"Yes, and so will Lacey, I hope. When do you expect him back?"

"It's hard to say."

The woman gave a provocative pout and stepped closer to the piano. "So, he has a new protégé?"

"Hardly. But he does let me use the music room."

"I have heard of you."

"Me?"

"Yes, you are accounted to be a most gifted young man, a writer, a musician . . . What else are you?"

Jenner was beginning to suspect Elaina's drift.

"A guest who has far overstayed his welcome. I go back to the country soon." Jenner tried to laugh carelessly.

"I see." Elaina raised one eyebrow. She strolled around the room, looking idly at the music scattered about until Edwards again opened the door to bring in refreshments. Jenner was stunned. She had pointedly not offered anything in the hopes of getting rid of Lacey's former mistress before Caroline returned. Either Edwards was acting on his own initiative or Miss Claridge had taken it upon herself to order Madeira as though she was still the mistress of the house.

Jenner wondered why this would set her hackles up so, until it occurred to her that she was jealous of the woman. She had always suspected that Lacey had been more attached to Elaina than to any of the others, and here she was in the flesh, as beautiful as ever. Jenner admitted that what she really wanted was to get rid of her before Lacey returned.

Elaina seated herself with a sigh as Edwards served her. Jenner caught him actually simpering and said, "That will be all, Edwards,'' in the most authoritative voice she could manage.

"It does appear that I will have to stay at the hotel for awhile yet," Elaina pouted.

"What do you mean?"

"Lacey will find a way to get rid of them, now that I am returned. Depend on it. He will merely fall into a fit of rage and send them away."

Jenner resented this statement, not just the easy confidence the woman had of her power, but her assumption that Lacey could be so heartless.

"Certainly not." Jenner laughed, seating herself sideways on the window bench and swinging one leg. "I think you will find Lacey much changed. He has turned respectable."

"That's not what I hear." She looked pointedly at Jenner's muscled thigh in the tight pantaloons.

"You should know better than to pay any attention to gossip."

"I have found that there is usually a seed of truth in a rumor," Elaina observed.

"A seed is a very small thing."

Elaina had just opened her mouth to reply when Lacey burst in, looked desperately from one to the other and said, "What the devil are you doing here?"

Elaina looked at Jenner as though she expected her to vacate the room, and Jenner had to laugh at Lacey's harassed expression in spite of her sympathy for his predicament.

"Perhaps I had better leave," Jenner offered. "You two must have a great deal to talk about." She stood up.

"No!" Lacey commanded so vehemently that she sat down again. "Elaina, what do you mean by coming here?" He limped over to confront her.

"Why, to tell you of my return. The war made travel so inconvenient."

"It would not have if you had not chosen to go to France."

"But, Lacey, I went to sing for the emperor. He is the most magnificent—"

"He is a madman."

"I did not come to argue with you."

"What did you come for?"

"To be reconciled, of course."

"Oh, no!" Jenner said.

Elaina turned to her in rage, but Jenner was staring into the street.

"Caroline and Stella are returning," Jenner warned. "I had better go deflect them."

Lacey did not stop her, but looked at her in mute appeal as she slid out the door and pulled it closed.

"Good. Now we can be alone," Elaina said lightly.

"I have nothing to say to you. When you decided to leave me that was an end to any love between us."

"Is that why my portrait stills hangs in this room?"

Lacey glanced at the painting and found himself wondering why it did still hang there. "You know what a sloppy housekeeper I am. I have simply neglected to remove it. Would you like it? I can have it sent round to you. Where are you staying?"

"I expected to be staying here."

"I told you it was over."

"It was just a fight. How did I know you would run off and join the army the next day?"

"That's not the way I remember it. You said you were leaving on tour. I must have been mad. I even offered you marriage."

"An offer I would now accept."

"An offer that is no longer open."

"I see. You have found someone else."

"No."

"I never would have thought it of you. He is rather pretty though." She turned to Lacey with a teasing look to be met by such a venomous glare that she doubted for a moment her power to charm him.

Lacey saw the doubt in her before it was veiled by her long-lashed lids. He decided to make any sacrifice to keep Elaina at arm's length. "He is also absolutely faithful."

"A hit," she said stepping back from him. "And I thought I had been so careful. But that was years ago. We can start over."

"Never. I will see you out now." He had heard the shopping expedition mount the stairs some minutes before, so he took Elaina forcefully by the arm and escorted her to the front door. When he had seen her safely away he went to Jenner's room. She was lying fully dressed on her bed, looking rather unwell.

"She's gone."

"Thank God." Jenner took her arm away from her eyes. "I asked Caroline what to do for a headache, and you should see the storehouse of medicines she produced."

"Did she cure your headache?" Lacey asked as he sat on the edge of the bed.

"I didn't actually have one, but I feel rather sick now, after the concoction she gave me."

"My poor Jenner," he said taking her in his arms. "I'm sorry you got caught in the middle of that."

"Me, too. Before I met Elaina I would have laid my money on Caroline in a standoff situation, but all I could think of was to shield her from Elaina. And you were as desperate to get rid of her as I was."

"Yes, and that is not at all what Elaina was expecting." Lacey laughed.

"Will she make trouble, do you think?"

"No more than I can handle. The timing is unfortunate."

"Will she accept that you do not intend to install her here in this house again?"

"I hope I have convinced her. It is hard to rebuff her too cruelly. I do owe her something for our years together."

Jenner sighed and rested in Lacey's arms for awhile. "I liked Elaina a lot better before I knew her."

"So did I."

"He's asleep," Caroline reported to Lacey some hours later as he sat alone in the music room.

"Jenner?"

"Yes. I think he pushes himself too hard. Up half the night at balls and gaming hells, then up early to ride, all the while still writing and working on his music. I don't know where he finds the energy. Perhaps he should stay in tonight."

"Perhaps we all should." There was an empty glass on the small table beside Lacey. Caroline followed his gaze to the portrait. Her expression was one of acceptance, not anger.

"I suppose you will be wanting us to leave now."

"What?"

"I heard that Miss Claridge is back in London."

"Good Lord! I beg you, don't leave now."

"Lacey?"

"I would not blame you if you did abandon me, of course. But your presence in the house was the only thing that prevented Elaina from arriving with her trunks." Lacey shook his head at his sister's bewilderment. "How unfair of me to use you like that. I think I have always done so and gibed at you for complaining," Lacey confessed.

"But I thought you were in love with Elaina. I would have accepted her if you had decided to marry her even though we don't like each other much."

"Swallowed your pride and accepted her for my sake?"

"I want you to be happy."

"You think marriage will do that for me?"

"I was happy while Henry was alive. Those were the best years of my life."

"Good, solid Henry. I miss him, too, even that disapproving stare." Lacey got up and hoisted down the painting. "I was just thinking we should have Stella's portrait taken this season. Not by this lying fellow, though. You find someone. I don't care what it costs. I should have Edwards wrap this and take it around to Elaina. That reminds me. I have a bone to pick with Edwards."

Elaina did not move in the same circles as Caroline and Stella, so there was no fear of meeting her at dinners or balls, but they did come across her while shopping and driving in the park and, of course, at the theater. They need not even exchange looks with her. Always she was with some gamester or half-pay officer to whom she whispered. Jenner could imagine the malicious tales she was spreading. Jenner actually did run into her in the hallway at the opera house on her way to procure ices for Caroline and Stella.

"You—boy!" Elaina hailed her.

Jenner came toward her in the hopes that others would not hear the exchange. "If you would but leave Lacey he would come back to me," Elaina said boldly. "I could make him happy."

Jenner could smell the gin on her breath and felt more repulsed by her than she would a man. "I am leaving, but I do not think that will help you," Jenner said as calmly as she could. "He loved you better than all the others. How could you betray him? He would have given you everything."

"Yes, even marriage," Elaina replied.

Jenner glanced at Elaina and could not suppress the amazement in her look.

"You are surprised. So was I. I was not ready for that. I would have had to give up my singing—everything—to be his wife, have his children."

"Are you willing to give it up now?"

"I am willing to compromise with him."

"That's a cold word, compromise, a word seldom used between lovers."

"A woman in my position must make sure of her footing."

"Then do not think of Lacey as firm ground," Jenner advised coolly as she walked away.

It mattered not that Jenner was so seldom seen with Lacey any more. Elaina's gossip, added to the rumors already started by Mowbray, would be taken seriously. Jenner had already noticed a more definite coolness toward her in some quarters, although the people she knew the best treated her no differently. For Jenner's benefit Lacey still seemed to laugh off the talk as easily as he laughed off the rumors of war. Jenner was so accustomed to being talked of she displayed a thick-skinned indifference. Caroline and Stella rode it out with aplomb. George was a rock. Only Dennis cringed at the snide remarks about his uncle.

It irked Lacey to have to avoid Jenner in public, but it was the price she asked for her continued, if temporary, residence in his house. Consequently Lacey accepted an invitation to a dinner at the home of Captain Turner and his dashing wife. He would not have gone if he had any idea Elaina was to be there.

Elaina sang and played quite charmingly all those ballads favored by the military set. Then she played the "Moonlight Sonata." It was one of Lacey's favorites. She knew just how softly to touch the keys to get the affect of night, of lovers, hesitation, hope and despair. It was so different from anything Jenner played. Lacey thought Jenner could never have handled the suspense of it.

"I must speak to you," Elaina said to him desperately when she had finished and was brushing past him out of the room.

His good sense warned him not to follow her, but the trouble in her eyes and the tender music had aroused a sense of past obligation in him, and in the milling about that followed the performance, he went into the hallway to see her beckoning from the small sitting room across the way.

"I don't want to speak to you," he said, entering and closing the door almost against his will.

"Have you any idea what is being said of you?"

"I have a pretty clear idea and I think I know why."

"Yes, because you obviously prefer the company of that boy to me."

Lacey had no answer for her.

"What has happened to you, Lacey? If I have killed your love for me, that is one thing..."

"You admit that you broke with me?"

"Yes, but I did it to release you. Do you think I did not notice you combing the papers every day for word of your friends? I knew you wanted to go. I just made it easy for you."

"You knew I wanted to join the army?"

"You and every other man in London. I spent three years agonizing over whether I had sent you to your death or not." Her handkerchief was a wadded mess by this time.

"I had no idea. I'm sorry if I misunderstood..."

"Do you really feel nothing for me?" She walked to him slowly, her arms outstretched in a plea. "If I had known what it would drive you to, I would have kept you with me somehow."

"If I misjudged you, I'm sorry, but things are different now." He straightened himself and thought desperately. "For one thing, I have my family staying with me now. I cannot ruin Stella's chances with an affair—" Too late he stopped himself.

"An affair with me would scarcely cause comment compared to what you are involved in."

"You don't understand, and I cannot speak to you about it."

"Oh, Lacey." She threw herself in his arms. "Don't do this. Is there no way I can get you back? Do you feel nothing for me?"

"No, I feel..." Her piled hair brushed his chin and the scent nearly suffocated him. He turned his head aside to escape the sweetness of the well-remembered perfume, so different from Jenner's clean-washed smell. Jenner would never enact such a tragic scene for him. She asked nothing of him, or if she did, she made her request openly.

When he glanced down at Elaina again he noticed her eyes under her darkened lashes were quite dry. He dropped his arms from the embrace as a sudden suspicion hit him. She clung to him more tightly, her arms snaking around his neck, her mouth seeking his, her eyes luminous under veiled lids. Yes, it was there, behind the desperation, a look of calculation. How could he be so easily manipulated, still? He grasped her wrists and pulled them away and held her off from him, looking at her intently.

"What is it?"

"You are lying. I think you always have lied to me. Perhaps every note you have ever played is a lie, and that is a horrible thought."

"I am trying to save you by any means I can."

"Jenner never lies," he said in unconscious comparison.

"How dare you compare me to him?"

"There is no comparison."

"If you don't give him up and take me back I will see you both ruined!"

Lacey straightened at the sudden threat.

"It can be like it was. I will do anything you ask." She softened again, but the fear of losing him had not left her eyes.

"It can never be like it was. You have not changed, but I think I have. At least I see a little more clearly now."

He left her crying real tears of frustration and rage.

Chapter Nine

George Marsh, with or without his mother, had become an almost daily caller at the house. Lacey complained of tripping over him everywhere. Jenner was more tolerant but no more glad to see the man. At best, George treated her coldly. In Stella's presence he positively scowled at her. To do him credit, George was provoked beyond what most men would suffer without complaint. Stella's apparently growing affection for Jenner, which she unfortunately chose to display in George's presence more than anyone else's, was making Jenner more than a little queasy.

George was doing a poor job of holding up a desultory conversation with Caroline when Jenner and Stella came in glowing from a drive. Stella had brought the team the whole way home unassisted and Jenner was just complimenting her on her progress. As they went into the morning room where Caroline and George were sipping coffee Stella whirled and grabbed Jenner's arm. Jenner just missed another passionate kiss by a matter of inches. At sight of the scowling George, Jenner began to sweat. Stella chatted happily as Jenner accepted some coffee and retreated to the farthest seat, replying briefly when the conversational ball was tossed her way.

"Someday I want to have a phaeton and team of my own," Stella said. "Do you think it is acceptable for a woman to drive herself, George, a married woman?"

Jenner glanced up, knowing what George's answer would be.

"Not alone, of course. What if there should be an accident?"

"A man might have an accident with a team, as well. Jenner will let his wife drive her own team."

"No!" Jenner almost shouted. "I mean, George is right. It is not safe without a groom. Who would hold the team if you had to get down for some reason, or you got pitched off?"

"Oh, I mean to take a groom with me. What sort of team would you buy for me, Jenner?"

"Stella!" her mother admonished as Jenner sloshed coffee into her saucer and looked in dread at the red and fuming face of her rival.

Lacey blundered into this explosive situation. "Hello, George, you here again?"

"I am just leaving. You will not be troubled with my company again."

"Do you suppose he means it?" Lacey asked of anyone as George stalked from the room like a large dog with his hackles raised.

"Oh, no, George will be back," Stella reassured him.

"I do wish you would not encourage the fellow," Lacey said. "I thought you had more compassion than that."

"George is like a rock. It is difficult to either discourage or encourage him."

"Tell him flat out he is wasting his time. I will do it if you want me to," Lacey offered.

"Oh, no, you must not," Stella said, gripping her uncle's arm. A slow smile spread over Lacey's face.

Stella's so obvious panic, and Lacey's reaction to it, planted a seed of suspicion in Jenner's jostled mind. She began to wonder if she had been so wrapped up in her own problems that she was oblivious to Stella's.

* * *

The next morning Jenner looked up in irritation as the door to the music room opened and, when it was obvious Edwards was showing someone in, her stomach turned over. But it was not Elaina, only George Marsh.

"Caroline and Stella are shopping, I believe," Jenner said absently, scribbling down a few more notes.

"I came to see you," George said ominously.

The bit of music she had been trying to get down flew completely from her head, so she rose from the piano, feeling that she really did not want to hear what George had to say.

"Stella will never think seriously about me as long as there is a chance you may ask to marry her."

"What?" asked Jenner, backing into a chair and nearly falling over it.

"She is in love with you," Lord Marsh said accusingly.

Jenner was looking at him in stark horror.

"By the end of last season I thought we had an understanding. That is not to be thought of now." The young man lowered brooding eyes and shook his head, discarding old memories. "I have just one thing to say to you. You had better treat her properly or you will have me to deal with."

"But I have no thought to marry Stella," Jenner blurted out.

"Not marry her! Then you have deceived her. If only I were related to her I could call you out."

"But if you were related . . ."

"What?"

"Nothing." Now Jenner was certain what sort of game Stella had been playing. Even at the risk of having to meet George, which she considered small, she decided not to ruin it for the girl. "Then you don't think I should take her to Italy with me?" Jenner asked uncertainly.

"Italy! If you loved her you would give her the protection of your name."

"But I have no name to give her. Jenner Page is just a name I made up."

George looked aghast. "To think that Caroline Langley would have you in this house."

"But it's not her fault. She knows nothing of my birth."

"The thought that Lord Raines, even with his reputation, would expose his niece to such an influence! I will speak to him about this."

"He does not know, either."

"If you have any shred of decency, you will tell him what you planned to do. I make allowance for your upbringing—or the lack of it. Perhaps Raines can make you see reason. I give you one week to tell him, or I will."

"Why, thank you, George. That's more than fair."

After George left, Jenner paced the music room plotting and chuckling until she could waylay Stella on her way back from her walk. She witnessed Stella arriving in a high-perch phaeton and being handed down by a dandy wearing unlikely lavender pantaloons while his tiger wrestled with the pawing team. Stella looked hopefully up and down the street, then at the windows of the house before bidding her acquaintance good day.

Jenner chuckled. It was almost too rich a sight to waste on only herself. She went into the hall and invited Stella into the music room.

"What is it, Jenner? Have you finished that piece?"

"No, I was interrupted. Don't you think it too much a sacrifice to have to be seen with such a fellow just to make sure your watchdog is still faithful?"

"You would always rescue me if I needed you, would you not?"

"I meant George Marsh."

Stella looked a little surprised and then frowned. "George is such a lump. He never does anything."

"He did today. He came to discover my intentions and threatened to call me out."

"Oh, if only he would ever do more than threaten," Stella groaned.

"Stella! I don't think I would have a chance with pistols, even against George."

"Yes, I know." Stella cast down her eyes. "Forgive me, Jenner, but I had to have some way of bringing him up to scratch. Otherwise it would be years before he screwed up the courage to ask me."

"Why didn't you tell me? I would do anything to help you."

"Oh, you have helped me. You have made him extremely jealous."

"So I see. But since he is at such a fever pitch, I think we may as well push on and get the job done. You are sure you want George?"

"Yes, of course! It's only his mother who makes him so indecisive. She has always thought for him. That will all change once we are married."

Jenner looked at her with the realization that this was true. Once they were married, Stella would think for George.

Upon being informed that Lord George Marsh was not dressed for receiving visitors, Jenner insisted that the matter was urgent and was admitted to his bedchamber. To Jenner's relief, he was completely dressed except for the arrangement of his cravat, but she had enough sense to hold her peace until Marsh declared the delicate operation a success with a curt nod to his valet. His man seemed reluctant to leave, but Marsh dismissed him rather ruthlessly. Jenner almost chuckled to think that her reputation would make men fear to be alone with her, but she sobered her face by the time Marsh turned to her.

"I have spoken to Stella and I think I have made her see reason," she commenced.

"What are you talking about?"

"I can't marry her. Now she understands why."

"You have stolen her heart. Now you jilt her. Why would you be so cruel?"

"There are several reasons. Foremost—"

"I have heard the rumors," Marsh said with an audible sneer.

Jenner had never seen his round face set in such stern lines before. If anyone could make something of Marsh, Stella could.

"No, not that." Jenner fidgeted with the single ring she wore, paced to the window for effect, then turned dramatically and said, "I have had a child with someone else. I have made Stella understand that I have other . . . commitments. But you must go to her now." Jenner advanced across the room, and Marsh wiped the surprise from his face.

"Now?"

Jenner could see Marsh's features soften and waver. "Don't you understand? She needs someone so desperately. I fear what will happen if she encounters another man in her present shattered condition. Get her promise now and all will be safe."

Marsh's face lit up and he said, "I will do it." He actually got as far as the door before he turned and said, "But I have not even spoken to her uncle or mother yet."

"Never mind that," said Jenner as she thrust him out the door and pushed him toward the stairs. "They will be so glad she is not marrying me that they will welcome you into the family with relief."

Jenner got him out of the house and thrust him into the hack she had left waiting while his face fluctuated between doubt and determination. "Best of luck, George. I will stay out of the way till you've done it."

A glance over her shoulder surprised several faces at the town house windows. Jenner wondered for a moment if she should have accompanied Marsh home, but trusted the momentum of her push would carry him within Stella's grasp. The rest was up to Stella.

Relief was not the word to describe either Caroline's emotions or Lacey's when they were informed by Stella that she was marrying George Marsh. The girl had the sense to save the news until George was hurrying safely away with an announcement for the *Gazette*.

"I won't have it! I won't! You could have had anybody. You are throwing yourself away on him. And he has no fortune to speak of."

"I'm sure we will get along quite well, Mother," Stella said proudly.

"You will get nothing from me," Lacey thundered in a patriarchal tone that made Jenner smirk. "Just what are you laughing at?" Lacey demanded. "Did you have anything to do with this, Jenner?"

"Oh, I may have given George a hint or the odd nudge," said Jenner, wandering to the sideboard and pouring herself some Madeira.

"Of all the meddling—really, Jenner, I fear I shall have to leave the room before I say something we shall both regret." Caroline stormed out under full sail.

"Well?" Lacey thundered at the abstracted Jenner.

"I was just trying to imagine what she was going to say."

"She couldn't think of anything bad enough to shock you," supplied Stella. "That's why she left."

"Just who asked you to interfere in my family matters?" Lacey demanded.

"Your family, is it now? If it were not for me, you would have left them on the street."

"That is beside the point."

"I asked Jenner to help," Stella said with her chin up.

They both turned toward Stella in some amazement. Jenner had not encountered a more challenging look in any opponent's eyes, and even Lacey sensed the implacability in the girl.

"You can't mean you are in love with this fop?"

"Yes, and I am determined to have him. I have planned it all very carefully and if you do anything to ruin it, I shall . . . I shall elope with Jenner."

Jenner choked on her wine and Lacey opened his mouth to speak twice, then burst into laughter. This only served to make Stella angry and even more insistent that she would marry Jenner to be revenged on her uncle. The more she insisted, the harder Lacey laughed.

"Stop it, Lacey," Jenner chided. "So, what would you like for a wedding present, Stella? You must go with me tomorrow and help me pick out something you would truly wish for."

"Oh, very well—" Stella pouted, "—if Lacey has no objections," she said pointedly.

"Oh, marry him, if you must," Lacey finally agreed, drying his eyes. "At least I shall be rid of one of my charges."

"If you will excuse me, then, I have to go convince Mother."

"Will she, do you think?" Lacey looked over at Jenner.

"I have no doubt of it. She is very determined, and she has much more energy than Caroline. Your sister doesn't have a bad heart, does she?"

"No. After all the battles we have fought, she cannot."

"Then I think we can in good conscience leave her in Stella's capable hands."

"You little vixen. I have learned to trust your judgment in most things, but George. Really! Will it do?"

"I don't see why not. In most relationships one partner is dominant. Perhaps Stella wants to make sure she is that one. But also, I feel she really does care about George."

"Poor George! His mother, and now this."

"You know, I think Stella may be the making of George if anything is. He came close to calling me out regarding her. And he can look so determined and rather manly when he speaks of her."

"George?"

"You will see. Women know about these things."

"I knew she would marry someday, but . . ."

"Confess. No one would be good enough for her."

"No, I suppose I do feel that way."

"How very fatherly of you."

"Stop making fun of me." Lacey pinned Jenner against the sideboard and took her chin. His advances were arrested by the entrance of Dennis, who merely looked at the frozen couple with a stony stare and closed the door behind him.

This brought on a fresh burst of laughter from Lacey, but Jenner was no longer playful. "We take too many chances, Lacey. At least I do not have Stella's future to worry about. Even if I am found out, she won't let George out of their engagement once it is announced."

"I wish it was our engagement that was being announced."

Jenner glanced up at him, not a little surprised. "You mean you would marry me, if it was possible?"

"Surely you knew that."

"I don't take anything for granted."

"Will you marry me?"

"Thank you, but you know I cannot."

"Which is to say I was perfectly safe in asking you."

This brought a misty smile from Jenner.

* * *

Not finding Lacey in his room early the next morning, Dennis went through the dressing room and opened the door to Jenner's room in a cold rage. He found exactly what he feared, Jenner curled up within the circle of his uncle's strong arms. It was the merest accident that Jenner was covered.

"So, now I know!" He said it loud enough to wake them both. Lacey's laughter sent Dennis off in a blind fury.

"Lacey, it's not funny. We have to tell him," Jenner begged.

"No, Dennis drinks too much," said Lacey as he slid out of bed. "He would be sure to give you away."

"I disagree. Dennis has never spoken of anything I have told him in confidence."

Lacey's eyebrows furrowed at this. "And what secrets do you have with Dennis?" Lacey looked superior at her speechlessness as he put on his dressing gown. "What does he know about you that I do not? It should be interesting to test his reliability."

"Lacey, that's not fair," Jenner protested as she slid into her nightclothes.

"Are you forgetting? The game we play has no rules." He came back to kiss her ruthlessly one last time. "You should be glad this has happened. It solves the problem of Dennis emulating me."

Had his mother and sister not been staying in the house Dennis would have packed and left. What could he do? Kill Jenner, and let the whole world know the rumors were true? Instead he plunged out of the house and walked the streets, ending at White's sometime around noon. He began drinking and playing cards and lost a packet, but made up for his losses at Brook's. As the day wore into evening, he lost himself in the gaming hells of London in the faint hope that his escapades would overshadow Lacey's latest scandal. Even Lord Coyle, who was used to Dennis' moods, thought his behavior dangerous. Dennis slept at Coyle's town house that night and into the next day, then began the rounds again. He lost heavily for hours at a time, but recovered enough to plunge into another day of heavy play and drinking.

After three days that Dennis thought legendary for their wantonness, he returned to a home that was much as he left it. Thanks to the lies Lacey had told on his behalf, there was no handwringing from his mother. The wind was a little let out of his sails that his uncle would not argue with him. Dennis supposed he would not dare, for fear of having his sordid little affair thrown in his teeth. Jenner could hardly face him. He could not know that Jenner had set Roland on to follow him and look out for him, or that his uncle sat up night after night brooding over the reports of Dennis' exploits. Still, Lacey would not disclose Jenner's secret, and he forbade her to confess. He used the argument that she would be interfering in his family matters again.

It was a somber party that gathered for breakfast the first morning after Dennis' spree. Three of them were scarcely speaking to each other. Stella was anxiously scanning the morning paper, so Caroline asked Dennis for the news from Europe to try to make conversation.

"Soult has accepted the office of major general under Napoleon," Dennis said slowly. "He will bring over any waverers. It means war for certain. Napoleon will have all his old troops back again, while half of Wellington's veterans are still in America."

Dennis looked at a frowning Lacey and seemed on the point of continuing when Stella interrupted, "It's here!

George put it in the *Gazette* just as I wrote it. I was beginning to be afraid his mother would convince him to cry off."

Caroline took the paper and read the announcement with a polite smile. "September. Very sensible, dear."

"Yes, Dennis said that would not interfere with any of the hunting. I want to be married at Kettering, if that is all right?" Stella looked hopefully at Lacey.

Lacey managed a smile. "Of course."

"Jenner, will you come?" Stella asked as she passed the folded paper over to Jenner.

"Oh, thank you for thinking of me, but I don't imagine I will be able to..." Jenner's eyes widened.

"What's the matter? Is it a mistake?"

"I think so. Not your announcement. This one farther down." She handed the paper to Stella.

Stella's happy flush died away. "Mother, you didn't!"

"What are you talking about?" Caroline wrested the paper away from her daughter. "Lacey, I thought you didn't mean to offer for Miss Dawson."

Lacey snatched the paper impatiently and read with growing choler. He slammed his coffee cup down so hard he made the saucer jump and Jenner was amazed to find none of the china broken. "If I can lay my hands on the person responsible for this... I take it none of you had anything to do with it," he growled as he looked sharply at them. They all looked back in sympathy, except Dennis, who winced at the shouting and put a hand to his aching head.

"Surely Miss Dawson would not have done it," Stella said.

"If she did she will be sorry."

"What about her father?" Caroline speculated.

"Possible, I suppose. At any rate I must see him." Lacey threw down his napkin as he rose. Jenner looked at him wide-eyed. "Don't worry," he said to her, "I won't let him trap me into anything."

Jenner looked at her plate, blushing furiously. This did not escape Dennis' notice, and he flung down his napkin and left the room. If she was not so deeply involved she might have thought it was funny. She did think it hopeful that Lacey was going off to confront his problem head on rather than trying to evade it.

Jenner was in the music room when Lacey returned. Caroline and Stella were turning out the latter's closet, planning her trousseau. They did not want to go out or receive any visitors until they knew what to say when people asked about Lacey's engagement. Dennis was hanging about the house apparently for the same reason.

Jenner put the violin in its case. "Was it one of them?" she asked.

"No, they think I did it, and that now I'm having second thoughts. The man as good as called me a liar."

"You mean they would have accepted the situation without another proposal?"

"Yes. I could not believe it myself." He slumped dejectedly into a chair.

"You don't think they were trying to force your hand?"

"Now they are. They say I cannot cry off. They don't know me very well."

"What date was it?"

"What is significant about the date?"

"Maybe nothing." Jenner read the announcement again from the now crumpled paper. "A month almost to the day after Stella and George's wedding. Just the sort of comfortable breathing space you would give yourself if you really intended to marry her." A momentary suspicion shook Jenner and she glanced at Lacey in surprise.

"Why do you look at me so?"

"You do know that if you really want to marry her I am no impediment. I have been trying to convince you—"

"How dare you!" he shouted, springing to his feet. "How can you think I would resort to such a cowardly ruse?" He flung a stack of music onto the floor.

"But it was not Stella or Caroline," Jenner said loudly as she rose. "I am convinced of that. Who else would know the date except George and his mother?"

"That just leaves you and—" He abruptly stopped pacing and whirled on her with a thunderous face. "You have been trying to convince me to marry and forget you. Did you really think such a trick would work?"

Jenner took a step backward, somewhat intimidated by his attack, but she answered defiantly, "I know you well enough to know it would not. I can see now it is a good thing I am leaving if we are to be shouting at each other."

"A very good thing indeed!" Lacey threw himself out of the room, slamming the door and colliding with his nephew in the hall.

"Sorry, Dennis. Jenner will be leaving."

"So I heard," Dennis said with amused consternation.

"See if sh— Would you ask him if he needs any help arranging for his journey?"

"Yes, of course."

Jenner was kneeling on the floor picking up and sorting the music and dropping a stray tear on it now and then when Dennis pushed the door open and asked what he could do.

Jenner bravely cleared her throat and, without facing him, said, "I shall need a crate to ship my books and such, but I suppose Edwards can find me one."

"I will see to it."

Jenner was in her bedroom and had nearly finished packing her papers and books when she heard a knock at the connecting door.

"It was not locked," she whispered to a repentant Lacey as she opened the door.

He held the violin case out to her. "I wanted you to have this."

"Lacey, I cannot." The tears started to her eyes again. "I was not even going to take Ebony with me."

"You must. I want you to have him." He came in and sat on the bed. "We have to talk."

"I do not think that would do any good."

"I have never apologized in my life before. Do you have any idea how difficult it is for me?"

Jenner laughed through her tears. "Yes, for I have the same problem."

"It was not you, of course."

"Not really my style," she said, walking over to him and laying the violin on the bed. "I'm sorry I suspected you even for a second." She held his head against her and he hugged her to him.

"If Caroline was a better actress I could believe it of her," Lacey said tiredly.

"Not now that she knows you don't care for the girl. Besides, she would know that you would never go through with it."

"It couldn't be a joke, could it?" Lacey asked in despair.

"I have no idea," she said, sliding down beside him. "But that might be one way out of it. A drunken friend, a wager. I have spent some rare evenings with these lads. Believe me, it is not at all unlikely. Could you pull it off?"

"Yes, I believe I might. Do you forgive me?" he asked, making it difficult for her to answer by kissing her.

"Yes, but I can't do anything about it now," she said with a laugh. "They are coming to take this box in a few minutes. Dennis is helping me."

"You are not still leaving? Can't we go on as before?"

"It must come to an end sooner or later."

"Another week, then. If it's all the time we are to have."

"A week, then."

"I thought Jenner was leaving," Dennis interrupted Lacey the next morning as he was cleaning one of his pistols in the book room.

"Not yet," he said, scarcely looking up.

"You just couldn't let him go, could you?" Dennis asked bitterly.

Lacey's hands were arrested in their movements over the gun. He looked up and then rose, slowly and momentously, so that he had the aspect of a demon rising up from Hades.

"You!"

"Yes, I did it. Someone had to bring you to your senses."

Lacey leaned over the desk and grabbed Dennis, who, to do him credit, did not retreat.

"By creating a public scandal?"

"You are a fine one to talk of that. You and your escapades with Jenner are the talk of the town!"

"Idle gossip," Lacey said, letting him go.

"You and I both know that is not true."

Lacey looked away, his eyes dazed. He was trapped. He could never tell Dennis. It was too risky. What right had he to rant at the boy? Dennis was only trying to save him. He shook his head.

"You don't even care what people think."

"All I care about right now is getting rid of the Dawson chit. I know! I will tell her I have a lunatic for a nephew."

"You have to marry her now."

"No one has ever made me do anything."

Lacey drove around to the Dawson house immediately. He was nonplussed to find the father and mother both from home and was torn between talking to the girl herself or coming back later. On the one hand, Susan would be easier to handle than her parents. On the other, it might be dangerous to be alone with her. While he was still debating with himself, the girl came into the room with those sharp small steps that made her look like an overnice mare out for an airing.

"Have you come to your senses, Lacey?"

"What?" He had detected that nagging tone he so hated in Caroline's voice.

"It's not exactly as I would have wished it, but now that the announcement has been made..."

"It was a joke," he blurted out.

"The date, you mean? I do want to change that."

"The whole announcement," he plunged on. "My nephew did it during one of his drunken sprees. He thought it would be funny to put it in the same day as Stella's. Well, he is regretting it now, I can tell you."

"You cannot be serious!"

"I am just telling you what happened. I shall write another notice. You can help me if you like..."

"No." She stamped her foot and tossed her head, again putting him in mind of an ill-trained horse.

"It's as plain as day we would not suit. What is the point of prolonging this farce?"

"I will not be laughed at!"

"Better that than spend the rest of your life ranting at me. You should consider yourself well-off to be out of it."

"I have no intention of crying off and you had better not do so either."

"And I have no intention of marrying you."

"We'll see what my father has to say about that." Susan Dawson flounced out of the room, forgetting, Lacey suspected, that she was in her own house, and leaving him to find his own way out.

"How did it go?" Jenner asked, as she looked up from the book she was reading. "Are you still engaged?" she asked with dread.

"I don't know." Lacey sank into a chair looking more tired than Jenner had ever seen him.

"Poor Lacey. This is all my fault. Yet I cannot bring myself to wish we had never met."

"I have been in worse scrapes than this. Perhaps I am getting a little old for this sort of thing."

"You are just tired out from worrying about Dennis. Would there be any harm in buying him an army commission now? If you truly believe Napoleon will be crushed so quickly this time, it might be just the thing Dennis needs."

"What brought this on?"

"He has always wanted to be a soldier like you. He has always admired . . ."

"I was never a soldier," Lacey said wearily. "I had no right to wear that uniform I bought for myself. I was only playing at it, like everything else I do. You have shown me that."

"Me?" Jenner asked, a little shaken. "And those medals Dennis told me about, they were for giving such a good performance?"

"I scarcely remember what they were for. Whoever that was who earned them, it was not me."

"If you are telling me you are not a professional killer, I can only greet that as welcome news. It bothers me that you had to kill even during wartime. That could not have been easy for you."

"Anyone can kill, given strong enough provocation. The frightening thing is not that it is hard, but that, after a time, it is so easy."

Lacey looked at her, his dark eyes filled with confusion, and Jenner felt a chill go through her. There was a part of Lacey she really did not know, the part the war had changed.

"What I am trying to say," he continued tiredly, "is that I do not know what I am. I used to think I knew, but I was only fooling myself. You saw through me."

"I only wanted you to stop thinking of yourself as a hardened rake," Jenner pleaded.

"But I have no other identity." He rose then before she could protest and left the room.

Jenner had not ridden with Lacey in weeks. And now Dennis had to be pointedly avoided. This was difficult and hurtful. She was doubly glad that she had hired Roland to guard her. He yawned prodigiously as they rounded Hyde Park for the second time.

"When did you last sleep? I was forgetting you were watching Dennis."

"It's not that. I've been chatting up one of the maids at that fellow Mowbray's lodgings. Seems he's been entertaining his uncle from the country these past weeks. He's been home less than usual. D'you want me to search his rooms?"

"What, and get yourself arrested? Certainly not. Besides, I can't think what good that would do."

"I might find something incriminating you could hold over him."

"If he paid someone to murder me, he'd hardly be likely to put it in writing and then keep it laying around."

"Aren't you even curious why he's trying to make off with you?"

"Oh, I already know why," Jenner replied absently.

Roland pulled his horse up short. "Well, for God's sake, tell me!"

Jenner shrugged and said as coolly as she could manage, "He raped my cousin and got her with child. The way I have been guarding Stella he is sure now that I know it was him."

"Has anyone asked him to support the bastard?"

"No. The child did not live. I do not think he even knew there was a child until I spoke of it."

"Then why would he try to kill you?"

"It makes no sense to me, either, but that is the only link between us." Jenner shook her head, going over the facts about Mowbray again.

"Why not take yourself out of harm's way, then?"

"I intend to, and soon. Of course, he may follow me," she mused.

"He knows where you live?"

"More or less, but that doesn't worry me as much as what he might do to my friends. Lacey was hurt. He might have been killed. According to you, Mowbray is now preying on Dennis. I have put them all in danger and I cannot be sure they are any safer if I run, not without knowing what is in Mowbray's mind."

"I see your point. P'haps it's time for a meeting with Mr. Mowbray to find out how things stand."

"Treat with him, you mean? How sickening! And I could never rely on him to keep his word." Jenner was surprised at how much she did sound like an outraged young man. "I must find out why he is so afraid of me. He would never just tell me that."

"What then?"

"Use it against him, if I can." She urged Ebony into a final canter before they left the park.

To do him justice Dennis never told Lacey anything Jenner asked him to keep in confidence, especially not when Lacey began interrogating him. Nor, it appeared, did Dennis tell Lacey the previous occupation of Jenner's groom. He might think Jenner mad to associate with such a fellow and might say so to her face, but he had not tattled. Up until he had found Lacey and Jenner together he had quite admired Jenner's recklessness and wished he had such a knack for adventure. Who else would think to pull such a stunt? It was not as though one could brag about keeping a tame footpad to heel. Certainly Jenner did not do it to impress him. Jenner never tried to impress anyone.

It was that quiet self-confidence that unnerved him. They were the same age, but Jenner had already made a mark on the world. Dennis found his own life to be somewhat conventional, perhaps even dull, compared to the untrammeled existence Jenner must have led. The thought that he was jealous of Jenner brought a halt to the silent truce that had existed between them for two days and he turned up at Cato's again in a reckless mood that sent Roland off to report his doings.

It was already late when Jenner said to a subdued Lacey, "I think Dennis will come home again when he hears I am gone."

"No, I won't have a pistol held to my head in that way."

"But Lacey, I'm worried about him."

"So am I."

There was a tap at the door and Roland slid in. "You'd best come, yer lordship. Yer nevvy is going down heavy at Cato's to that Mowbray fellow and I doubt if it's a fair game."

"Go order my carriage." Lacey rose decisively.

"Yes, sir," Roland said as he left the room with amazing alacrity for one of his size.

"Not you, Jenner," Lacey said, pushing her back into the room. "Not this time. I will take care of this. If you are there I will have two of you to worry about."

"But I hate waiting."

"Promise me you won't stir from this room. I won't be any longer than it takes to get him out of this mess." Lacey stalked to the door with his walking stick in hand.

Jenner was trapped. To tell Lacey why Mowbray was after Dennis was to pit him against Mowbray to the death. To follow Lacey to Cato's would play right into Mowbray's hands. She paced the room, but she did remain there, not so much because of her promise but because of some inherent confidence in Lacey. As passionate as he was, Lacey impressed her with his competence. If anyone could extricate Dennis, Lacey would know how, even though he was not fully recovered himself.

She considered how different were the men she knew and the roles she played for each of them. For Rob she had been a nurse and protector as well as a lover. With Roland she was as bluff and cold-blooded as she could be without laughing at her own impudence. For Dennis she was now forced into an absurd role that might have been comical had it not affected him so badly. But with Lacey, she played to his lead as naturally as though they had rehearsed all their conversations ahead of time. She could not help thinking that they could have done rather well on the stage together.

Was that all her life amounted to, playing role after role? It was the very thing she had accused Lacey of. She became rather shaken to think that, like him, she might have no real identity at all. Even for her aunts she had acted the devoted niece, all the while carrying on an affair that anyone else would have considered sordid. But she could not regret those years. With Rob she had come close to revealing herself. Now, when she was alone with Lacey, she was her truest self and he did not despise her for it. And she was quite willing to let him take care of her as no one else had ever done.

She was peering out the window for the hundredth time when Lacey's carriage pulled up in front of the house and a shadowy figure slid up to the door. She snuffed the candle the better to see. Why would Roland come alone unless something had gone tragically amiss? She ran to the door and let Roland in herself.

"You'd best come, lad."

"What's happened?" she whispered desperately. "Are they hurt?"

"Not badly. There was a bit of a fight, but they didn't get the worst of it."

"Roland, there's blood on your face. Where are they?"

"In the lockup. Have you a bit o' money by you?"

"I will get it."

Jenner was up the stairs and down again quickly and silently so as not to wake anyone.

"Now tell me what happened," she demanded as they were being driven to the jail.

"His lordship saunters in, cool as you please, and doesn't do more than raise an eyebrow at the stack of paper in front of Mowbray."

"Dennis must have been drunk to play with him again."

"Langley wasn't the only one in tick to Mowbray. That young Coyle had lost heavy, too."

"Oh, no."

"His lordship watched the roll of the dice for awhile, then he gets himself into the game. Once he hefted those dice two or three times he could tell. Mowbray made another bet and threw the dice. Without any warning his lordship swings up that heavy walking stick, not that I believe he needs it, and smashes the dice."

Jenner chuckled nervously. "What happened then?"

"Well, I asks you. It was as plain as your face Mowbray was a cheat. Lord Coyle picked up the stack of i.o.u.'s and threw them in the fire. I never heard such a bellow. Mowbray was like a wounded bull. He would have killed Coyle if his lordship hadn't stopped him. There was that tall fellow . . ."

"Poulton."

"Ah! One or two others stood up for Mowbray, but the rest of them were on Coyle's side. They pretty well tore up the place between them."

"I would wager that's not the first time that's happened. Are you sure they're all right?"

"A bit the worse for wear, but it would have done your heart good to see them fighting shoulder to shoulder like that, and his lordship seemed to take particular delight in beating on Poulton."

"I'm glad. Are we here then? You had best wait in the carriage."

Jenner had a vague idea from Rob of how to go about freeing Lacey and Dennis, but his description of the inside of a roundhouse had not prepared her for the atmosphere of stale gin that pervaded the place. If anything it smelled worse than Cato's. She encountered Lord Coyle trying to persuade his father to extricate the others as well as himself, but he gave up the argument as soon as he saw Jenner.

"I'm glad one of your friends, at least, knows how to stay out of trouble," the old lord grumbled. Jenner smiled uncomfortably as she was introduced to Coyle's father.

After Jenner had paid the fines of everyone she knew, Dennis plodded sullenly out to the coach. Lacey was grinning sheepishly.

"Perhaps I should have brought a doctor," she said, taking in Lacey's split lip and Dennis' bruised cheek.

"How did you know where to find us?"

"Roland came for me," she said, climbing in beside her smug groom.

"What a fellow to have by you in a fight," Lacey said bracingly. "I'm glad you got away, Roland. You are a good man. I hope Jenner has the sense to hang onto you."

"Unfortunately Roland proclaims himself a creature of the city," Jenner said, looking at her puffed-up retainer. "He won't agree to come north with me."

"Then I shall hire you. What do you say, Roland?"

"Lacey," Dennis intervened, "I don't think—"

"It's only fair to tell yer lordship, this is my first job—as a groom."

"What were you before, a highwayman or something?" Lacey asked playfully.

"Well, yes," Roland admitted as Dennis groaned.

Jenner had the treat of seeing Lacey struck speechless. Then his eyes danced and he rolled on the seat in peals of laughter. "I might have known," Lacey finally managed.

Dennis looked at him with disfavor. "I might have known you would think it was funny."

"Dennis, how did you keep your peace?"

"I do not interfere in other people's affairs."

Lacey raised an eyebrow. "At least not while you're sober."

"Quite right," Roland agreed.

With a start Jenner realized she had overstayed the week she had promised Lacey, and it looked to be as hard as ever to tear herself away. On the one hand, Dennis would not be satisfied until she was gone. On the other she hated to leave Lacey in such a mess.

"How goes it with Miss Dawson?" she asked Lacey as he entered the music room and collapsed into one of the chairs.

"I have been to see her father again. The upshot is, they won't let me out of it. They have threatened a breach of promise suit."

"There was never anything in writing, except that notice in the paper."

"Yes, but everyone knows I did propose to her once."

Jenner was thoughtful for a moment. "How bad is she, really?"

Lacey looked up with a weary smile. "She's a shrew. I couldn't live with her a week. What amazes me is why I was ever attracted to her. I must have mistaken avarice for spirit."

"Can you afford to pay them off?"

"I suppose, but it goes against the grain, especially when none of this is my fault."

Jenner stared fixedly at the fire for a few minutes. When she turned to Lacey she was wearing an amused and thoughtful expression, as though she was about to tell one of her stories.

"You have an idea. What is it?"

"No, it's too absurd. Caroline would never agree to it."

"Tell me. If Caroline won't like it, you know I would be bound to."

"Since you cannot break off the engagement, Miss Dawson will just have to cry off."

"Why would she do that now that she has her hooks into me?"

"Embarrassment. She is a proud girl. You have only to look at her to tell that."

"If she is not embarrassed just being engaged to me, I can't see what more I can do. According to you I have lived my whole life in an effort to keep respectable women at arm's length. You see what a waste it has been."

"Which would be worse for Caroline, the lawsuit or you taking a mistress?"

"The former, I would say. She is used to my affairs by now."

"And which would cost less, the lawsuit or a house and furnishings?"

"The house, of course. But what are you getting at? The last thing I need right now is another woman in my life."

"You said to me once that you thought you owed Elaina something. Set her up quite publicly in this house as though it is to be a permanent arrangement."

"That sort of thing usually happens after the wedding."

"I know, but you cannot afford to wait. If that does not gag the Dawson chit, nothing will."

"Then what?"

"Then we throw your engagement dinner—and invite Elaina to sing. That should throw some sparks."

Lacey laughed. "More likely it will be fur that will be flying. It's perfect. Why didn't I think of it?"

"There is still Caroline to convince. How much time do you need for your part of it?"

"Three days—not more."

"You are very sure of yourself," Jenner teased. "In three days you have to charm Elaina back to you, talk her into a house other than this one and get it properly furnished for her. In the process you might be seen with her as often and as publicly as you can manage."

"I shall sit in her pocket. Besides, you have the harder task, convincing Caroline."

"Here's the guest list for the dinner Lacey wants to give." Jenner held the paper out to Caroline as though it might burst into flames of its own accord. "I worked out a seating arrangement that should create the maximum amount of tension."

"Tension? What are you talking about, Jenner?" Caroline's sharp intake of breath made Jenner smile. "You cannot be serious. The Dawsons and Elaina Claridge? They will think we are purposely trying to insult them."

"Precisely."

"What are you up to?" Caroline furrowed her eyebrows in an expression that reminded Jenner of Lacey.

"Getting Lacey unengaged and getting Elaina off his back at the same time. But we cannot manage it without your help."

"But, really! Do you realize what you are asking me to do?"

"Do you really like any of them?"

"No, but the talk."

"People very seldom relate stories that discredit them. The only thing is, will George be offended? We shall need him for a witness."

"You will be lucky if he even realizes what's going on. It's positively disgusting the way he dotes on Stella."

"I think it's rather sweet. Well, what do you say? Think of it as a challenge, a problem in social logistics. If you can pull this off, it will be the greatest success of your career."

"More likely the greatest disaster," said Caroline, taking the paper, "but I will do it for Lacey."

"Elaina, there is something I want to show you," Lacey said to Elaina as he caught up with her in the park. "Will you come with me?"

"Why should I?" she asked, looking scornfully at him in his phaeton. There was nothing she wanted more than to be taken up beside him in this most public of places, but she wanted to make him pay, to beg a little, at least.

"You said I would be sorry for the way I treated you and you were right. It appears I have a conscience after all. I only want to make it up to you. It will take an hour of your time, no more."

"Very well." She extended her hand to him and he pulled her lightly up beside him, not relinquishing her gloved hand until he had kissed it.

"Lacey, have you been drinking?"

"Bit early in the day for that, love."

"What do you think?" Lacey asked ten minutes later as he wandered around the front room of an empty house, his voice echoing slightly between the bare walls. "It's a new square of houses, but bound to be fashionable. Your portrait would look well here and the light is good for your music." Lacey walked to her.

"What if I prefer the house in Grosvenor Street?"

Lacey was prepared for this. "No, that is all spoiled now." He showed her only his pouting profile.

"Lacey, what has happened? What has that boy done to you?"

Lacey's frown was real now. "Rejected me. He is leaving, just as he always said he would." He tore his gaze away from her and walked toward the tall windows on the east side. He had picked the house because its layout was so similar to that of his London home.

Elaina came up behind him and laid a hand on his shoulder. "Tell me what has happened."

"No, I won't speak of it again," he said petulantly, very much like his old self. "Here is the key. The deed will be in your hands in good time." He pressed the key into her palm and held it there as though he was afraid she would drop it. "If you refuse, I will understand," he said very bravely.

Elaina had dealt with Lacey dead drunk, even violent with rage, but she had never seen him shattered before. If she could be said to have a heart still, Lacey touched it then, but what she wanted was to be his wife. All in good time, she thought. This was a start. "I don't know," she said, feigning uncertainty.

"After the way I have acted, why should you trust me. Let me assure you that you will be under no obligation to me. I want to make a place for you. I owe you that much consideration. You may cast me off next week and it will be no more than I deserve."

He glanced at her and guessed by her frown the calculations going on in her mind. He sighed. "I had one of the bedrooms furnished already. You could move in whenever you like. You would want to hire your own staff, of course, and the furnishings need a woman's touch. I am at your disposal for the next few days if you want me to help you choose things. What do you say?"

* * *

"Dennis," Lacey called as he saw his nephew skip by the door of the book room. Dennis ducked his head inside the room.

"Yes?"

"I shall require your presence at a dinner party Caroline is giving for me tomorrow night—"

Dennis was looking mulish.

"For Miss Dawson and her parents." Lacey continued writing at his desk so he could only guess at Dennis' change of expression.

"Yes, of course," Dennis agreed. "Who else will be here?"

"Just the family, a few friends, and George, of course."

"Very well."

Had Dennis been thinking more clearly he would have been suspicious of Lacey's easy compliance. As it was, he could only think his uncle had come to his senses, and even began congratulating himself on being the one to give Lacey the push he needed in the right direction.

George and the Dawsons were chatting stiffly with Lacey and the Langleys while they waited for the last of the guests to arrive.

"Why did Lacey send you to fetch me?" Elaina asked Jenner as a startled Edwards took her cape.

The butler looked from one to the other and opened and shut his mouth several times before Jenner said, "Pull yourself together, man. You know Miss Claridge. Now go and announce her."

"In there?"

"Of course, in there. And stop acting a fool."

Elaina raised an eyebrow at Jenner.

"He was stuck here with his other guests but he thought you might feel more comfortable not arriving alone."

"So he sent you?"

Elaina was still looking scornfully at Jenner as she entered the room and the door was closed behind them. Suddenly she saw the trap into which she had stepped.

"Elaina, my dear," Caroline said warmly as she got up to embrace her sworn enemy and kiss her cheek. "I am so glad you could come."

Elaina did not know whether to be more shocked at the Dawsons' presence or Caroline Langley's odd behavior.

Since Lacey rose at that moment and gave his hand to Miss Dawson to lead her in to dinner, Elaina had the notion to bolt, but she had more stage presence than that. She also wanted to know what was going on. She had thought an invitation to dine with Lacey's family meant she was being accepted, but why then had he bought her a house? None of it made any sense.

She took Jenner's arm and walked into the dining room, her eyes glittering with suspicion. Her reaction was mild compared to that of Mr. and Mrs. Dawson, who knew very well she was Lacey's past—and probably current—mistress. Amelia looked to be about to pick up and go home, but her husband steered her to her seat. He had no intention of letting Raines off the hook, no matter how much they were provoked.

Suddenly it occurred to Elaina that Lacey must be intentionally trying to insult the Dawsons and break his engagement. Then he could marry her, but why had he not warned her?

Stella had thrown herself into the plot with an unexpected passion. Dennis rolled his eyes at Lacey, who only smiled benignly at him. Dennis was seated next to Elaina. Lacey sat at one end of the table between Elaina and Susan, Caroline was at the other end between Jenner and Mr. Dawson. Stella smiled at Lady Amelia across the table and

Dennis faced the impassive George, who did not seem to be even faintly aware of the social crisis that was occurring.

"Have they all run mad?" Elaina asked Dennis under her breath.

"So it seems," Dennis said sympathetically. "Do you want to leave?"

"No," she said stubbornly. "If this is some kind of contest, I do not mean to be bested by that chit of a girl."

Jenner, sitting close to both the Dawsons, conversed with less embarrassment than she normally felt. Surely Mr. Dawson had heard the rumors about her and Lacey, for he looked at her with cold disgust. Lady Amelia glanced down the table toward Lacey from time to time as though she expected him to start raving.

Partway through the meal Jenner began to wonder if she was doing Lacey a favor, parting him from two women both of whom were eager to marry him, when she could not. Was she that jealous of them that she would rather see him alone since she could not have him herself? But she still hoped he would meet someone else. After all, Rob had, and he seemed quite content. When she tried to picture someone for Lacey, she could only manage to conjure up a younger version of herself—the girl she would have become if so much else had not happened to her. She wondered at her own audacity to plan such a scheme. If she had ruined Lacey, he had certainly changed her, as well. She smiled to think how shocked her aunts would be if they found out what she had been up to.

She looked across at Lacey and he grinned at her. He was at his best when excited like this, riding the edge of disaster like a young colt about to explode. The air was charged with something. Everyone could feel it, even the innocent Susan and the dull George Marsh. Remarkably enough, Caroline and Stella were enjoying themselves, as well. For all Dennis' attempts at recklessness, he was the only truly conservative member of the family.

When the meal ended and the ladies rose to leave, Jenner remarked, "We are hoping you will sing for us tonight, Miss Claridge. Remember, I have never heard you."

"Oh, yes, please," said Stella in a sisterly way. "Let us go choose some music. Either Jenner or I will play for you if you like."

Because of the presence of Mr. Dawson, Dennis could still not ask Lacey what the devil he was doing. Conversation ground to a halt, and Lacey made no effort to keep it going. George rambled on in his aimless way, eliciting an occasional response from Dennis or Jenner. Lacey leaned back in his chair, observing each of the actors around the table. When his eyes passed to Jenner, she smiled faintly in a private way. Dennis pushed his glass away in disgust.

"Shall we join the ladies?" Lacey asked, rising as though at a signal.

When they entered the music room, it was obvious that some insult had been offered to Elaina. Her color was high, but that had not dissuaded her from singing, since she and Stella were at the pianoforte. It was equally obvious that Mrs. Dawson had found somehow an opportunity to apprise her daughter of the situation, for the girl looked like she could cut Lacey's heart out and eat it. Lacey winked at Jenner and took a seat where he could get the best view of Elaina. Jenner went to turn the music, surprised that she could have engineered a situation that would make so many people in the same room acutely uncomfortable.

Elaina was in voice in spite of everything. Jenner played some ballads as Elaina sang, then Jenner and Stella played a duet. It was with something of a shock that Jenner realized she had become one of these people, whoever else she was. She didn't lie, precisely, but she let people take things in a certain way and make incorrect inferences. If she stayed here much longer she might come to dislike herself even more than she had originally disliked the people of the ton. Somehow the realization made her coming exile more bitter.

But there was no alternative, not for the remembrancer in her story and not for her. It was time for the game to end. It was destroying Dennis. And at any moment it could ruin Caroline and Stella. And Jenner now cared about them almost as much as she loved Lacey. She had one more social commitment, the opera tomorrow night. She would leave the next day.

The impromptu concert was quite good but the Dawsons did not appreciate it. Lacey asked Miss Dawson to sing. She rose and came up to him, but only insisted in a fierce whisper that she must talk to him. As Lacey led her into the adjoining salon, Stella laid out some more music and Dennis moved around behind his mother's chair to demand what the devil she thought she was about.

"Dennis, do not be so dense," was all the reply she made him.

Jenner and Stella had just agreed on a piece and persuaded Elaina to do the vocal part when the door opened and Susan stormed back in.

"That is the last straw!"

"But what about . . ." Lacey faltered.

"There is no engagement!" Susan spit at him. "And I want to go home," she said, bursting into tears. Her father was smoldering, but Amelia Dawson gave vent to her pent-up feelings with a vengeance that impressed everyone and left her gasping. Mr. Dawson shepherded them out.

George was still looking owlishly surprised and offered Lacey his condolences. Elaina walked over to Lacey. "Is there something you wanted to say to me?"

"Only that you were magnificent, my dear, far better than I even hoped. But, no, I am not going to marry you, either."

"You used me!"

"Yes, how does it feel?" He caught her hand as she was about to strike him. "You still have the house. I owe you that much but no more."

"I want to leave."

"I will take you," Dennis said, supporting Elaina to a chair.

Lacey rang and commanded the carriage to be brought around, then congratulated Caroline and Stella on their excellent performances, as well. George was looking confused, but that was often his expression since he had begun to frequent Lacey's house.

Caroline was feeling very full of herself. "Tell me, Lacey dear, what was the last straw?"

"First she scolded me fiercely for asking Elaina here tonight. Then she caviled at me for buying Elaina that house, not that I did it at all, but that I had the bad taste to do it before the wedding. She thought there should be some decent interval of wedded bliss, although I don't know exactly how long she expected that to be."

"Do you mean that was not enough to give her a disgust of you?" Caroline demanded, ignoring the angry Elaina.

"No, it was when I said I intended to set Jenner up in a house as well—"

Caroline snorted with laughter in spite of herself, Stella giggled, and George looked cross.

"You are disgusting, the lot of you," Dennis said as he took Elaina out of the room.

Jenner flushed. "You must have been fighting in the last ditch to resort to that."

"It was a near run thing in spite of all our work," Lacey admitted.

"See here, you meant to trick that girl into crying off?" George concluded finally.

"Why not? She tricked me into an engagement."

"And I must say you were magnificent, George," Stella said in obvious adulation.

"Me?"

"Yes, you played your part to perfection just by being yourself. We could not have brought it off without you. You won't give us away, will you?"

"Good heavens, of course not. I am very nearly a member of the family."

Caroline looked at him and said, "You know, in some ways, George, you remind me of my late husband, Henry."

George looked a little dubious until Stella said, "That's good, George," and patted his arm.

"You are a good man, George," Jenner said, "and I hope your worthy influence on Lord Raines and the Langleys makes the family a little more stable."

"I shall do my best."

Chapter Ten

Jenner sat up writing that night, half expecting Lacey to creep into her room. But the sound of regular breathing from his bed told her that he was getting a much needed rest, so she did not disturb him. She got so involved in her story she scarcely noticed the clock chiming three. It was the stillest part of the night. Jenner often wondered if she was the only one who bridged the gap between the night world and the day world, part of both and not really belonging to either. She was about to snuff her candle and seek some sleep when something rattled against her window. She did blow the candle out then and cautiously pulled aside the drape. Roland's large bulk was clearly recognizable, and she raised the window to whisper to him. He merely pointed toward the stable and she nodded.

"What is it, colic?" she asked as she joined him outside the back door.

"What do I know of such things? But there's a chap here I thought you would be interested to meet. I've seen him watching the house more than once. Tonight, as I was up anyway, I managed to hobble him."

Roland led her to an empty horse box where a burly fellow was tightly trussed and hanging upside down from a

bridle hook. Even by the dim light of the shuttered lantern
Jenner could see the fellow was nearly purple in the face.

"Good Lord! How long have you left him hanging like
this?"

"Not more than an hour. I wanted to make sure everyone else was asleep."

"Best cut him down before he dies of heart failure."

"What do you want to ask him?"

Jenner thought for a moment. "Just what his orders are,"
Jenner said brusquely.

"Here, you!" Roland growled, grabbing the man by his
ragged coat collar. "Mowbray, what did he hire you for?"

"Ah dunno any Mowbray," the man complained.

"Poulton, then," Jenner prompted.

The man snapped his mouth shut like some giant fish and
Jenner took a closer look at him. "I think this is one of the
thugs who attacked us in Jermyn Street. He might be the
man who half killed Lacey."

"This is river slime, not like an honest footpad. What was
you paid to club a couple of gents outside Cato's?"

The ruffian sent a calculated glance from one to the other
and Jenner regretted being merciful enough to worry about
his heart. He obviously did not have one.

"He's not going to talk. Shall I kill him for you?" Roland
asked with a wink.

Jenner looked the man in the eye as coldly as she could.
"Let me think a moment." She paced the length of the stable and back. "No, best not," she said in a disappointed
tone. "There's no place to dig hereabouts." She noticed the
man twitch. "We would have to get the body the whole way
to the river," she said, nodding toward the Thames. "And
we might run out of time."

"True enough," Roland said in disappointment. The ruffian slumped with a sigh. "I suppose we could turn him over to the watch for assault," Roland offered.

"What would he get, do you think?"

"Couple of years if it's proved. But he's got enough low-lying friends to alibi him."

"Can we keep him shut up until tomorrow night?" Jenner asked. "That would give us the whole night to get rid of him." Jenner kept her eyes on Roland but she could see the helpless thug glancing from one to the other of them.

"Too risky. I know, I'll just break his arms." Roland's gruff voice sounded convincingly serious.

"Really! Can you?" Jenner asked as the fellow moaned.

"Easiest trick in the world."

Roland left the man's feet trussed together but rolled him over and cut his arms free so he could demonstrate.

"Wait! Wait! He never paid me to take that."

"He paid you enough to nearly break someone's leg." Jenner turned her head sideways to stare at him meanly and this time the sharp edge to her voice was genuine. "It was Poulton, was it not?"

"Yes. Ow."

"And what are you here for now?" Roland twisted his arm until he cried out again.

"Watch the 'ouse. Watch 'im coming and going," he said with a nod at Jenner. "Tell Poulton if anyone is going on a trip—carriage and baggage, that sort of thing."

"What else?"

"That's all, I swear."

Jenner paced again for effect.

"Cut him loose then."

"What? Not even one arm?" Roland asked as he slid his knife between the man's grimy stockings.

"Oh, very well." Jenner gave in as to a child begging for a treat.

The ruffian screamed, wrenched himself out of Roland's grasp and clawed his way out of the stable. They listened to the sound of his scrabbling footsteps die away before they bent double with laughter, but one thing he had told them sobered Roland.

"You know what this means, lad?"

"Yes," Jenner agreed, wiping her eyes. "He will not be content to drive me from town. He means to have me killed one way or the other." She gave a heavy sigh.

"I can see you safely away from here, but if he has an idea where you live you will never be safe from him."

"I know, and what is worse, I will carry the enemy right into my own camp. Well, there is no help for it. The damage is done." Jenner was surprised that this knowledge did not upset her more than it did. If she did not fear for her aunts, the prospect would have been almost exciting. To be on guard the whole rest of her life—not a dull existence, at any rate. It was the kind of thing that would appeal to someone like Lacey or Roland. What would Mowbray find if he pursued her to Thetford, a girl who looked very much like her? No, even he would realize they were one and the same and would be vindictive enough to spread the tale.

"What will you do?" Roland asked as he put out the lantern and picked up the ropes.

Jenner thought for a moment. If Mowbray came north to cut up her aunts' peace she would have to deal with him. "We have lots of places to dig where I live."

Roland whistled and Jenner shrugged, for she did almost mean it. If it came to killing Mowbray or letting him harm her aunts the choice would be easy.

By the time Jenner got back to her room, Lacey was there looking worried, his scrambled hair hanging across his brow.

"Where in God's name have you been?"

"I thought I heard something in the stable."

"Why didn't you wake me?"

"You were sleeping so peacefully, and you have not been lately."

"I thought I heard someone scream."

"No one we know, and all is well among the horses."

Jenner undressed in front of Lacey, which generally excited him, but tonight he only held her and drew her into bed with him.

Lacey watched Jenner sleeping innocently, her head resting on his arm, quite amazed that she could look so carefree after all she had been through. But then, her conscience was clean. She had never broken faith with anyone. She had certainly never lied to him. She had told him at the start she would leave and she meant to do it.

He wondered what her hair would look like longer than the curly crop she favored. He wanted to spend the rest of his life watching her. He had no doubt about his own commitment this time. He would never grow tired of Jenner, never want to escape from her. It was his punishment that she was one woman he could not keep.

She smiled and he ran a hand down her side to arouse her. But when she opened her eyes a sadness came into them that belied the smile.

"You cannot leave me," Lacey said lightly.

"Don't speak of it," Jenner whispered.

She locked her legs around him and pressed him into her with a hunger that was insatiable. They twisted together, gasping in a desperate struggle to satisfy, to give everything. When their muscles relaxed in warmth they came up for air, panting and heaving like two swimmers in a deep sea. Jenner was as close as she had ever been to losing all control, to slipping off with Lacey to someplace where they need never see another human soul.

But such places do not really exist, she reminded herself. There is always the morning, the cold kind light of day to bring you back, the faithful valet with a tea tray, and a need to wake up to the real world. There was a strange kind of comfort in hearing Collins in the other room, an assurance that whatever happened he would take care of Lacey as he always had.

One might do some quite extraordinary things once in a great while, but the main part of your life was the daily routine of meals, conversation and the day's work. And Jenner's was about to shift back to what it was before. If she could continue, then Lacey could, as well. He was not so fragile as she had feared.

At breakfast Dennis was conspicuous by his absence.

"He did not come home last night," Caroline said to Lacey's look of inquiry.

"I am sorry, Caroline," Jenner admitted. "Elaina will try to take Dennis now to be revenged on us."

"I know, but it was a risk we had to take. And I must say I enjoyed myself. Lacey, I don't know how I could have imagined you married to Susan Dawson. She has no countenance. As for Dennis..."

"A short affair will do him no harm right now," Lacey decided. "In fact, it may keep him from more dangerous pursuits. And I expect he will get over Elaina much quicker than I did. He is, in all things, more moderate and sensible than I have ever been.''

Upon being asked her plans for the day, Jenner said, ''I have some business to settle before I leave. I promised I would tell you when I planned to go.''

''When?'' Lacey felt his chest tighten.

''Tomorrow after lunch. I will stay a night on the road to rest Ebony.''

''You must write to us, Jenner,'' Stella said.

''I will do that, at least.''

This was not how Lacey had imagined it would be. He had thought they would be alone, and he would convince her to stay, or to let him go with her. For now, he could say nothing. All the joy of the previous night was drained out of him and he felt empty at the bleakness of the future before him.

There was no chance to be private with Jenner that day, even after dinner, for she was going to the opera to help deflect Lady Marsh's tongue from Stella. George had come to rely on Jenner to braggle with his mother on these occasions, and Jenner had developed a mutual antagonism with the old woman. Jenner almost cried off. She had no relish for such a trying evening when she could spend those hours with Lacey. But she also knew Lacey would try to convince her to stay, and it would not take much to shake her resolve.

Lacey was passing into the card room at the Stiltons' rout party when he sensed a certain coldness. He had only come out of boredom and from a strange reluctance to stay home and brood. Usually he provoked disapproving stares, sly glances, whispered confidences behind fans. That had always been a delicious feeling. This was something else. He was cut by half a dozen people before he made it across the room. He made a mental note of who turned his back on him, which men and women looked at him speculatively and which tried unsuccessfully to look as though nothing had happened.

This was what Jenner had meant about being alone. He had never felt it before. He stared at the mass of them as he realized he had nothing in common with even those he had fought beside in the army. None of them knew him. Realizing how little he cared for the opinion of anyone present freed him suddenly from the oppression and he gave a harsh, majestic laugh as he passed from them for the last time. He would not go among them again, not because he couldn't face them, but because they bored him and he didn't really care. But he was alone. He did know it now. He left with the determination to go with Jenner and shake the dust of London from him forever.

The party arrived well before the opera started. Stella and George sat in the front of the box, holding hands and conversing in low whispers. George was slightly flushed by this public display of intimacy, but Jenner found it quite touching that he tolerated it so well. Jenner watched Lady Marsh settling herself on her left and turned to smile at Caroline, who shook her head ruefully. Caroline was accepting the engagement in better part than Jenner had hoped. So long as George never lost his awe of his mother-in-law, Jenner thought they would get on quite well.

There was no question of her living with the young couple, of course. She and Lady Marsh did not much more than tolerate each other, and Caroline had her duty to Lacey. Someone must keep house for him until he married, then she would set up a small household for herself, in Bath, perhaps. Jenner was trying to picture Caroline content to run a small house when the voice she had come to dread pierced her reverie.

Mowbray! What in God's name brought him here to ruin her last evening? She started involuntarily when she saw who was with him in the box across from them. Mowbray was laughing and chatting to Lord Gawlton. Jenner moved her head so that George blocked a direct view of her face, but Gawlton was absorbed in Mowbray's discourse about the performance, which showed only that Mowbray had read the playbill. As she gradually recovered from the shock of seeing both of them, the strangeness of seeing them together began to take hold of her. Lady Marsh followed her look. "That must be Mowbray's great-uncle come to town," she said querulously. "They say Mowbray will inherit a sizable estate when Lord Gawlton dies, if he manages not to disgrace himself again. There are no other heirs."

"So that's it!" Jenner said just as the musicians began to play. She ducked her head behind George again when Mowbray glanced anxiously at Lacey's box. It all made sense now. That's why he was so desperate to get rid of her. If she went to the straitlaced Gawlton with her story he might choose to disinherit his nephew. Gawlton's rare trip to town had nearly spelled her doom in more ways than one. Now she knew why Mowbray was so desperate to hide a crime that his contemporaries would merely shrug off, some even laugh at. Lord Gawlton was the one person in the world to whom it would matter.

There was one good thing. Unless Mowbray wished to persecute her friends from sheer maliciousness, she thought they were no longer in any danger—provided she got away from them. It was a comfort in a way to have a definite reason to go even if she could not tell Lacey what it was.

There was the possibility that Mowbray would come looking for Jenner Page and the girl he had ravished and try to shut them up. And he would know exactly where to find them. Jenner gave a small shudder of rage at the injustice done to the now vanished child that she had been. It was almost as though she was now another person. There was certainly no going back to that time of simple innocence, and she realized with a start that she would not wish to. If not for Mowbray, she would probably be married with children, still as ignorant of life as when he had shattered her paradise. If not for him she would never have known Lacey. Or, she reminded herself, the pain of giving Lacey up.

She felt very strange with her heart pounding as she sat there perfectly still wanting every minute to choke the life out of the simpering fool who was clearly irritating his uncle by whispering to him during the performance. This must be what Lacey meant when he said anyone could kill with the right provocation. As soon as his first comrade fell he must have become fantastically dangerous. If it were not for the danger to Lacey's family, the temptation to confront Mowbray would be overwhelming.

Jenner had herself under some sort of control by the end of the first act, but the task of avoiding Gawlton's gaze kept her so preoccupied that Caroline asked if she was quite well. She confessed to a slight headache and then had to suffer listening to Lady Marsh and Caroline arguing over the best remedy all through the interval. If she was in a tight spot she drew some comfort from the spectacle of Mowbray sweating it out across the way as he continued to look nervously into the shadows at the back of their box. Suddenly it occurred to her that it didn't matter if Mowbray saw her. It might encourage him to take his uncle away. Just as the second act was about to start, and Gawlton's attention was focused on the stage, Jenner pulled her chair forward and Mowbray caught sight of her. Mowbray drew back with a horrified start and immediately began trying to persuade Lord Gawlton to leave.

Jenner's chuckle drew an inquiring look from Stella. She enjoyed herself torturing Mowbray throughout the second act. At one point she smiled at him and looked significantly from him to Lord Gawlton. Mowbray sent her such a venomous stare she could taste the hatred. At the second interval Lady Marsh said she must have some air so Jenner took her to walk up and down the corridor where she met a crony of hers. She had no qualms about dispatching Jenner to procure lemonade for them. Jenner guessed badly and turned right down the corridor, only to confront Mowbray before she reached the stairs. She hesitated before saying as coolly as she could, "Is Lord Gawlton enjoying the evening?"

"He would come here, damn him! As for you, if you say one word to him, it will be your last."

"In front of witnesses?" There was a continual coming and going from the boxes, not to mention Lady Marsh within earshot.

"There won't always be so many people about you. You have been lucky so far."

"I have been careful. I can see my man was right. I should have called for a meeting with you instead of playing this game. It grows rather boring. Besides, I do have to go home, and I would not want you to think I'm giving up."

"What are you talking about?"

"I will not tell Lord Gawlton that you are the man who ravished my young cousin, if—"

"I accept no conditions from you. I said I would kill you and I will."

"But by then the damage will be done. It is an old wound anyway. But I need to know you will never do that to another child. So long as you behave yourself in that respect your secret is safe."

"What do you want? My hand on it?" Mowbray sneered at her.

"The word of a gentleman should do..."

Mowbray's eyes shifted sideways, calculating.

"But in your case I will set someone to watch you. I have a man watching you now. It's a job he is well content with, and I will not mind paying him to do it until you are too old and infirm to be a danger to anyone." Mowbray lunged at her and she stepped back.

"Jenner, you troublesome boy," Lady Marsh shouted imperiously. "You have stood talking through the entire interval and not brought us any lemon water."

"Just going, Lady Marsh."

"Never mind now. I'm ready to go back to the box."

"As you wish." Jenner smiled at Mowbray and backed away from him. It was rather like playing with a cobra. She saw him rejoin his uncle and sit in surly silence through the final act. He looked to be close to exploding with frustration. She did not think it made up for what she had suffered, but it did her good to enjoy his embarrassment—even if only for a few hours.

She turned over in her mind what would happen if she told Lord Gawlton the whole story. He might disinherit Mowbray, but she had a grudging respect for the lonely old lord. In spite of her uncle's differences with Gawlton over the enclosure bill, she knew that Lord Gawlton prided himself on doing the right thing. What purpose would it serve to make him miserable?

It then occurred to her that she might have Mowbray for a neighbor in a very few years. The thought was not as disquieting as it should have been. After Lord Gawlton was gone, Mowbray would have no need to silence her. Until then, she could live very much as she had been doing. And when Mowbray came to occupy the estate—she rather thought he was not the sort to be living in the country—but if he did, he would be made more uncomfortable by the situation than she would. She could picture any number of ways to put him out of countenance.

When they returned from the opera, Jenner noticed a light in the book room and went there to seek out Lacey. He was lounging in one of the chairs, pulling sluggishly at a brandy. The nearly empty decanter was beside him on the table.

"Collins? Oh, Jenner. Back so soon?"

"It's after midnight. Coming to bed?"

"I'm too drunk to go to bed." A stranger would not have known Lacey was drunk, but Jenner sat down patiently to wait for him.

"I wish I had not left you tonight. We could have been alone for hours."

"I felt it tonight, what you spoke of, that terrible isolation. I went to the Stiltons' party. I don't know why. Just to see who was there. And this wave of silence preceded me through the rooms, not like before, when they would chuckle at my imbroglios. The best of them were merely sorry for me." He looked at Jenner to see the silent tears running down her face.

"I have ruined your life, just as Dennis says."

"I had no life before. I was just playing at it."

"I must go tomorrow. I told you from the beginning I couldn't stay."

"Let me go with you."

"And have them all say we have run off together, which would be no more than the truth?"

"I don't care what they say. They are nothing to me."

"What about Caroline, Stella and Dennis?"

"They will understand."

"I meant leaving them to face the scandal alone."

"You have trapped me!" he growled in anguish. "You say you have ruined me. That is more true than you know. Having once been so close to you, having really loved you, to have you leave me means I will always be alone. At least I didn't see myself before."

"What do you mean?" Jenner gasped.

"I have always thought myself rather hardened, but now I see that is not so," he said in amazement, sinking back into the chair.

"Perhaps that was just part of your disguise. What is the matter with that?"

"It's hard to explain. When you take off your boy's clothes you are still someone—the same person. Now that you have shown me what an actor I am, now that you have stripped off all my masks, there is nothing left."

"That's not true. You are a person and quite a lovable one. Caroline, Stella and Dennis see that as easily as I do."

"Do not define me in terms of what I am to other people, least of all yourself," he nearly shouted as he pounded the chair arm.

"But I love you. Who could not?"

"And still you will leave me?"

"There is no other way."

"You cannot doubt that I love you."

"The best someone like me can hope for is to live so as not to do any harm. I have done far too much already. I had rather not see you again than watch your love die, watch you come to hate me like you came to hate the others."

"That is not possible."

"Let us not speak of it." She led him up the stairs and dismissed Collins. She put him to bed herself and held him as he slept the night through. They made love in the morning, not with the heat of passion, but with a deliberate slowness, knowing it would be the last time. Every move, every second they stretched out with their enjoyment, sealing each feeling away in their minds against the lonely years ahead. When Collins' tentative movements in the other room could no longer be ignored Lacey rose and left wordlessly.

Jenner did not like the way Lacey was taking the parting. If he had ranted at her in that spoiled way of his it would have been different. But this morose drinking alone worried her. He might very well drink himself to death if he did not pull out of it. She decided she would have to trust Collins with her direction in case Lacey got very bad. It was a lot to burden the man with, but she trusted Collins' loyalty to Lacey. She had come to trust a great many people; Collins, Roland, Coyle, Dennis, not to mention Stella, George and Caroline. It was remarkable considering what a loner she had been. Lacey was not the only one she would miss.

"Collins, I wanted to see you." Jenner caught him on the landing.

"You are not leaving?"

"Not quite yet. I have to call in at Roberto's. Here is something for you." She handed him some envelopes. "And something for the others."

"This is not necessary."

"Neither was looking after me. I just wanted to say thank you. I have not told him who I am or where I live. I think a clean break would be best for him. But here is my direction in case he should fall ill . . . or be wounded . . . I don't know what I'm saying. Use your own judgment, Collins. I'm sure it is better than mine right now."

"You will see him before you go?"

"Of course. I shall be back in an hour or two. I have had most of my things shipped except for a few clothes. I have decided to ride Ebony home, after all. It's not all that far if I take my time, and I should do much better than in a carriage."

"So long as you don't run into any fog."

"Right." She laughed weakly as she strode down the stairs.

Dennis appeared from the music room and loomed over her as she hesitated at the bottom of the steps. She had never realized before how tall he was. It was a good excuse not to look him in the eye.

"At least Lacey has no idea where I live. Apparently you have kept that to yourself. For that I thank you." She turned her hat nervously in her hands.

"You almost sound as though you want to escape him."

"I must. I must!" she said fiercely as though to herself. Jenner glanced up at him then and saw the shock appear in Dennis' eyes and the suspicion of compassion knit his brow.

Jenner collected herself and determined to turn his mind the other way. "Do not go thinking of me as the victim just because I am younger. Whatever has happened here is my fault. I have caused all of it. You must contrive to keep him from following me." She said it in her firmest, boldest voice, though she was far from feeling either of these.

Dennis' jaw hardened. "I will keep him here if I have to tie him up."

"He won't soon forgive you for that."

"I don't care."

"I am sorry, Dennis."

"Where is Jenner?" Lacey demanded of Collins when he jerked awake again in his own bed.

"She went out early, but she is coming back."

Staying in bed was not delaying Jenner's departure. Lacey rose and began to shave and dress. Collins had just turned to pick up a neck cloth when Lacey, seated at the dressing table, caught sight of himself in the cheval mirror that stood beside it. He quite deliberately smashed the glass. Collins said nothing. He merely folded the neck cloth into a bandage and bound it around Lacey's bleeding knuckles.

Caroline opened the door without knocking. "Lacey, what was that crash?— Oh, so Jenner is truly leaving?"

"If I thought you had anything to do with it..." Lacey half threatened. Collins left discreetly.

"I asked him to stay, Lacey."

Lacey looked up from nursing his knuckles.

"Sometimes, dear, it is better to ride these things out than to fly from them."

"I suppose you would know. What do you usually do when I make a scandal?"

"But this time it is unjust. I feel like staying and fighting myself."

Lacey called to mind a picture of a much younger Caroline defending his behavior to his stern and arrogant father.

"I know I should have warned you, Lacey. But it seemed so preposterous. I even hinted at a match between Jenner and Stella to create a diversion."

"Jenner is right. I have treated you horribly."

"I helped to spoil you, so it is no more than I deserve." Caroline laid a hand on his shoulder. "But you are still young..."

"Not any more." He patted her hand. "You had best leave me alone in my book room today. I won't be fit company for quite some time."

Dennis had determined to see Jenner off himself rather than let his uncle alone with the boy. To that end he sat in the music room with the door open, guarding the hall and the approach to the book room. So when Lord Gawlton came to the front door asking for young Mr. Page, Dennis thrust Edwards aside. "He is out."

"May I wait for him?"

"He is leaving today. I would rather you did not. It might disturb my uncle."

"But I must see Jen. It has taken me all this time to find out what name—to find out where he is staying."

Collins was just then bringing down Jenner's small valise.

"Collins, have you any idea where Jenner went?" Dennis demanded.

"Friday is his regular day for Condez's lesson. He meant to go there today, as well."

"Where is that?" Gawlton asked. "If you can direct my driver I would be much obliged."

"I will take you there," Dennis offered. "I want a word with you, anyway."

"That's not necessary."

Dennis studied Lord Gawlton as he got into the hackney beside him and told the driver to go around to Hedge Lane just before Charing Cross.

"How do you come to know Jenner?"

"We are neighbors." Gawlton eyed Dennis warily.

"You have known Jenner a long time then."

"Yes, all her—that is, ever since—I mean, quite a few years."

"He has been creating quite a stir here."

"So I have heard. I want Jen to come back home with me. I worry..."

"You are not related then?"

"No, but I do care what happens. I do not know if Jen will listen to me."

"Why should he? He doesn't listen to anyone else."

"Jenner has had a very hard life, one way or another. You must not blame the boy too much."

"Which does not give him the right to ruin my uncle's life."

"I have heard that rumor. If you knew the truth of the matter..."

"I know enough. I want nothing to delay Jenner's departure today."

Lacey let his breakfast grow cold on the tray they had brought into the book room for him. He had begun to systematically clean and oil his pistol collection. None of them were in need of cleaning, but the mundane task helped him think.

His mind kept running in the same tired circle. If only he had not flaunted Jenner all over town, there might be some hope of marrying her. It was his fault they were in this fix, not hers. And yet he had the feeling that she only used that as an excuse. He would gladly forgo the pleasures of London for as long as it took for her face to be forgotten. There was something else, some private cross she bore that prevented her giving in to him. It hurt that she would not confide in him.

After two hours the only conclusion he could reach was that he would have to let her go. But he could not imagine himself without her, living alone with Caroline and Dennis. Dennis would not tolerate it. He would leave. What if he had no one? As much as his family had plagued his existence, they had always been there. For a few minutes he sat totally alone in the quiet house, then deliberately loaded one of the French dueling pistols.

But that would be stupid. What was he thinking of? Such an act would destroy Jenner and his family. But he might need a pistol if he followed her north. To save himself, he pretended he was going with her. Why not? Even if she would not permit it, she could not stop him following her. Once he knew where she lived he could insinuate himself with her aunts somehow. He was good at that sort of thing. How could she stay angry with him? He had a way around women.

He stopped. Not Jenner, though. His only hope was that her resolve would not hold. He laid the pistol aside. He might need it anyway.

He resumed his work while he waited for her. She said she would tell him face to face when she was leaving, and she had never lied.

He had always accepted what happened to him as his just due for past crimes. If he was being punished, this was the worst that could befall him. He should accept it with a good grace. Or was life just a series of accidents, as Jenner believed, and you controlled it as best you could by picking up the pieces and going on?

If he held to his own philosophy he was immobilized, like a slave cowering under the lash. Only Jenner's road held any hope. She had fallen into his life by accident. He had made a mess of a situation she tried hard to control. The pieces that were left were the two of them. Very well, then, he would follow her.

Once the decision had been made he stopped beating himself against the wall of his despair and the black mood lifted from him. He ate his cold breakfast ravenously and sent for Collins.

"Pack clothes for me and put them in my curricle. You and Hawes take it and the chestnuts on ahead to the George at Halstead. I know the way that far. Have Lancer saddled at the same time as Ebony. Hawes can take charge of the horses at Halstead. I will drive from there on. Let me know when Jenner returns but do not tell her what I plan to do."

"What is that, sir?"

"Abduct her, if I have to, but don't worry. I won't run her down again." Lacey smiled tiredly.

Collins brightened at the sudden decision in Lacey.

Jenner scarcely noticed the half dozen young blades practicing or lounging about the fencing salon, for Rob was nursing a cut ear. It bled profusely on his white shirt and she was about to bind it up and chide him on his clumsiness when she realized his opponent, Mowbray, was still standing there. She knew a moment's dread. It must have shown in her face for Mowbray sneered at her, and all her old, aching anger returned as destructively as ever. For the first time she noted with satisfaction her enemy's bruised face and the bandage on his hand.

"Boy, practice with me," Mowbray growled. "Condez has had his fill."

"No!" Rob protested.

Jenner wondered for a desperate moment if Mowbray had divined a connection between her and Rob. If so, Rob could be in the gravest danger.

"Why not? I came for a lesson," she said lightly, but the veneer of calmness she had restored to herself after the interview with Dennis snapped like an overtaut bowstring.

Mowbray threw her a sword and she caught it. It was heavier than the foils she and Rob usually fenced with. Mowbray did not give her time to don the padded vest one normally wore when practicing with such a blade. His first onslaught backed her halfway across the room as she studied his technique. She did no more than defend herself for some minutes, getting used to his pace, which was not even, but full of rushing onslaughts and gasping pauses. He was old, but not past the point of being dangerous, and if his bruised hand impeded him she was not aware of it.

"Afraid?" Mowbray taunted when he recovered his breath.

"Not of you, old man," she said, keeping her eye on him as she circled, half-crouching. There were chuckles behind her from the younger men.

Rob looked on grimly, throwing her an occasional hint as any good teacher would. She listened to him with half her mind, but Mowbray was distracted by Rob's sharp orders. She got under his guard and slit his sleeve, then nearly disarmed him. She backed off when he clutched at his chest, then cursed herself for her stupidity when his fresh onslaught forced her across the room where someone nearly tripped her.

Mowbray's blade ran down the underside of Jenner's forearm but she spun and blocked his next thrust. The collective groan at her opponent's unfair play had barely died away when she saw Rob with a knife to Poulton's throat. At

least she thought it was Poulton, but his face was a ghastly
mess. From the blackened eyes she decided that Lacey must
have broken his nose. Mowbray rushed at her again, and she
defended with the same series of forehand and backhand
blows as before. There was a pattern to each of his onslaughts, and one he was not aware of himself.

Then she saw Roland leaning against the wall with a hand
in his pocket. She would not give a groat for Mowbray's life
if he did manage to kill her. This made her laugh, which was
not at all what Mowbray had expected. She was still fresh,
just starting to breathe hard, and he was very nearly spent.

"Your credit is no good in this town any more," Mowbray taunted. "No matter what you say, no one will believe
you now."

She thought he was merely trying to distract her, but her
mind was moving at lightning speed. She said slowly, as
though she was telling a story, "I am not a gossip like you,
but I know what I know. Do you expect me to be complacent about it?"

He backed her into a table and she shut up and concentrated on his blade.

"If you ever dare to mention it, I will cut your tongue
out."

The coats and white neck cloths of the observers flashed
by her side as they circled each other. Rob, Poulton and
Roland were frozen now in anxious silence.

"What? Not simply murder me as you have been trying
to do these past weeks? I couldn't make out why until last
night when I saw you with Lord Gawlton. To think that I
very nearly left London without knowing."

"Hold still, you little coward." Mowbray was out of
breath and less able to defend himself verbally than physically. Was it like a woman, she wondered, to try to outtalk

him? But she did not feel like a woman just then. She felt like what she had pretended to be all this time. Accidents were nothing new to her and she never gave them a second thought. But she had often wondered what she would do if an act of courage was actually required of her. She was surprised to find that she had flung herself into the situation as carelessly as Lacey would have done. They were more alike than she had thought possible.

"I am surprised you challenged me today. Usually you prey only on weak and innocent women."

"I am surprised," Mowbray panted, "that you dare to show your face here since it is known what you and Raines are to each other."

"That affair exists only in your imagination, you seducer of children." Jenner took advantage of his distress to beat him back. "Yes, I know all about what you did to my cousin. You didn't bother to discover she was only fifteen, or that she nearly died along with your child." Jenner had raised her voice and Mowbray rolled his eyes to see who was listening.

"Have you ever even wondered in all these years what became of her?" Jenner continued. "Or was she just one among so many that she didn't even count to you. But my face, so like hers, brought it all back to you, didn't it? And you wondered if I knew. Your very actions made me suspect you. All that scheming to get rid of me, including that farcical story about me and Lacey. That told me more surely than anything that you are the one. I wrote for particulars. She has described you too well. Old men don't change that much in eight years." Jenner took advantage of the shock her verbal onslaught produced to disarm him with an opportune twist of her sword. Mowbray backed against the wall, sweating as she held the blade to his throat.

"Tell them it was a lie about Lacey. Experience the novelty of telling the truth for once. It may be your last opportunity."

She deliberately pressed the steel into his throat until a trickle of blood ran down his neck.

"I lied."

"Louder!"

"I lied. I know nothing against Raines."

"Very well, you may live for all I care." She stood back from him. "As for your crimes against my cousin, your disgrace will cover that. I would estimate you have no more than two days before this story is spread all over London. I would look for another country if I were you."

Mowbray caught up his coat and fled in public and undignified haste.

"I knew you could beat him." Rob grasped her hand.

"And I only came to say goodbye. Have a care, my friend," she said, shaking his hand warmly. "I am a dangerous person to know and you have others depending on you now."

"Yes, I know. I have been thinking about selling this business and starting over somewhere, perhaps America. But I'm not a farmer."

"Have they no cities in America yet?"

"There's a thought."

"I must go. I would say write to me, but you may be safer if I don't know where you are."

She turned to discover that the two men she least wanted to see in London had witnessed her performance. Dennis gave her one fuming look before he turned on his heel and left. Lord Gawlton stared at her dumbly.

"You didn't know, did you?" It was more of a statement than a question.

"Jen—I always suspected, but he denied it." He hung his gray head in shame. "Will you have him arrested?"

"And stir all that up again? I think not, even if I could. It's better this way. For a man like Mowbray, the fear is always worse than the reality."

She left him standing there and walked through the dozen or so spectators the fight had attracted, wondering if he would give away her identity. She thought not. But she did know that feeling Lacey described, of risking everything on one throw of the dice. He had gotten her used to living on the brink of disaster. She only hoped life on the farm would not be boring after all this.

She was barely conscious of one or two of Dennis' friends saying, "Well done!" and clapping her on the back. She looked at Coyle in some surprise when he grasped her hand. "I must admit you had me a bit worried there for a moment. But I expect you do this sort of thing all the time. That is why you take it so much in stride."

"If you want to know the truth of it, I'm a bit embarrassed to fight an old man like that. What will people think of me?" This caused the young group about her to laugh and push her out the door and toward one of the clubs for a small celebration.

As soon as she could free herself of her comrades, she bid them goodbye as lightly as though she expected to see them all again in a few months, and ran down the steps of the club to find Roland waiting with a hackney.

"That was a close run thing, by the looks of it," Roland remarked gruffly, glancing at the bloody handkerchief wrapped around her coat sleeve.

"Closer than you suspect."

"Why didn't you kill him?"

"I suppose I didn't need to. Saying all that, letting someone else know about it, watching him sweat, that was enough. Besides, he is an enemy I now know. I might miss him."

Roland gaped at her. "I will never understand you. The way you make up names you could have slipped off into another life if you'd run him through. No one would have ever found you."

"Yes, that has been my goal, but I am satisfied. As for you, your trials are nearly at an end. That is, unless you've changed your mind about going north with me."

"A fish out o' water is what I'd be in the country."

"In that case, saddle Ebony for me as soon as we reach the house. I leave within the hour. Here's your pay for this week and a few more. If London should ever get too hot to hold you, go to my cousin at Fallow Farm near Thetford. Miss Parkening will help you."

"Lacey, let me in. I must speak with you." Dennis knocked persistently on the book room door.

Lacey finally opened the door still carrying a pistol. "You know I am not to be disturbed in here. Has Jenner returned yet?"

"I left Jenner at Roberto's. Those two are pretty thick. Are you sure..."

"Never mind that. Is that all you came to tell me?"

"Mowbray was there, and challenged Jenner to a match, he said, but everyone in the room could see he meant to kill the boy."

Lacey swung on him abruptly and grabbed him by the shoulder.

"Mowbray! Where is Jenner now—hurt? My God, did you do nothing to stop it?"

"A scratch on the arm is all. I wish to God he had been killed. Then this mess would all be over."

"Don't say that!" Lacey turned away and his eyes darted around the room in a hunted way.

"I was almost forgetting," Dennis said coldly. "You are in love."

"You don't understand. Leave me alone. I have to think."

"Jenner's quick, I give him that. Quick on his feet and with his tongue." Dennis closed the door and leaned against it with his arms folded. "He came out with a tale so pat I almost believed it, all the while fighting for his life. Whatever else he is, he's not a coward."

"No, he's not." Lacey was sweating and shivering.

"He threatened Mowbray with some past rape. Seemed to actually scare the man. I don't know why. Surely he won't be prosecuted for that after all these years."

"Would you take such a crime lightly if it happened to Stella?"

"No, I suppose not." Dennis looked at his uncle in some concern. "Jenner called Mowbray a seducer of children—I take it he meant the girl, not himself. And when he had his sword at Mowbray's throat he made him admit he had lied about you two."

"Did anyone believe him?" Lacey asked vaguely.

"All they believed when Jenner was done is that Mowbray is a coward and that Jenner is devoted to you. He may have done more harm than good."

"I don't care about that, so long as she—his cousin has been revenged."

"What is this nameless girl to you?"

"Never mind that now. Leave me alone."

"How can I when I see what he is doing to you?"

"Don't blame Jenner. It's all my doing."

"I have known you all my life. I have always looked up to you. How can I believe that?"

"Perhaps it's time you didn't look up to me."

"That's not the way I want it."

"You are so young, Dennis. You see only black or white. No one is entirely good or evil. When you are older . . . you may understand."

Dennis turned and left in some puzzlement. Lacey locked the door.

"Where's Lacey?" Jenner gasped, flinging the front door open.

"He is not at home." Edwards drew himself up.

"Don't lie to me, Edwards. I have to talk to him. I have to warn him."

Dennis had come out into the hall to bar Jenner's way and handled her rather roughly when she tried to brush past him.

"Sir, the boy is hurt," Edwards remonstrated, trying to get between the two.

"At least give him a message. Let him know what to expect."

"I already told him what you did, you idiot. By now half of London knows about you two."

"Well, where is he? What did he say?"

"Nothing to any purpose. Just locked himself in the book room with his pistols."

Jenner gasped, "What? You left him in that state of mind with a pistol?"

A shadow of doubt crossed Dennis' face and he strode to the door to knock and call to Lacey. There was no reply.

"Break it," Jenner ordered. "Quickly."

Dennis put his shoulder to the door only once before the molding gave way and he half fell inside. Lacey was sitting behind the desk with a raised pistol in one hand and a look of genuine surprise on his face. Jenner dashed across the room, slid over the top of the desk and grasped his arm. The pistol discharged harmlessly into the bookshelves behind Lacey.

"Jenner!" he gasped, as he picked her up from the floor behind the desk. "Dennis said you were hurt. Is it really just a scratch?"

"Yes, I'm all right. Of all the idiotic stunts to think of. I'm now convinced you are more deranged than I am. Is this what I have driven you to?"

Lacey looked at her in confusion until it dawned on him that they all thought he had been about to shoot himself. He chuckled in relief. Then as they all looked on him with the concern one reserves for someone who is about to go raving, he sobered himself and ordered his butler and nephew from the room.

"I won't go!" Dennis shouted. "I won't leave you with him."

"As long as I am still alive," Lacey said with some of his old strength, "I am master in my own house." He moved threateningly toward them. "Get out so I can talk to Jenner." Lacey shut the door on them and leaned a chair against it.

"They have a perfect right to hate me. I have completely ruined your reputation. He told you about the fight with Mowbray?"

"Yes. Let me see your arm." Lacey undid the bandage and stripped off her coat as she desperately tried to explain.

"When he said that about you in front of others I could not let it pass. Not to fight him would have been an admission of guilt."

"Whereas vanquishing him exonerates me, I suppose."

"I didn't even think of that, I was so angry," Jenner admitted with desperate tears in her eyes. "You once told me killing was easy. I can understand that now, but I don't think it was so for you."

"Yes, because I expected to die. So I thought it didn't matter. In a way living is a worse punishment to me since I now have all those lives on my conscience."

"It was war. You did what you had to, what anyone would have done in your place."

"You?"

"Perhaps more so than another woman."

"You let him provoke you into a fight. You could have been killed."

"He's old and slow, although he does have one or two tricks I was not expecting."

"So I see," Lacey said as he bandaged her arm with his handkerchief. "It seems you put me in the position of having to leave London. And since we are both leaving, we may as well go together."

Jenner opened her mouth to protest.

"You know what my alternative is," he threatened her with a glance at the pistol on the floor.

"No!" She hugged him to her. "Come with me then. We can live together in the country until they have forgotten about you and me."

"They won't forget. It is inconceivable that any woman of breeding would accept an offer from me now, not that I would dare to make one. However, if I returned from the country in a year or so with a loving wife on my arm, I have a feeling that would put down a great deal of the talk."

"I had not thought of that." Jenner looked at him with the faintest glimmer of hope. "But who can we get to..."

"You, my little idiot. For a teller of tales, you are losing your grasp on this plot. It will make a great ending."

"But people will guess. My face is too well known."

"And you bear a striking resemblance to your cousin. What is her name, by the way?"

"Jennifer. Do you forget what I clearly stated Mowbray did to her? You can't use her—me—to save your reputation."

"Oh, I imagine we will be talked about behind our backs for years. It's quite a delicious feeling to have every eye in a room on you, to have women whisper about you behind their fans, old men shake their heads. When we come back we will take the town by storm. We will be the hit of the season."

Jenner laughed weakly and dashed her hand across her eyes.

"Poor Caroline and Stella. Even Dennis will suffer."

"They will either get over it or they won't. Caroline should not have thrust herself and the children on me if she did not want them embroiled in my scandals."

Jenner turned to him a tragic face. "But Lacey, I was forgetting. You have to marry someone else."

"Why?" He searched her face for the answer. What else could she be holding back from him? Surely he knew everything.

She looked away with pain in her eyes. "I should never have tried to impose my philosophy on you. It does not work for you. And I am limited in a way you are not."

"Because you are a woman?"

"Because I am not really a woman anymore."

"You make the most passionate love to me that I have ever experienced and you have doubts about your identity?"

"A wise man said that everyone should plant one tree, write one book and raise one child. I cannot do all this. There is no reason for you to fail at life. You have so much to pass on. Not money, but love and understanding."

"What are you talking about?"

"Don't you remember? I can never give you any children."

"Is that what this is all about? Have I ever asked for any puling brats from you? I don't even like children much when they are someone else's. I'm sure I would detest my own."

"You say that now. How will you feel in five or ten years?"

"The same. Besides, it will give Dennis something to anticipate. And if you should discover you must have a baby, there are plenty of orphans we can adopt, as many as you want, so long as they stay out of my study. Now, will you marry me?"

"Yes, but I don't see how to manage it."

"First, I mean to take you home and let your aunts make you well again. Then we shall enjoy a traditional courtship and a country wedding—my side not attending. We can live on your farm or travel as we please until your curls grow out some. I think we should arrive in London from Italy or some such place. I leave it to you to invent how we met. I suppose that disreputable boy, Jenner, introduced us."

"Lacey, have you ever thought of writing?"

Chapter Eleven

Edwards knocked on the door to report that the horses were waiting.

"You have a few moments to say your goodbyes to Caroline and Stella. I must speak to Dennis before we go." Dennis was still waiting in the hall and entered belligerently as Jenner went in search of her hostess.

"Before you go running off you may as well know that I mean to enlist as a regular. Don't think you can stop me," Dennis threw at his uncle.

"Is this because of me?" Lacey asked tiredly.

"Not entirely." Dennis' manner softened a little. "I have to get away for awhile. I need something of my own."

"Can commissions still be purchased?"

"Yes." Dennis watched in amazement as Lacey sat down to write him a check and a brief note of recommendation. "Why now, when you refused before?"

"Before, my need to get away was greater than yours." Lacey handed him the check. "I'm not leaving the country. Not going much farther than Kettering, in fact, so you needn't worry about Stella and Caroline."

"I'm surprised you trust me with this after what I did."

"You have never disappointed me, Dennis. I wish I could say the same about myself. I have used you damnably. I don't ask you to forgive me."

"You don't have to ask. You do realize that once Stella is married, you will be alone with Mother?"

"Yes, it will be quite as it used to be, her bullying me into things I know I should do. Perhaps I can provide her with a companion, someone to lend a more sympathetic ear to her than any of us ever has."

"Lacey, you sound almost sorry."

"I tried to imagine what life would be like without Caroline—damned boring. I need her to liven things up when I am getting too complacent."

"She will do that for you. You know I never coveted Kettering. It always made me feel tied down."

"You may come to a time in your life when that feeling is not so unpleasant."

"She won't stop trying to marry you off, you know."

"I don't expect Caroline to change. I expect I will."

"Then I advise you to marry, and if you must keep Jenner by you, find a place for him where he will cause the least scandal."

Lacey's eyes opened wide. "That doesn't matter to you? You accept the situation?"

"Yes, but if you have to have him, can't you at least keep him someplace out of the way and out of trouble?"

Lacey looked at Dennis rather strangely. "Jenner is not the sort of person one keeps. He has a life and plans of his own."

"Yes, I know."

The curricle and pair that pulled up in the stable yard at Fallow Farm looked so imposing even Aunt Bette, who was hard to impress, left off schooling the green colt and gave him into the charge of a stable lad. Thinking it might be someone wishing to purchase a horse, she turned over in her mind which of her pets was ready to go. It was hard enough for her to part with any of her beasts, so that her clientele had to pass the strictest scrutiny of their horsemanship.

"Aunt Bette!" Jenner shouted as she jumped down and ran to her. "There's someone I want you to meet, and please be nice to him."

"Does he want to buy a horse?" she asked loud enough for Lacey to hear.

"No, he wants to marry me." The tall woman eyed her niece skeptically. "This is Beatrice Fallow—Lacey Raines. He is an excellent rider," Jenner confided to her aunt breathlessly as though that were the only credentials needed to get Lacey into her good graces.

"I see. Does he know what a hoyden you are to be capering about in those boy's clothes?" Bette asked sharply. She was herself attired in a riding habit of distinctly military cut.

"Yes, he knows all about me. Please don't say you'll object, for we need to live here for awhile until we make our plans."

"Well, Mr. Raines, so long as Jenner wants you and you are willing to do your share of the work, I certainly have no objection. This will be her place someday, but that day is fair and far off, so if you expect to feed your servant and these horses at our trough you will have to pull your own weight."

"Yes, ma'am." Lacey touched his hat in what was almost a salute and handed the reins over to one of the grooms. He cuffed the smirking Collins on his way past and followed Jenner and her aunt in the back door. A small sweet little woman was counting eggs in the kitchen when they entered, and merely looked over her spectacles.

"Milly, this is Mr. Raines. He wants to marry our Jenner. What do you think?"

"Forty-seven—yes, yes, please tell cook and have Horton set another place for lunch—forty-eight—"

Jenner laughed and bent to kiss the lady's cheek.

"Forty-nine," she continued, as they went through the room and toward the door. "Oh, Jenner, dear, you had better change your clothes before we sit down to eat or Horton will be frowning and grumbling all through the meal. You know he disapproves of you dressing like that even for riding— Oh dear, where was I now?"

"Forty-nine, and yes, I will change. It's like I have never been away," she confided to Lacey.

"You may as well take Geoffrey's room," Bette said, preceding them up the narrow stairs. "I will send the maid up to dust it later." She went to the window and drew back the heavy curtain as Collins came in with Lacey's valises. "Jenner, come with me. I want to talk to you." Jenner left in Bette's wake with a mischievous grin.

Lacey rattled down the stairs sometime later to discover Aunt Milly watering plants in the large sitting room. She was having difficulty with a fern on a stand and Lacey volunteered to take the heavy watering can and finish the job.

"Did you say you are going to marry Jenner?" Milly fluttered.

"Yes, it took me some effort to convince her, so I hope you are not going to disapprove."

"Oh, no, it would be the very thing for her, especially if you like horses. Perhaps Jenner will even settle down a little. Bette and I have let her do as she pleases since she came of age. She has so little enjoyment and no friends. Always so restless, always riding or walking somewhere. Of course, we could not quite like her going off to London alone, but her letters were all so cheery, she sounded to be having a lovely time. And the books she sent back! It will be years until we read them all. Did she write that you are getting married? I can't remember."

"No, she didn't have time."

"Oh, I thought I might have missed something. I do so often, you know, miss the most important news when I am concentrating on something else. My mind seems to be so crowded at times I can't keep track of all I need to remember. There is one thing I don't quite understand."

Lacey looked at her inquiringly.

"Was she dressed that way the whole time?"

"Yes, everyone in London knows her as Jenner Page."

"Oh, dear. That is just the sort of thing she would do. Is that why you are marrying, because she . . . ?"

"I love Jenner. Nothing else matters any more."

"Well, that's all right, then," Aunt Milly said contentedly.

Lacey had a feeling Aunt Bette's approval would be much harder to gain.

Bette came downstairs looking imposing, and no less military, in her severely cut walking dress. "Has Millicent thought to offer you some sherry or brandy?"

"Or raspberry wine," Milly suggested. "We make our own."

"I hardly think Mr. Raines would like that sweet stuff."

"I would like to try it, and please call me Lacey. Everyone does so."

"Good. I shall fetch a bottle," Milly said. Bette was on the point of telling her sister to ring for Horton instead, but thought better of it and let Milly leave the room.

"Do you know about Jenner?" Bette asked Lacey abruptly.

"I know her whole life story."

"And it doesn't matter to you?"

"It makes me love her more."

"You are an unusual young man."

"Jenner is an unusual girl."

Lacey was sipping his wine, which was actually quite good, and undergoing an interrogation from Aunt Bette, while Milly smiled contentedly. He heard quick footsteps in the hall and turned to see a young girl in a blue muslin dress. Long brown curls fell from a topknot nearly to her shoulders. Though he was expecting to see Jenner in a dress he stared openmouthed at her for a moment. She blushed and looked over her clothes to make sure she hadn't forgotten something. Lacey stood belatedly and came to take her hands.

"Amazing!"

"Oh, the hair. They had to cut it when I was sick, but they saved it and made it into a fall. It's quite convenient to have it detachable."

Lacey laughed. "I can't believe it."

Milly smiled wider, and even Bette was looking kindly on the besotted Lacey.

"What happened to your arm?" Bette demanded suddenly when the shawl Jenner had negligently thrown over her shoulders slipped to reveal the bandage on her forearm.

"That's just a scratch."

"I know you. I will see that scratch after lunch. How did it happen?"

"It's rather a long story."

Horton came in to announce luncheon. He glared at Lacey on general principles, but cast a more kindly look at Jenner.

"Oh, a story," Milly said. "We have not had one in such a long time."

"How did it happen?" Bette demanded relentlessly of Lacey as he seated Milly and then Jenner in the small dining room.

"Actually, she was fighting a duel—to protect my honor."

"I see," Bette said as she drew her own chair up to the table. "Perhaps we will wait until tonight to hear all this," Bette said as Horton came in with the soup tureen. "Raines," she began, changing the subject. "I met an Honoria Raines once."

"Yes, my mother. She is dead now."

"She had her daughter with her in London—Caroline, I believe."

"You have a remarkable memory, Aunt Bette. Lacey is—"

"Caroline's younger brother," Lacey interrupted with a significant look at Jenner.

Jenner and Lacey spent the afternoon walking about the farm and the surrounding lanes and woods. She took him as far as the ruined cottage where she had first found Rob.

"Why did you stop me telling them you are a lord? Now they are thinking you some penniless younger son."

"Just this once I want someone to like me for myself."

"Don't you think I do?"

"I think you would take me in if I were a murderer on the run."

"You are right, of course, but I am glad you are nothing so desperate."

They walked back by way of Lord Gawlton's wood.

"This is where it happened, is it not?" Lacey asked gently.

"How did you know?"

"Your face. It suddenly went quite sad."

"Yet I can't help thinking that if not for that misfortune, we would never have met."

"No. We would have been drawn together somehow."

"Still so religious, Lacey. At least you are beginning to think your destiny is not to be so tragic."

"You still believe that everything is an accident?"

"I believe that people can make their own destinies, if they are willing to be a little flexible."

"On this, we will never agree."

"Then we will never be bored with one another."

Epilogue

"How do I look?" Jenner asked.

"Beautiful," Lacey replied calmly.

"You have to say that now that we are married. I mean am I different enough?"

"We are about to find out."

"Stop the carriage!"

"What?"

"I need some time to think. Make them let us out here. Tell them we want to look at the view."

Hawes disapproved of keeping the sweating horses standing while his master walked his new lady out into a meadow, but he knew how to follow orders. Jenner paced back and forth with her rather mannish stride, then went to Lacey.

"What did you write to Caroline?"

"That I had fallen in love with Jenner's cousin and married her. She seemed surprised, but there was not one word of rebuke in her letter."

"The news of your marriage—to anyone—would probably be welcome compared to what we put her through in London."

"She asked me to bring you to Kettering. She wants to meet you. And now that she has heard Dennis is alive, she doesn't seem to mind what I do."

"I'm afraid," Jenner said, desperately twisting her gloves.

"I have never known you to lose courage before," Lacey laughed, "even in the face of real danger."

"Don't you see? This is what I was dreading all along. It is almost as though we have been swept to this point by something outside our power, even though I could see far enough ahead to know it would come to this."

"Why Jenner, how fatalistic of you."

"A sad lapse I must admit. Stella would not care, but I cannot help feeling that I betrayed Caroline. And she does love you."

"I know that now, but only because of you."

"I want to tell them the truth, Lacey," Jenner said with sudden decision. "I cannot bear the thought of lying to them all our lives. At least let me tell Caroline and Stella."

"If that is what you want."

"Yes, and as soon as possible. How will they take it do you think?"

"It doesn't matter."

"Yes, it does— Oh, what are you doing?" Lacey had swooped down on her and picked her up.

"We cannot stand about disputing in a field all day. Hawes, drive on to the house. We will walk." Lacey smiled at Jenner and his quiet confidence flowed into her.

"You are mad. Put me down," Jenner commanded without making any real effort to escape his arms.

"My land begins at that stream. I am carrying you over the threshold so to speak."

She clung even tighter to his neck and he paused to kiss away the last of her fears. "Don't worry. If they disown me, we still have each other."

And with that, he carried her, unresisting, into their awaiting future.

* * * * *

Harlequin® Historical

We hope you enjoyed your introduction to our March
Madness authors and that you will keep an eye out for
their next titles from Harlequin Historicals.

Castaway by Laurel Ames—A British shipowner gets more
than he bargained for when he becomes ''heir-apparent''
of a large and zany family.

Fly Away Home by Mary McBride—The story of a half-
breed Apache and the Eastern-bred woman who proves to
him that their love can conquer all.

Silver and Steel by Susan Amarillas—The western
expansion of America's railroads serves as the backdrop
for this tale of star-crossed lovers who can't escape their
destiny.

The Unicorn Bride by Claire Delacroix—A young woman
finds herself married to an enigmatic nobleman veiled in
secrets and legends in this French Medieval setting.

**Four stories that you won't want to miss. Look for
them wherever Harlequin Historicals are available.**

HHMMAD

Following the success of WITH THIS RING and
TO HAVE AND TO HOLD, Harlequin brings you

JUST MARRIED

SANDRA CANFIELD
MURIEL JENSEN
ELISE TITLE
REBECCA WINTERS

just in time for the 1993 wedding season!

Written by four of Harlequin's most popular authors, this
four-story collection celebrates the joy, excitement and
adjustment that comes with being "just married."

You won't want to miss this spring tradition, whether
you're just married or not!

AVAILABLE IN APRIL WHEREVER HARLEQUIN
BOOKS ARE SOLD

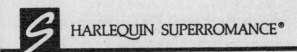

HARLEQUIN SUPERROMANCE®

HARLEQUIN SUPERROMANCE NOVELS WANTS TO INTRODUCE YOU TO A DARING NEW CONCEPT IN ROMANCE...

WOMEN WHO DARE!
Bright, bold, beautiful...
Brave and caring, strong and passionate...
They're unique women who know their
own minds and will dare anything...
for love!

One title per month in 1993, written by popular Superromance
authors, will highlight our special heroines as they face unusual,
challenging and sometimes dangerous situations.

Discover why our hero is camera-shy next month with:
#545 SNAP JUDGEMENT by Sandra Canfield
Available in April wherever Harlequin Superromance
novels are sold.

Where do you find hot Texas nights, smooth Texas charm and dangerously sexy cowboys?

COWBOYS AND CABERNET

Raise a glass—Texas style!

Tyler McKinney is out to prove a Texas ranch is the perfect place for a vineyard. Vintner Ruth Holden thinks Tyler is too stubborn, too impatient, too...Texas. And far too difficult to resist!

CRYSTAL CREEK reverberates with the exciting rhythm of Texas. Each story features the rugged individuals who live and love in the Lone Star State. And each one ends with the same invitation...

Y'ALL COME BACK...REAL SOON!

Don't miss *COWBOYS AND CABERNET* by Margot Dalton. Available in April wherever Harlequin books are sold.

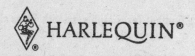

THE TAGGARTS OF TEXAS!

Harlequin's Ruth Jean Dale brings you
THE TAGGARTS OF TEXAS!

Those Taggart men—strong, sexy and hard to resist...

You've met Jesse James Taggart in FIREWORKS!
Harlequin Romance #3205 (July 1992)

And Trey Smith—he's THE RED-BLOODED YANKEE!
Harlequin Temptation #413 (October 1992)

And the unforgettable Daniel Boone Taggart in SHOWDOWN!
Harlequin Romance #3242 (January 1993)

Now meet Boone Smith and the Taggarts who started it all—
in LEGEND!
Harlequin Historical #168 (April 1993)

Read all the Taggart romances!
Meet all the Taggart men!

Available wherever Harlequin Books are sold.
